"My brother might have hired you, Mr. McCord, but I run the stables, and I don't go for all that horse-whispering mumbo-jumbo or your sense of humor."

Jake cocked his hip and set his hands on his belt buckle. "There's a saying that you can't step into the same river twice. Once you step in, you alter it, you affect its flow, you transform the soil and water mixture and you make a mark. It's a changed river. When I'm finished with Diablo, he won't be the same horse he was when I got here. I'll guarantee that, Ms. Colton."

He leaned in. He couldn't help it. Alanna was so attractive when she was setting her boundaries. Tangling with her was more dangerous than French-kissing a rattlesnake. He should heed his instinct, but it wasn't in his nature to back down, even though it was in his best interests.

* * *

The Coltons of Texas
Finding love and buried family
secrets in the Lone Star State...

HIGH-STAKES COLTON

BY
KAREN ANDERS

First Published in Great Britain 2016
By Mills & Boon, an imprint of HarperCollins*Publishers*
1 London Bridge Street, London, SE1 9GF

© 2016 Harlequin Books S.A.

Special thanks and acknowledgement are given to Karen Anders
for her contribution to the Coltons of Texas series.

ISBN: 978-0-263-91944-8

18-0916

Our policy is to use papers that are natural, renewable and recyclable products and made from wood grown in sustainable forests. The logging and manufacturing processes conform to the legal environmental regulations of the country of origin.

Printed and bound in Spain
by CPI, Barcelona

Karen Anders writes a suspenseful and sexy mix of navy and civilians investigating murder, espionage and crime across a global landscape. Under the pen name Zoe Dawson, she's currently writing romantic comedy, new-adult contemporary romance, urban fantasy, syfy and erotic romance. When she's not busy writing, she's painting or killing virtual mmorpg monsters. She lives in North Carolina with her two daughters and one small furry gray cat.

To cowboys and lawmen.
God bless them.

Chapter 1

This county was probably one of the prettiest places on earth, as far as Texas Ranger Jake McCord was concerned. And he'd been to a few. Rolling grassland was carved by deep gullies and dotted with copses of oak and pine. It was so damned beautiful with the prickly pear cacti, emerald green color and blue sky.

He squinted slightly as he reached for the thermal coffee mug on the dash. At least the road was decent, largely due to the influence of the wealthy Coltons who owned and lived on this one-hundred-thousand-acre, billion-dollar spread: Colton Valley Ranch. The ranch was his current destination and located just outside of Dallas.

He was fortunate to woo a wealthy woman, Darla, and after purchasing the land and beginning what would become his vast ranch, Eldridge Colton, now also an oilman, had amassed a substantial fortune.

The road made a sweeping curve over the rise, and before him lay a piece of flat land, the cut banks along the southern boundary giving it a plateau effect. Beyond the trees, ranch buildings came into view, and sunlight glinted off a running horse weather vane atop a huge arena. Various outbuildings and five stark white barns with red X's on the doors. The apartments for the hands built out of a former barn and steps from the working barns were situated right in the center, the space between blocked into paddocks. About a mile away the big rear of the mansion loomed with more paddocks and pastureland, along with another stable, most likely where the Coltons kept their family horses as the arena and barns were at least a mile away. He felt immediately at ease here, the spread reminding him of the ranching he'd done before his stint in the Texas Highway Patrol and getting accepted as a Texas Ranger.

His expression sobering, Jake braced his elbow on the window ledge and absently rubbed his thumb against his mouth, thinking that he hadn't been on an undercover operation in quite some time. He had recently spent his time at the Texas Department of Criminal Justice French Robertson prison, or the TDCJ French Robertson, training chase horses for manhunts for the Texas Rangers.

Nearing the approach of the long lane, he signaled for a left turn and slowed to a crawl, checking the side mirror as the horse trailer tracked into the turn, the whole outfit rocking as Valentine, his roan gelding in the back, shifted. He kept his speed to a crawl as he drove across the cattle guard, and he checked the side-view mirror again. Once clear, he accelerated slightly, the bright sunlight bounding off the shiny hood of his midnight blue 4x4.

There were two entrances onto the property, a service road from the highway that he was currently using and the more formal drive up to the vast mansion. The first floor was where Eldridge and his second wife, Whitney, had their suite, with the second floor occupied by his children with Whitney: Thomas or more well-known as T.C., and Reid. Also occupying the second floor were his two adopted stepchildren from the marriage with Whitney, Marceline and Zane—who also lived with his new pregnant wife, Mirabella—and another adopted daughter, Piper. That left Eldridge's children with his deceased first wife, Darla. Fowler Colton had his residence in the left wing along with Alanna Colton. Jake's main mission was to get close to the family and find out what they were hiding.

Alanna was the manager of Colton Valley Ranch Stables, a huge equestrian center that exclusively bred, raised, trained and sold top class cutters and award winners.

She was probably still asleep in her posh king-size bed, all cozy and warm as it wasn't quite six yet. The little princess most likely supervised from her high horse named along the lines of Emperor or Rembrandt.

His mood reflective, he absently rubbed his thumb across his mouth again, his gut tightening. He wasn't exactly sure accepting this mission was the smartest idea his superiors had. He wasn't the most tactful guy. Granted, he was touted as the best horse handler in the Rangers, and it was bandied about that he was an honest-to-God horse whisperer. But he tended to be blunt, and rich folks weren't keen on an outspoken employee.

His gut was suddenly in knots. He felt as if he was a hair away from disaster. All he knew was that for the last four and a half months, he'd been kicking himself hard over the death of Tim Preston, a rookie Ranger. The gnawing only got worse and every time he went to sleep, he'd see the whole scene played over in Technicolor. The headshrinkers called it occupational burnout. Jake just called it doing his damn job. Came with the territory, but he'd been relegated to the TDCJ French Robertson prison after he had rushed into a hostage situation. A street thug on the lam from police had run into a resident and her child. Knocked the mother down and took the girl inside with him. Jake had gone in, stared the guy down and saved the girl without bloodshed. He was sure the guy was never going to give up and he would have killed that little girl. Negotiations would have been a waste of time. He'd trusted his instincts and been reprimanded for it.

His superiors weren't happy, and his psych test told them he "was unable to cope fully with the stress." No kidding, Sherlock. He'd cope just fine once he found the bastard who had killed Preston. He should have gone with his gut and realized there was something off during that case. Now he had a dead man haunting him and a bad guy who'd gotten away.

When Sheriff Troy Watkins had requested assistance from the Rangers for someone to infiltrate the ranch and spy on the wealthy Coltons, he was the likely candidate. It seemed that their patriarch, Eldridge, was missing and foul play was involved. The sheriff had so far not made any progress on finding who had been behind the kidnapping, hitting a dead end. On the recommendation of the sheriff, Colton Valley Ranch's new foreman, Buck Tressler, hired Jake to tame a blooded but unruly stallion named Zorro.

It was considered a low-stress mission and tapped into Jake's expertise—blending in seamlessly with his ranching background and taming horses as though he knew their special language.

So, he got tagged.

A big sign said COLTON VALLEY RANCH STABLES indicating with an arrow that he should go right at the next turn.

He parked the rig in front of the big white clapboard arena with a sign outside that read Abilene, then tossed his sunglasses on the dash. Settling his pearl gray hat on his head, he grabbed the halter lead in the passenger seat and got out of the truck. Two border collies came around the back of the truck, and he reached down and ruffled their ears, grinning when one nudged his leg begging for a deeper scratch.

He wasn't sure he agreed that this was a low-stress assignment. He couldn't seem to trust himself and his time in the Rangers had been tumultuous. He was born to be a Texas Ranger. It was in his blood with the long line of Rangers in his family. Both he and Matt, his younger brother, had been groomed to carry on the family legacy. With Matt's memory came the sense that he'd let his little brother down. Dead at sixteen from an overdose. His brother's death made him question his instincts. Instead of pushing his little brother, he should have supported him. There was no reason for him to change now. Why did every day add to this belief that he was dying inside? He pushed away those thoughts. He was just going through a bad patch.

He straightened and stretched his long legs. He went to the back of the horse trailer and clicked his tongue as he unfastened the locking mechanism and pulled the back open. Standing to the side as Valentine sidled, he slipped his hand over the roan's rump and made his way to the animal's head. Clipping on the lead, he clicked again while pulling slightly on the halter. Valentine, one of the best horses he'd ever met with the heart of a lion and the disposition of a lamb, obediently backed out.

Once the big gelding had all four hooves on the driveway, Jake took him around a couple of turns to get him used to the environment and to work the kinks out of the trailer ride.

Valentine raised his head and flicked his ears forward at the sound of whinnying in the distance. Look at that. He was already making friends. Valentine returned the call. He had excellent manners.

Leading the gelding, he went through the big open doors. Once inside, he had to wait for his eyes to adjust to the dim interior. The skylights were placed every few feet in the arched roof, flooding the arena with faint, early morning natural light. Only the center row of mercury vapor lights high above the arena area were on, and Jake suspected it was a bid to save electricity.

Shoving his hands in his jeans pockets, he skirted the arena wall, watching the two riders who were working a small herd of cows inside the four-foot-high cambered plank wall. Realizing he wasn't all that visible in the dim light, he rested his arms on the arena wall and watched a buckskin gelding perform, the horse's movements quick, sharp and highly tuned as he prevented the wheeling, running steer from returning to the herd. A good cutting horse was poetry in motion as far as Jake was concerned, with the horse and rider as synchronized as man and animal could ever get. The horse's athletic ability had to be top caliber for it to work and the animal had to have cow sense. When it really came together, it was showstopping. And his pulse sped up when he spied the gorgeous blonde putting a horse through his paces.

But it wasn't just the highly trained, athletic ability of the horse that he appreciated. It was the woman's stillness, her grace, her oneness with her mount that made his pulse hit overdrive. She was something to see on a horse, especially one working like this one was. It was almost as though she were an extension of the gelding, her hands motionless, the hard, fast, twisting action of the horse barely shifting her in her seat. The lady could stick to a horse like lint; that was for damned sure. He allowed himself a small smile. And she looked mighty fine while she was doing it. He could see why Colton Valley Ranch had a top-notch reputation.

Resting his forearms on top of the wall, he stared at her. She had on blue jeans and tan suede shotgun chaps, and a cinnamon-colored tank top showing off her tanned, toned arms. Her deerskin gloves were darkened with age and use, and she had her golden-blond hair pulled back and braided, but hair had escaped and wisped around her face. A straw maize hat with a multicolored scarf was tied around the crown on her head. She had sawdust in her hair and a big smudge of dirt on her cheek, and by rights she should have looked like a mess.

But not this dynamo.

She looked like she had just walked out of some fashion magazine. Boy howdy, those long legs in tight chaps were enough to make a man forget his good intentions about keeping his hands to himself.

She worked the horse another fifteen minutes, then dismounted, handing the reins to another young woman, then took the reins of the horse the other rider had been warming up. She had just mounted when Jake stepped out of the shadows and started toward her.

About halfway there, he got quite the jolt when he recognized the looker.

It was the princess herself. Alanna Colton.

"Would you get a load of that?" Tamara LaCross said. "Holy cow."

Alanna Colton, perched in the saddle of one of the cutters she was training, followed the trajectory of her assistant's gaze. In the distance, a man was striding toward them, leading a gorgeous blue roan. The horse had a black face, mane, tail and stockings, the coat a blue sheen and a leopard-patterned body.

Feeling strangely breathless, she watched him advance. She glanced at the cowboy and a strange flutter unfurled in her midriff. The man wasn't so bad, either.

He was tall, six foot two at least. The cowboy literally radiated an aura of strength and masculinity. He was powerfully built with heavily muscled shoulders, but beneath his unquestionable virility, beneath his physical toughness, there was something…some indefinable quality that drew her. She wondered what kind of person really lay beneath his alpha image.

He looked as if he had just ridden off the range. He was dressed in faded blue jeans and a dark blue Western-style shirt that fit him like a second skin. Threaded through the loops of his jeans was a wide hand-tooled belt that sported an engraved silver buckle, and on his feet he wore a pair of scuffed brown cowboy boots. His face was heavily shadowed by the broad brim of his gray Stetson, but even that couldn't conceal the strong jawline.

"Excuse me, ma'am," he drawled.

"Yes, how can I help you?" Alanna felt vaguely suspended as she met his steady gaze.

"Good morning, ma'am," he said, grabbing the brim of his hat and giving it a tug. "I'm looking for Buck Tressler."

"Buck's on an errand in town. How can I help you?"

"He hired me to work with your stallion Zorro. Name's Jake McCord."

Oh, shoot, this was the horse whisperer Fowler had agreed to hire to work with that damn rogue stallion he had foisted on her without speaking to her first. Sure she had agreed they needed to infuse the stables with some blooded stock, but she hadn't expected him to pay way too much for an unmanageable stallion. Fowler wasn't the most patient person when it came to working with horses. In fact, Alanna liked it much better when her brother spent his time focused on Colton Incorporated. Since their father's disappearance, Fowler had been on edge for the last couple of months with he and Zane fighting over his longtime girlfriend, Tiffany and her possible involvement in their father's kidnapping. Her family seemed more fractured than usual.

That all seemed to be resolved now with Zane blissfully happy with his administrative assistant, Mirabella, now his wife. Alanna liked and admired the willowy redhead, and was pleased to welcome her into the family.

But with Fowler's interference in her domain, she now had to work with this tantalizing man. She didn't go in for that horse-whispering mumbo jumbo and was skeptical of the practice that promised near-miraculous results that were misleading at best and damaging at worst.

Now he'd hired this phony. Jake the Fake, as far as she was concerned.

"Alanna Colton," she said as he extended his hand toward her. "Welcome to Colton Valley Ranch." She pulled off her glove and placed her hand in his. She was bombarded by disturbing new impressions and the tantalizing warmth of his callused palm sliding over hers. Handsome? No, not exactly, but there was a compelling attractiveness about him, an attractiveness that was unfeigned and indestructible. Dark eyebrows arched over blue eyes, flecked with gold and amber, and the thick long lashes accentuated their hypnotic intensity, the stubble of beard along his jaw a dark, sexy shadow.

There was something very intriguing about his face, something that touched her in the most profound way. It revealed a depth of character, an inner strength, but it also revealed an imperviousness that had been carved by disillusionment. It was the face of a man who had forged on alone, a man whose sensuous mouth had been hardened by grim determination. And, against her will, Alanna felt an immediate affinity for him that she had never felt for another human being. Her keen awareness of him as a man had an immobilizing effect on her, and she was conscious of nothing except the warmth of his touch and his unwavering gaze.

He was a man of contradictions, and he confused her.

"Thank you kindly," he responded.

Alanna didn't want to let go of his hand, and she reluctantly withdrew it from his grasp. Impatiently, she thought this was damned inconvenient. No way did she need another alpha male in her life who told her what to do. Not to mention, she was wary of anyone who professed to "have a way with horses." She'd already had her brother undermine her, and before his disappearance her father just couldn't let go of control of the stables even though he often told her she was in charge. She felt like an island surrounded by sharks and if she ever tried to leave, she would drown. She was at the very worst undermined and at the very best ineffectual. Along with running every aspect of a busy and thriving stable, training cutters for market, and now dealing with a dangerous and untrainable stallion, Alanna was working with her new outreach project. Colton Valley Ranch Gives Back was a program for inner-city kids that taught them how to handle horses and provided a safe environment to learn about responsibility, leadership and community. "Tamara, continue working Samson."

Swinging her leg over the saddle and dropping to the ground, Alanna turned. "Yes, ma'am," Tamara said, taking the reins from Alanna's outstretched hand.

"Let me show you your lodgings and where you can stable your horse," Alanna said. The sooner she put distance between them the better. She still had a full day. But Buck wasn't due back for at least another thirty minutes, and she didn't want to delegate this task to anyone else. Jake was an employee and new here. She did want to make him feel comfortable, even with his questionable profession.

"Valentine," he said.

She approached the roan. Jake watched her with an unsettling steadiness that made her knees a little weak. Reaching out, she rubbed Valentine's forelock, and he pushed his nose into her hand with an exhale of air. Then nudged her as if he wanted to make friends. Charmed by the gelding's soft blue eyes and friendly temperament, she couldn't help herself, she slid her hand down the animal's smooth neck. "Really, that's his name?" She smiled, moving around Valentine, her hand running over him. Valentine stood still and calm. "And, I can see why. This marking on him is heart-shaped."

"It's a birthmark, but even though he can't perform, he still loves the ladies."

"He's gorgeous, and you've taken good care of him."

"Yes, ma'am, he's a fine partner."

The horse nuzzled her again, and she ran her hand over his velvety nose. "You're a lover not a fighter, huh?" Valentine nickered softly and flicked his ears forward.

"This way, Mr. McCord." He stepped to the side, making way for her to pass him, and with a gentle guide to the small of her back, his hand big and warm, he dropped back to allow her to pass, but the brief touch had been electric.

She headed for the back of the arena and the big double doors. They exited through into a wide corridor with a row of box stalls to each side, closing the doors behind them. Walking side by side, she led him around the side of the arena, and Valentine pranced, his head up again, this time a loud whinny splitting the quiet air. Several mares in the paddock they were passing trotted over to the fence. She didn't blame them. He was quite the handsome specimen.

She laughed at his antics and was impressed with the way Jake settled him down with an ease she'd never seen on any horse person she'd worked with, not even some very competent old-timers. It was a sense of balanced energy that radiated out of him as natural and as basic as Jake himself.

"I guess you weren't exaggerating. He is quite the ladies' man."

He scrutinized her intently as if he had already made up his mind about her, but had to switch gears. Not a surprise. A lot of people pigeonholed the Coltons into fancy folk slots, but getting her hands dirty, working the horses, running the stables wasn't just what she did for the ranch, it was her life. Her father had steered her toward jumping, but it was barrel racing she'd loved and competing was her guilty pleasure. His contemplative tone tinged with an undercurrent of amusement, he said softly, "I don't exaggerate, ma'am."

"Unless there's a campfire and some tall tales to be told," she quipped before she could stop her wayward mouth.

He slid a sidelong glance her way, some of that cynicism fading with the twinkle in his gorgeous blue eyes. "I don't tell tall tales," he said. "You know, unless there're some greenhorns to sucker."

She laughed as they came out to the main thoroughfare between the barns and headed toward the farthest, newest of the buildings.

She turned left and led him to the wide-open doors of the barn closest to the apartments. Walking into the interior, Valentine's hooves muffled against the black, rubber floor mat over a shiny brick floor. Curious by nature, many of the horses in the barn stuck their heads out into the main hall and with an eerie stillness they watched Jake with interest as if he exuded something irresistible…a silent communication. She frowned. That was interesting. She'd never seen that before. What was it about this man that made not only the horses sit up and take notice, but seemed to excite the very air around him?

She noticed a stable hand had Firecracker crosstied at one of their two wash racks. The prized pure white horse was an excellent broodmare for their cutters, but Alanna suspected she would be better at throwing foals suited to barrel racing.

Firecracker started to get antsy and Jake stopped short. His gaze went to the horse. As the stable hand untied her, she broke away.

Jake dropped the lead line to Valentine and ran toward the horse. Firecracker came to a stop and danced until Jake got to her. He whispered something, took ahold of the halter and immediately turned the horse in a tight circle, touching the quivering horse's neck, quieting her immediately. The stable hand approached and Jake said, "Probably got a whiff of a stallion and it excited her. Just be aware if she starts to get anxious again, untie and lead her around a few times until she quiets down. I know it's an extra step, but will ensure she doesn't bolt."

The stable hand nodded and thanked Jake.

He came back to the docile and quiet roan and picked up his lead line. "Lead on," Jake said. Alanna had to absorb this new information about Jake. It was obvious he knew what he was doing, but horse whispering was just a fancy name for natural horsemanship. It was true Firecracker was aptly named, but Alanna had never seen her respond so easily to someone.

She stopped at the end of the barn and indicated a corner stall. "You can use this box stall which is cleaned daily. Our horses are fed four times a day with fresh water daily. If your horse requires special needs you can speak with the stable manager for this barn. His name is Billy Jones."

"Valentine is fit as a fiddle. No extras required."

She nodded. "All right. He can answer any questions or feel free to ask me."

He pulled open the sliding stall door with the black steel half grill across the length of the gleaming cedar planks. Guiding Valentine in, he unclipped the lead rope and slid the door closed. Valentine tossed his head and blew and snorted as he explored the interior of his temporary new home.

Alanna noticed how big, strong and sure Jake's hands were as he handled the large roan with ease. Obviously a man who had been around horses his whole life. She pushed back her curiosity. She wasn't going to ask. Getting personal with him wasn't on the agenda. Although, her questions burned in the back of her skull.

"The yoke…" He trailed off, looking at how to open it so Valentine could poke his head out. "He's a curious cuss and will want to stick his head out to survey the area. He doesn't bite at all."

She stepped up to the grill and turned to him. "The latch is right here," she pointed out. Jake got close, so close she got a whiff of him flavored with a woodsy, citrus scent that made her want to turn her head into his chest and breathe deep.

"Where?"

She reached out and captured his wrist, guiding his hand to the latch. His skin was smooth and warm. The double combination of smell and touch sent her heart into overdrive, pounding with a hard beat. "Right here."

"Of all the newfangled…" He fumbled around, then made a gotcha sound. "There we go," he said as he slid the cover to the side and latched it.

He was still standing too close and her gaze connected with his. Alanna experienced that same flutter as she fell victim to the laughter in his eyes. She had a sudden and nearly overpowering urge to touch him again, but she drew a slow, measured breath and deliberately hooked her thumbs in the waistband of her chaps.

He was watching her with that unsettling steadiness again. She made herself back away just to be out of his disturbing presence.

Her voice was only slightly uneven when she said, "I assume you brought your own tack."

He smiled, his eyes crinkling at the corners. "Yes, it's in my truck parked up at the arena. I'll unload it later."

Okay, more devastating when he smiled. It disarmed her even more. "Let me show you the tack room."

"You have a chandelier in a barn," he drawled, stopping and looking up.

She smiled. "Yes, there's no reason we can't be elegant and refined, even in a barn."

He shook his head. "Yes, ma'am."

It was clear he didn't agree. "We have a heated tack room, two wash stations that include hot water, a heated viewing area for our customers, and an upper level split loft area for hay."

Five minutes later she took him over to the apartments, leading him through the great room with its comfy furniture and TV, past the tricked-out gourmet kitchen with two old-fashioned big farmer's tables where a dark-haired woman who looked about the same age as Alanna stood at the stove, her back to them.

"Hi, Ellen," Alanna said.

The woman turned and smiled, her hazel eyes warm and infectious. "Hello, Miss Colton."

"This is Jake McCord. He's going to be working

here taming Zorro. This is Ellen Martin. She's your cook."

Her brows rose, and her eyes went skeptical. "That's a tall task. Good luck with that. Breakfast is at 8:00, lunch at noon and dinner at 5:00. Coffee is always hot and pie plentiful. Snacks on demand." She smiled, and Alanna was aware of just how pretty the single mother was. She might have sixteen-year-old Daisy, but she was only thirty-three. She didn't want to think about Ellen and Jake in any romantic situation, not that it would happen. Why did that bug her?

Jake tugged his hat again. "Pleasure to meet you, ma'am."

Alanna stopped at a small office and opened a metal lockbox hanging on the wall. Searching through, she extracted a key. Climbing the stairs up to the third floor of the remodeled barn, she took him through the door to the largest of the apartments.

"Home away from home," she said, opening the drapes to reveal a balcony patio. "Fowler requested you be given these accommodations. Parking is in an underground area below the apartments."

"This is very generous of you, ma'am. Thank you."

Alanna walked back toward the door and Jake stood just inside the foyer. She had to slide past him. "Fowler thinks you should be as close to and have as much access to Zorro as possible. You will need a comfortable place to come back to." Her voice lowered. "Zorro is…dangerous. He's been mishandled in the past and, coupled with a fighting spirit, he is unpredictable. I would ask you, for your safety, to be very careful."

Jake studied her for a second, then leaned his shoulder against the wall. A heavy measuring look settled on his face, and she got the impression once again that he carried a considerable burden. "Horses don't live in the past or the future. They live in the moment. People are the ones with an agenda, timetables, time limits, goals. Makes for a major disconnect with their horses. Dwelling on the past brings baggage, and focusing on the future can bring anxiety." The way he looked was incongruent with his sage response. Awareness churned through her, making her heart jump and she was struck by a paralyzing fascination to know what it was she saw in his eyes. "I work with horses in the present. No need to worry. Zorro won't hurt me."

He could hurt you. She thought without reason or comprehension, and Alanna was very good at protecting herself. She had to in a family with more politics than the US government and just as much backstabbing as ancient Rome. With a father who had been rumored to be a former bank robber, a serial killer uncle, Fowler and Marceline scheming to create trouble between everyone, her stepmother's histrionics, growing up on guard with an inner layer of steel was warranted. She wasn't going to find out about Jake. Vulnerability was too risky. She had her own burdens to bear, stress and anxiety to handle. Best to steer clear of anything too complicated when her attention needed to be elsewhere. Even with those thoughts, she felt something had tilted beneath her as if everything had just been thrown out of sync. The bleak look in

Jake's eyes did awful things to her heart, and she shivered, hurting for him. And not even knowing or understanding why.

Chapter 2

She cleared her throat and stepped back. "Why don't you get settled?" She looked at her watch. "Buck should be back in about fifteen minutes and will be at the arena. Meet us back there when you're ready."

Ha. Sage advice from him about horses. They did live in the present. Too bad he couldn't apply it to his own life. Too much of his "present" was mired in stuff that had happened in the past. The loss of his younger brother, Matt, to gangs and drugs, and the loss of the rookie that still made the guilt mount, caused sleepless nights, the heat that had fueled his meltdown and burnout. But he wasn't here to dwell on baggage. Alanna was waiting for an answer and he nodded. "I'll be there as soon as I unload."

She handed him the key. "You're expected to handle the daily upkeep, but there will be a maid that comes through every week."

"Will do." She left and closed the door behind her. This two-bedroom apartment was smaller than his modest house, but definitely more expensively furnished. The floor was hardwood and the colors russet, gold with burned orange accents. The small kitchen was compact and complete with a microwave. The living room looked comfortable and inviting with the leather couch and stylish chair and ottoman along with a rugged coffee table, small stand and wide-screen TV.

It didn't take him long to walk back to his truck and drive the rig over to the stables and unload his hand-tooled saddle, the saddle pad and bridle. He rolled his eyes at the chandelier. He found a peg in the well-organized and very clean tack room of the barn identified with a shiny bronzed plaque that read Cisco. Looked like all the barns on the property were named after cities in Texas. That was very... Texan.

He parked his truck, then unhitched and stored his trailer in an area designated for them. Back up in the apartment he brought in his suitcases and unpacked.

Taking a quick shower to wash the grime of the road off, he put on a clean set of clothes and headed back over to the arena.

He realized with wariness he was excited to see Alanna again, and it had nothing to do with the case and everything to do with the way she looked in those shotgun chaps.

It wasn't lost on him, evidenced by Ellen the cook's comments and Alanna warning him that Zorro was dangerous, that neither woman believed he would succeed in rehabilitating the stallion.

"I love Fowler, but he's wrong about that horse. I

don't believe he can be tamed, and I don't want any breeding program I'm endorsing to contain genes from a horse with his disposition." Jake overheard Alanna speaking to a tall man with broad shoulders, salt-and-pepper hair and eyebrows, impressive handlebar mustache and stubble on his cheeks. The man straightened when he saw Jake walk up, clearing his throat, but Alanna had already stuck her proverbial foot into her beautiful mouth. "Whispering won't do any good. I think Jake is just a plain old cowboy who knows how to manipulate a résumé and reputation. I don't believe he's any more a horse whisperer than I am a ballet dancer."

Jake stopped and put his hands on his hips and the man she was talking to cued her that she'd better button her lip and turn around. When she whipped around, she faced his gaze head-on without flinching. Damn but he liked a flinty woman who knew how to stand her ground, and he wasn't surprised she was skeptical of his skills. He got the feeling she wasn't too keen he was here, but now he was certain it wasn't only the crackling sexual tension between them. He couldn't mistake that for anything than what it was.

"You better tie up your pointe shoes. I think I hear the opening to *Swan Lake*," he drawled.

The man choked on a laugh, and it was clear not many people talked to Alanna Colton that way, but he didn't give a damn. There was a small part of him that felt a bit of the ego bruise she'd apparently landed. The rest of him was just much too turned on by this fascinating, contrary woman who ran this stable like a well-oiled machine. He was damned impressed on many levels.

Too bad he was here to delve into her motivations and reasons for possibly masterminding the kidnapping of her own father. Was this slip of a woman capable of that? She was a Colton, so he would have to say yes, but did he feel it in his gut? He wasn't quite sure that was accurate. Snap judgments were something he'd honed over his time in law enforcement. Alanna discombobulated him.

She folded her arms over her chest and narrowed her eyes. He reached out his hand, "Mr. Tressler?"

"Yep, that's me." His handshake was firm and quick.

"Jake McCord. The horse whisperer," he said, and got the expected reaction from Alanna when she stiffened and huffed out a breath. "I'd like to get acquainted with Zorro if that's convenient for you right now."

"I'm free—"

"Just a minute," Alanna interrupted and turned to her foreman. "I need to have a word with Mr. McCord."

Buck gave him a sympathetic look and said, "I'll be right outside when you're ready." It looked as if Buck thought Jake might be a mite sore after getting his hide stripped by Alanna.

Jake faced the pretty, agitated blonde and waited. She dropped her arms and her fists clenched. "I don't believe you can tame that horse with magic and moonbeams, Mr. McCord. Just so you know I have no compunction telling you straight to your face." He went to speak, and she held up her hand. "I believe he's ruined, unpredictable and dangerous and even a rugged cowboy, all hopped up on his sage wisdom, can't pull off a save. That's my honest opinion."

"I had no doubt you are an outspoken woman, Ms. Colton. I will do my damnedest to show you that I don't doctor up my résumé or my reputation. Pretty much what you see is what you get. No subterfuge." He realized he was here undercover, but he was being completely straightforward about who he was. What she saw was what she got.

"My brother might have hired you, Mr. McCord, but I run the stables, and I don't go for all that horse-whispering mumbo jumbo or your sense of humor."

He cocked his hip and set his hands on his belt buckle. "There's a saying that you can't step into the same river twice. Once you step in, you alter it, you affect its flow, you transform the soil and water mixture, and you make a mark. It's a changed river. When I'm finished with Zorro, he won't be the same horse he was when I got here. I'll guarantee that, Ms. Colton."

He leaned in. He couldn't help it. She was so attractive when she was setting her boundaries. Tangling with her was more dangerous than French-kissing a rattlesnake. He should heed his instinct, but it wasn't in his nature to back down, even though it was in his best interests. Getting attached in any way to a suspect was asking for trouble and getting mired in emotions was certainly not something he needed to add to his already burned-out attitude. She was…refreshing, though, and it was his job to get close to her. Get her to reveal any secrets she might be storing in that pretty head of hers. Getting just close enough, but not too close was his game plan. A little wooing was necessary and he was finding it more enjoyable than he'd planned. "I take your meaning, but my sense of humor might grow on you. And, Ms. Colton, I do all kinds of whisperin' and reckon it works like a charm, no complaints so far. Let me know if you…" his voice dropped an octave "…need any samplin'."

He turned on his heel and left her standing there with her mouth open. With each step he felt buoyant, not that he wanted to; he couldn't seem to help himself.

When he cleared the doors and stepped back out into the sunlight, it was going on seven thirty. "Your hide looks intact, and you're walking pretty good there, cowboy."

"This ain't my first rodeo," Jake said and grinned.

"Yeah, it takes a strong man to stand up to that lady. Hats off to you."

"Let me take a look at this devil horse and see what we've got."

"I'm with Miss Colton on this." He started walking over to a two-seater golf cart. Jake looked at it skeptically and Buck grinned, his demeanor open and warm. "Not exactly what cowboys normally ride around on, but this is a big area and it's fast transportation. I'll give you the breakdown as we go."

"Fair enough." Jake slid into the seat and Buck started up the engine.

Buck settled his hat tighter to his head. "You also think Zorro is a lost cause?" Jake asked as the foreman put the little vehicle in gear.

"Yes, I'm afraid so. I've been riding and ranching all my life. I've never seen such a rogue horse. He belongs in the wild with his own herd. Gelding him would be the other choice, but I don't think he'll ever be a top-notch cutter or agreeable barrel racer. Fowler is adamant the horse would enhance our bloodlines, and I disagree. He's got everything else going for him conformationwise. No doubt. But breeding a horse with that disposition seems like a disaster in the making."

"I haven't met Mr. Colton yet. I hear he's not a tolerant sort."

Buck chuckled. "Fowler Colton doesn't suffer fools well, or anyone for that matter. But he and the family are under enough stress."

"You mean with Eldridge Colton missing."

Buck shot Jake a look, his expression contained with an undercurrent of censure. "I wasn't here when it all happened. But I'm sure it is a source of stress no doubt, but the family is weathering his disappearance as best they can. Best to leave that to them and Sheriff Watkins."

"Sure, I understand. It's been in the news a lot lately. Hard to miss."

"The media is as hungry for news as a newborn calf is for its mama's milk," he said, his message clear. He didn't gossip about the Coltons. Jake had to admire that and wondered if it was just Buck's character or something in Alanna that inspired such loyalty. "The stables behind us house the sale stock as well as the indoor arena, as you've seen, and includes a viewing area as well as the forty stalls."

He drove until the apartments were in sight, then made a right to go around. "These are the two barns that house the cutters. Cisco is where we keep the horses we're training and the studs. Jasper is where we keep the mares, foals and yearlings."

"How many head you got?"

"Altogether, we've got about two hundred or so depending on sales and such. We're about to have an auction for the new crop of fully trained horses."

He looped around and pointed out the next set of identical barns. "Spur and Dallas house mostly training stock. I believe that's where your mount is, correct?"

"Yes, sir. Name's Valentine. Blue roan."

"I have a soft spot for roans. Had me one when I was just a tyke." He gestured ahead. "Each of the service barns holds forty horses with two wash racks and tack room. The mare barns also have sleeping accommodations when mares are foaling in case Alanna or the vet want to catch some shut-eye."

"It's an expansive and impressive operation Miss Colton is running."

"Yes, she has the staff to help her, but she's pretty tireless and always on top of things."

As they passed, Jake noted each of the barns had a paddock adjacent to the structure opening out from the stalls.

Buck pulled the small cart over and parked. He got out and Jake followed. "Time for breakfast. Don't want to miss Ellen's cinnamon rolls."

"You're both right on time," Ellen said, her gaze lingering a little longer on the foreman. "It's nice to have you back, Buck."

"Good to be back, Ellen."

"Any luck?"

"Yep, two new mares."

"Very good. Have a seat before the masses arrive and all hell breaks loose." Ellen waved them to chairs. She returned with cutlery, two steaming cups of coffee, a pitcher of cream and a pan of cinnamon buns. She set them down in front of them, then went back for a napkin dispenser and a bowl of sugar from the lazy Susan. "Have at it," she said with a smile.

They dug in and Ellen had been right. People started to arrive. More than he could learn the names of in the first sitting. But it wasn't until Alanna walked in that for him, all hell broke loose.

She was cordial to everyone, but reserved. When she met his eyes, she didn't shy away. He liked her self-possession, but he was a master of body language, partly from being a cop and partly from his ability to work with horses. Alanna Colton didn't trust easily. Who could blame her? If it wasn't her controversial and backstabbing family, it was the media trying to get dirt on them. Getting close to her was his job. There was no getting around that. But his ability to professionally detach himself from any situation involving the criminal element seemed to elude him. Didn't mean she wasn't guilty.

When Buck rose, Jake went with him, setting down the mug, Ellen quickly picked it up and set it into the sink. Jake donned his hat and tipped it as he left. Alanna didn't give him much of a response.

Later, on the backside of the barn was where he got his first glimpse of Zorro. Jake climbed the fence and the horse turned his head to look at them. He stiffened into an alert stance, his nostrils flaring as he caught Jake's scent. He could see why Fowler had bought the stallion and why it would enhance both the cutters and the barrel racers. His lines were excellent with all the makings of a stellar all-around stud.

"Thanks for showing me around. I'll spend some time getting acquainted."

Buck nodded. "Good luck, Jake," Buck said as he jumped down from the fence. He stopped and looked at the stallion, then at Jake. The horse had moved closer to the fence where Jake was perched. Not exactly friendly. Jake simply made eye contact and slowly sank down into himself, holding the animal's hostile gaze. Some people who watched him called it The Zone, but for Jake it was a thought-free state beyond being present but in touch with presence itself—the natural state of being for horses. How they lived life. In the moment.

Out of the corner of his eyes, he saw Buck's lips part and his brows rise, but Jake kept all his attention on Zorro. The horse's ears flicked forward, then went back. He took another step forward. There was a noise from inside the barn and Zorro whirled and trotted to the end of the fence. His message was clear. It was going to take more than a positive attitude to gain this animal's trust.

Buck said softly, "Well, I'll be jiggered and left."

"I'm not paying you good money to stand around and stare at him," a sardonic voice said from Jake's left. He turned to meet the cold blue eyes of Fowler Colton, dressed in a pricey Stetson and a charcoal-gray business suit with Western accents across his broad shoulders, his brown hair neat around his ears. The oil baron dabbling in horse-trading. It was an interesting prospect since Fowler had no interest in the stables previously.

"I think I left my fairy wand in my other jeans."

Fowler's eyes narrowed. "Is that supposed to be funny?"

"No, it's to remind you miracles don't happen overnight. You hired me to do a job. Let me do the job."

"Not many men stand up to me without consequences, McCord."

Jake had never been a yes-man. He'd been his own man and stated his opinion. He often worked in a system that ate a man whole and spit him out. He realized he shouldn't have been so flippant, but Jake recognized something right away. Fowler respected a man who could hold his own and would most likely trust someone who wasn't a kiss ass. "But you come highly recommended, so you get one pass."

"It takes time to rehabilitate a horse, Mr. Colton. If you aim to breed him with the best results, you'll give me the time and patience I need to give you the value of that good money you paid."

Fowler stepped closer, his wintery eyes assessing Jake and recognition flared. Yeah, that's right, Jake was an alpha, too. "Is that so, son? I'd say get on with it. I'm not in the business of throwing away money and that stallion was pricey. Make it work."

"In good time."

Fowler turned to go, but almost collided with a pimply-faced teenager leading a mare. "Watch where the hell you're going!" Fowler said, and the teenager quickly apologized.

"What is your name?"

"Mike, sir."

"Well, Mike, I'll have you off this spread so fast your head will swim."

"He deeply apologizes, sir. Don't you, Mike?"

A tall, good-looking cowboy intervened just before Jake was about to open his mouth and try to smooth it over.

"Yes, sir. Deeply."

Fowler gave both of them one more glaring look and strode off on his pricey hand-tooled boots.

"Better get Jo back to the barn now, Mike."

They had a quick conversation about being more careful, even though it was Fowler who wasn't looking where he was going.

The older guy faced Jake and said, "Hey, there. Saw you at breakfast but didn't get a chance to say howdy. Dylan Harlow and that's Mike Jensen. He's one of Alanna's troubled teens. Good kid."

"Jake McCord."

Dylan took off his hat and ran his hand through his dark hair, then jammed his hat back on. "Whew, still a mite warm for September."

"Figure it is."

"You the guy they hired to handle Zorro?"

"I am that man."

"Boy howdy, you got your work cut out for you and I don't just mean Zorro. Good luck," he said as he sauntered off.

Jake nodded, looking in the direction Fowler had taken. Jake was sure the CEO of Colton Incorporated wasn't done breathing down his neck.

At the end of the day, feeling the effects of the heat, the dirt and the slow start with Zorro, Jake headed for his apartment and the meal he was sure Miss Ellen would be cooking. After the initial meeting with Zorro, Jake found the rest of the afternoon to be frustrating as he tried to get closer to the animal. But it was as if he was off for some reason. He wondered if it could be Alanna. She did knock him for a loop.

As he approached, the aroma of beef and other delectable scents hit him as he entered the apartments. Ellen was at the stove and she waved to him as he climbed the stairs, his stomach grumbling.

In his newly appointed apartment, he stripped, opened the linen closet and discovered there were no towels. There was a knock at the door and he hastily pulled on his jeans, zipping them but in his hurry forgot to button them.

When he pulled open the door, Alanna Colton burst into the apartment toting a stack of fluffy brown towels with her tail on fire.

She came to a stop and bemused, he followed her. She was a combination of edgy sweet and bossy princess. She turned and that direct gaze slammed into him. Hoo-boy, she was riled. "I understand you had a run-in with my brother. What happened?"

"He wanted me to hurry up and fix the horse. I left my fairy wand in my other jeans."

Her mouth dropped open and her eyes widened. "You didn't actually say that."

"I did."

A soft laugh escaped and she shook her head, a gleam of admiration there. "And, you're still here?"

"Left my fairy dust at home, too."

That made her laugh out loud as if she was picturing him as Tinker Bell. "You had a full day pissing off the Coltons, huh?"

"Setting my boundaries is all."

"I'd say they're set. Not many men can or are willing to cross swords with my brother. That sets you apart, Jake." His body leaped in response to her softly spoken compliment, urging him to do something—anything—about it. Hard to keep telling himself this was supposed to be a fake wooing when the sexual tension between them was clouding up his mind in a thick fog.

He nodded, taking a breath, shifting to accommodate the sudden lack of room in his jeans, deciding they needed a benign topic. "The towels are welcome," he said in the sudden silence. Alanna had just realized he was bare-chested. The way her startled green eyes drifted over him set his teeth on edge, the very air vibrating with tension. On undercover operations where he had to get close to a suspect, he hadn't worked this hard to stay detached. But she intrigued him.

He stepped over and slid his hand on top of and under the stack, and their fingers accidentally brushed across one another. She pulled her hand away, and stepped back. Her sudden uncertainty was so at odds with her bold nature. They were still standing close and something tightened in his chest. She was so innocent-looking, angelic even with her honey skin and tawny hair now loose and free, cut into tapered layers. But it was her face that did him in, every time. As a man he was acutely aware of her body, but he was a fool for that face, the innocence and the beauty of it never failing to turn him inside out.

"I saw the maid with them and I wanted to talk

to you about Fowler. Let you know he's…particular. He's also out of his element and that makes him—"

"Confrontational?"

"He's that on a good day. I was going to say nasty. But he's handling the situation the best he can."

"With your father's disappearance," he asked, not having to feign the slight roughness to his voice. Did she have any idea the effect she was having on him? Probably not. He didn't fully understand it. But tell that to the rest of him, which was having no problem at all responding to her. Why he felt protective of her was anybody's guess.

Think about why you're here, boy, and rein in that hunger.

She blanched a bit and looked down, then nodded. If he wasn't mistaken, that was true pain and worry in her eyes before he lost her gaze. If he was to go by what he'd just seen and felt, he would swear on a stack of Bibles that Alanna Colton had nothing to do with her father's alleged kidnapping. But he wasn't here to make snap judgments. He was here for facts.

Her bowed head and the glimpse of this angel's pain worked against his cynicism. He leaned in, reacting on instinct, breathing her scent. Which was dangerous, given his current state of mind—and his tight jeans—but an impulse he seemed helpless to curb. She had been training horses all day and by rights she should smell like a barn. Only she didn't. And standing this close, he noticed how smooth and soft-looking her skin was. For someone working such a physical job, exposed to the sun and wind, he'd expect her to look a bit more…worn.

Then it was that slight overbite. It was cute, and

she wasn't the cute type. She was no-nonsense and wore her confidence as easily as she did her shotgun chaps. What she was, drilling it into his head, was off-limits at least for where his male brain automatically took him. Give her what he suspected she was lacking…a shoulder to lean on. There wasn't anyone in her family she could turn to for comfort and that made for a lonely existence. He knew that too well. It was something he was here to exploit.

He'd started this and now Alanna Colton was going to make this much too real.

But he would do his job, regardless of how the Colton princess was getting under his skin.

Chapter 3

Alanna had always used physical work as a means to keep her own ghosts at bay. If she kept busy, she wouldn't think about how totally worried and upset she was about what had happened to her father.

But work wasn't going to help here…now. Not with Jake's voice so soft and deep. Not when he was so enticing, half-naked, with those sinfully tight jeans, unsnapped and showing off all that muscle in his hips.

The waning afternoon light angled over him, defining the solid ridge of muscles across his shoulders and up his torso, thick and hard across his chest, casting his deeply tanned skin in a patina of bronze. The strong angle of his jaw was highlighted by a stubble of beard, the burnished skin across his cheekbones drawn smooth. He looked like a heavy weighted anchor, not even an earthquake could shake him. The kind of anchor she craved in the deepest part of her where that little girl who had grown up so alone lurked.

It was an unspoken rule that Coltons did not talk to outsiders about family matters. Alanna had grown up an heiress, stood to inherit a large sum of money from all of the Colton holdings, it naturally made her wary of anyone who got too close.

And Jake was too close.

Not only in proximity.

But when Fowler had growled and said Jake's last name like it was a swear word, she couldn't get over here fast enough to find out what had happened. Now she was standing here with a loaded question regarding her father's violent and mystifying disappearance. She lived in an environment where she always had to watch her back, even from her family members. The police seemed to be at a dead end after first clearing Fowler, then Zane. The turmoil the family had been through the last couple of months would rival a soap opera. Then who could trust Marceline? She hated Eldridge and had been acting so secretive and…well… guilty. Did she have something to do with his disappearance? Then there was her stepmother, Whitney. Her insistence and dedication to finding her Dridgeypooh seemed real, but was she a good actress, really worried and upset, or did she hire someone to murder her husband? But if her dad was dead, where was his body? A painful contraction clutched at Alanna's heart.

The need to talk to someone was an aching pressure against her breastbone, holding in the worry and the despair as each day passed. The fact that there was no news wore on her, tearing at her armor.

But Jake was an outsider, an unknown. His reputation aside, she couldn't trust anyone, not inside her family circle or outside it. Not to mention, he'd also undermined her this morning with his refusal to take her seriously over Zorro.

"I suspect your brother isn't the only one struggling with it."

His voice was quiet and full of understanding as if he knew all about the kind of suffering that took chunks out of her. He tested her sense of balance. This bond they seemed to share was as unexpected as it was unwanted. At least on her end. The fear of giving in to that need for comfort was just as strong as her attraction for him. The problem was she hadn't determined if he was friend or foe. But even if he was the former, she couldn't risk it. At this point, she had no control, nor did Fowler believe she had what it took to be the decision maker for the stables. He'd told that to her face once it was clear he was now in charge. He and her father were one in the same mind about her abilities.

Jake would probably be just the same and letting an alpha get closer to her would be tantamount to jumping off the side of a cliff. She might as well give up. Besides, his time was limited. Once he realized Zorro was a lost cause, he would quit. All she had to do was resist temptation. Very potent temptation.

"We're doing the best that we can," she said, her response flat. It was time to turn tail and run.

She wasn't too worried about him being inappropriate. Her worry was all about *her* misbehaving. Jake was potent enough and with his face and body and the sense that he was carrying the kind of pain she was made it all the more enticing to unburden herself to someone who would understand it. The pull of that was magnetic.

Either she wasn't quick enough or he had the instincts of a predator as he blocked her attempt to leave by simply stepping into her path and setting the towels down on the coffee table.

"That's all we can do," he murmured. "The best we can."

There was something in his voice that resonated with her big-time, like he knew what it was like to fight against something, as if constantly climbing a hill. She didn't want this…connection with him. But against her will, it was there.

"I should get going," she said, thinking to get out of his presence would be a good thing. "There's still a lot of work to be done." She should have curbed her impulse to come dashing over here after she'd seen the result of her brother and Jake meeting for the first time.

"You do work hard here."

"You say that as if it surprised you."

"Maybe it did. I expected you to be the queen, I guess. Not the worker bee."

"You really can't believe everything you read in the media, Mr. McCord."

"How about I open my mind and you start calling me Jake?"

Did he want to be friends? Or more? She was getting the vibe that he wanted more, but now she wasn't so sure. Maybe she was just projecting her own wishful thinking.

Curious about his background was an understatement. "How did you get into...horse whispering?"

He shrugged. "Fell into it. Had the knack and something that came naturally."

"Which is really all it is. A fancy and manipulative way of labeling natural horsemanship. There's nothing mystical about it." She had a deeper conviction before she'd seen him calm down Firecracker, but she still held the belief that it was all science, not magic.

She paused to see if he would elaborate, but he said nothing more, and she took that to mean her line of questioning was over. Perhaps for the best. Information was fine, but in hindsight, the more he offered, she supposed, the more she owed in return. Maybe the less they had to talk about, the better.

As if to prove her point, he said, "You were the force behind Colton Valley Ranch Stables. How long have you been working with the horses?"

She stilled briefly, surprised he knew about her past. Not that it was a secret. Alanna knew reports of her work history out in the public domain were pure fluff. It could be that the people who worked for her talked, but it was discouraged. Still, it was more than a little unsettling to think he'd been checking up on her, or asking about her. Her guard increased. "I was the one who brought it up to my father when I was younger and had gotten into barrel racing. He was all about the cattle, but I loved the horses." Still, she found it hard to maintain direct eye contact in the face of Jake's rather intense focus. She doubted he missed much, and after dealing with Fowler's surprise purchase of Zorro and her father's sanctioning of it, her guard was in need of a bit more shoring up before handling this kind of test.

"I'm guessing you're an island here."

Her heart took a jolt. "How so?"

"It's not easy to buck traditions, especially in a male-dominated industry."

Those softly spoken words wormed under the armor she had just been shoring up. She blinked a couple of times, forcing herself to maintain steady eye contact, but it cost her. She could only pray he didn't see how his words affected her down to that seething, frustrated woman deep inside her.

"This is a man's business," she replied, feeling it was a pat and safe answer. There was no denying that ranching and the cowboy way were squarely in the male-dominated arena. Especially in Texas where the men had big, strong personalities, called their women "little ladies" and pampered the hell out of them.

"I got a feeling men in general and Colton men in particular don't have a clue about your strength and staying power."

She had to relax and respond as if this was just a normal getting-to-know-you conversation, which it likely was. She was so used to keeping everything to do with outsiders, hell, with her own family, super-ficial. She didn't want anyone getting to know her, that was all. Especially not this man, with his crystal eyes and overwhelming intensity. He made her nervous and made her pulse race, all at the same time.

She grinned. "That is for sure."

"Discounting you is a mistake, Alanna. I'm sure you'll rub their noses in it before all is said and done."

She tried to maintain a casual air, but his comments made her wonder if he was simply innocent and supportive. Could he really be working for Fowler? Against her? It wouldn't be the first time Fowler would stoop to underhanded ways of gaining information. Was Jake pumping her for information? With all the backstabbing going on, that was not out of the realm of possibility.

She had to consider it and keep Jake in her sights until she could discover if he was here to train Zorro or be her brother's snake-in-the-grass spy.

Or could he have his own personal agenda. She couldn't discount he might want her money or to bed the Colton heiress or both.

Usually she could spot a fake a mile away, but even with her convictions about horse whispering, he was hard to read.

"You gotta play to win." Her lips curved a little, despite the nerves jumping around in her stomach.

"Maybe you can tell me about it sometime."

Damn, he was unnerving and it was unnerving enough, just standing so close. Jake didn't strike her as the kind of man who would work for her brother against her. But, she couldn't underestimate Fowler. She loved him, but he would do what was best for the Coltons' business interests, even foil her attempts to get her way.

She wanted to expand into barrel racers and open a training facility, as well. It would diversify the business and use the expertise of her current employees. But Fowler couldn't possibly know that. She hadn't trusted anyone with her ideas, not even her father. She'd drawn up the plans, scouted all the stallions and broodmares, and projected all the costs and the revenue. This was her baby and she'd sink or swim on her own. That's the way it would be.

Jake was standing far too close—at least, that was the excuse she used for taking a slight step back. He didn't allow the escape, minor though it was. A small step and he was even closer to her than before.

"Maybe," she responded noncommittally. He cocked his head, and there was interest in those blue eyes, but she couldn't be certain exactly what the source of it was. When he turned it on, the heat was so intense, she felt scorched clear down to her toes. She had muscles quivering in places she'd normally have to be naked to have quivering, and he hadn't so much as laid a finger on her.

And, God help her, in that moment, she certainly wanted him to lay fingers and a whole lot more on her.

Trying desperately to shake herself free from such a spellbinding haze, she broke away from his intent gaze and sidestepped around him. Unfortunately, it required her to slide and put her hands briefly on his chest since they were in such close quarters. Without warning he settled his arms around her and spun her toward the door, not letting her go immediately.

His skin burned beneath her palms and the look in his eyes sent weakness through her, her nipples were so tight they hurt.

His head dipped, but he didn't move any closer. The twitch of his lips was more of a real smile now, one that made it all the way to his eyes, crinkling the corners. And wasn't that just lethal and oh so sexy. "Maybe, huh? Don't be too worried about setting me in my place. I can handle rejection."

She couldn't help it. She smiled back. "I'm taking

a shot in the dark here, but I bet that doesn't happen to you often if at all."

He lifted a shoulder, but didn't respond.

She still didn't believe the interest wasn't just a cover for something else.

"I won't keep you any longer." It was his voice, she decided, as if he was hypnotizing her the way he did horses. The timbre of his voice when he said "keep," how it dropped an octave, melted her. "Oh, thanks for the towels." The twinkle resurfaced, as did the eye crinkling. "And for the concern over your brother, but I can handle him." He was intensity personified, which she was clearly struggling to resist. She really didn't need him to be charming, to boot.

"Thank you for the compliments."

"All true."

She was looking straight at him—like she could look anywhere else, even if she wanted to—and she could swear he was telling the truth. Maybe she was paranoid. Maybe he really was simply here to train Zorro and to kill some time flirting with an heiress.

But being paranoid was what had kept her one step ahead of her father and brother, the press, businessmen who thought she was a pushover, and blue-eyed flirts who thought she was starved for attention and might be an easy lay. She couldn't afford to be anything but an island.

But he made it easy to respond to this verbal foreplay he'd so effortlessly begun. Like, even if she didn't have bigger things to worry about, she'd want the attentions of a guy who may be anywhere from a low-down spy to a bedpost notcher.

"You wouldn't be trying to get us both into trouble, would you?"

His lips curved. There was a flash of white teeth. "Maybe," he said before he closed the door.

She stood there for a moment, then realized she was in the hall. How she'd gotten there escaped her.

Maybe she was starved for attention and maybe he was cowboy sexy wrapped up in a gorgeous, well-muscled package with all kinds of sidetracking possibilities.

But everything about her upcoming coup d'état had to stay hush-hush. She was going out on a limb with her plans, going against her father's wishes and now against Fowler's.

She was an island all right. One surrounded by shark-infested waters.

She couldn't trust a soul. Or could she?

Was Jake one of those hungry sharks or was he that lone rescue ship on the horizon?

A few days later, things weren't any better. She'd tossed and turned every night thinking about Jake and his hot body and tame-the-savage-beast sexy voice.

Currently, she was grinning as she stood behind the open stall door and watched Clay Ford, one of her kids from the community project Colton Valley Ranch Gives Back lead Lotus out. She had no worries about the horse acting up. Excluding Clay doing something totally unusual, Lotus would go through the motions on autopilot, as she'd done a million times before.

Other than overseeing the breeding, shoeing and general upkeep of the stables, Alanna had kept pretty much to the arena and away from Zorro's paddock.

She didn't want to come into contact with Jake. Hopefully, he could do his horse-whispering magic, then go back to where he came from.

Just because she took the time to put on makeup and a little lip color or take care to put on some skinny jeans with a black tank and a short-sleeved checked shirt tied under her breasts and a pair of really cute black boots when she normally wore ratty working clothes and worn brown boots didn't mean a thing.

She certainly didn't need to worry about Lotus misbehaving. The one she needed to worry about was herself. In any near vicinity, Jake was potent enough. Up close in any personal proximity, he was downright intoxicating. He was intensity, charm, humor with the kind of focus that made her want to smooth her hair back and moisten her lips. Hell, if she was honest he made her want to do a whole lot more than that. There had been moments where she could have sworn he was thinking the same thing. Thank God there had been plenty of interruptions.

Even if Jake wasn't the enemy she feared—and she wasn't certain about that yet—he wasn't an ally, either. Of any sort. Couldn't be, not in her current circumstances. She just hadn't counted on that bothering her so much.

She closed the stall door as soon as the horse was out, then walked on ahead of them, toward the crossover to the other aisle.

"What if she doesn't go?"

She turned and smiled when she found him still standing just outside the stall. "No worries, Clay. She's quite the lady and will be fine. You did say you wanted to learn to ride."

He nodded, his whiskey-brown eyes still wary of the mare which wasn't a bad thing. A healthy respect for animals that weighed tons of pounds and could with a flick of their head or a movement of their body do some serious damage. He was a handsome kid, one who had that bad boy vibe going and the chip on his shoulder, using a disarming grin to get by. He'd gotten into some trouble with the law over shoplifting, but it was because he was living on the street.

It was satisfying work—more than satisfying, she thought, as she replayed some of the kids' reactions today as they spent time around these magnificent beasts.

In the few months since she'd worked to get the program going, it had never ceased to move her, the way the animals brought out so much in jaded teens who were otherwise so closed off, mostly due to forces beyond their control and largely terrible situations and circumstances. She wasn't sure if she could save any of these kids, the system was a tough place to be, but she hoped she could give them some values and responsibility, show them what it was to work hard for a good cause. Give them a purpose for now and maybe…just maybe they would find something they could use for their continuing journey into adulthood.

She wanted to enrich their lives, giving them windows of opportunity to express and enjoy themselves in ways that conventional therapy methods could not. Oftentimes, the look on a teen's face made it clear how vitally important their being here really was.

It was invigorating, but also exhausting. A whole lot of emotions were being expended into the air of

Colton Valley Ranch Stables every single day, and it did zap a person, even if it was for the very best of reasons. Today had been one of those days. She'd debated even working with Clay, not wanting to risk him or Lotus picking up on her less-than-sharp reflexes, or worse, her tension. Tension that really had nothing to do with the day she'd put in, and everything to do with the man who had invaded her world. But the day she'd put in made hiding those feelings a little tougher. And she needed all the stamina she could muster to make it through this lesson.

She heard some stamping down the aisle and saw it was Mimosa getting shoed. Ah, bad timing. That horse was ornery on her best days and nasty on her worst. She didn't recognize the farrier with a stable hand. He must be new here.

Torn between teaching Clay and calling their lesson quits to deal with the unruly mare, she was just about to get Lotus back into her stall and postpone the lesson when Jake appeared. That man seemed to know exactly when a horse needed to be gentled or soothed. And, just like before, Mimosa calmed as if by…magic.

All up and down the row of stalls, equine heads popped out. Lotus turned and with a soft nicker greeted Jake as if he was one of their own. It was eerie and uncanny. He stood framed in the light, his gray broad-brimmed Stetson casting his face in shadows, his plaid shirt open at the neck, tucked into a pair of worn jeans as he stood with his thumb hooked in the front pocket. The hair on the back of her neck rose and she found that she was holding her breath.

Oh, for the love of God, she wasn't going to buy

in to it, but she was beginning to suspect Jake had some skill which only made her want to run in the other direction.

Then Jake looked up and Mimosa sidled, the look on his face was thunderstruck, pain rolling across his features like a tidal wave. She followed his line of vision right to Clay.

Clay, standing in profile while his attention was on the horse, sensed something, too, as he looked over his shoulder at Jake. Clay's head whipped back around and he took a quick breath and it looked for a moment like fear in his eyes as if he saw the long arm of the law reaching for him.

Her attention went back to Jake, sensing his sudden withdrawal, as if walls had suddenly gone up, Mimosa settled once again.

With Jake's expression fixed and shuttered, there was a grimness around Jake's mouth that made her stomach drop.

Their eyes held, her stomach twisting, feeling as though she had witnessed something, very personal, and so painful.

The farrier finished and Mimosa was led away. Jake settled the gray Stetson onto his head like he was going into battle, and headed toward her and Clay.

She couldn't help but wonder what had put that look of bitterness in his eyes.

Chapter 4

Jake was still reeling from his first glimpse of one of Alanna's teens. It was as if he'd seen a ghost. He resembled Matt so closely that in the dim light of the barn, he thought for a minute it was him. But of course, reality sunk in. Matt was dead. Jake had failed him.

The emotions about his brother's death had been contained, but were still volatile and he reined in his guilt and shame at being unable to help Matt when he really needed Jake the most.

As Jake approached, the look in Alanna's eyes compelled him to put up a wall. He couldn't give in to the pain that still lurked and hit him when he least expected it. The sound of a laugh, the whiff of peppermint or the strum of a guitar. Matt's presence was gone, but the memories of him lingered like long-lost ghosts.

He shook off the effects of his lapse in control, which got easier as he neared Alanna and the kid.

Clay looked at him like he was a cop and Jake relaxed into projecting calm, just as he had with the pretty sorrel mare. Jake recognized the wide eyes, the nervous disposition. Street kids had a sixth sense when it came to the law. He recognized all the signs he'd seen in his kid brother. But Matt was gone and he had a job to do.

"Good afternoon," Alanna said, and there was something about her voice that tangled him up every time. "This is Clay Ford. Clay, this is Jake McCord."

Jake stretched out his hand and noticed how Clay's curiosity replaced his fear. "You're the guy who's supposed to train that crazy black horse."

"One and the same. Are you the guy who's going to get some lessons from Alanna?"

"Yeah, what of it?"

"Nothing. Just being nosy."

That look came over the kid's face again.

Jake turned to find a man walking toward him from the opposite end of the stable. He had a halter and lead rope in each hand and dragged his right foot, just a tad. A memory niggled at him and he studied the man harder. A jolt shocked through him. It was the slight drag that tipped him off. This guy reminded him of the man who had killed Tim Preston. Jake was sure of it. It had been dark and he hadn't gotten a really good look at his face, but that slight drag. He chased the guy but couldn't get a hand on him. He'd disappeared, but that limp stuck in his mind. He'd scoured the area for the perp afterward and looked at every mug-shot book available, but was never able to identify the drug dealer. He would remember his voice for sure. He'd heard it through Tim's mic.

The man came alongside them and Jake watched him. Out of the corner of his eye, he saw Clay stiffen and look down. Jake heard the gunshot again in his mind, the sound deafening in the quiet night. The anguished sound Tim made as he was hit, then the thud of his body as he'd fallen to the concrete. The sound of running footsteps. Then Tim's labored breaths. He'd whispered through the pain, "Tell Jen I love her." Then one long breath as he'd died.

The horse, Thundersparks, made a soft whickering sound, bringing Jake out of his thoughts. He'd endured a lot within the last few years, losing his brother and then the rookie. This job was bringing up a lot of baggage.

Henry drew closer and she dropped her head to snuffle around at his hands.

"Treats after you work a bit, my pretty," he said. Jake thought Henry's voice, the deep nasal quality of it, seemed familiar. Could he be the guy who had *killed Tim*? Jake would have to keep his eye on him. He was undercover and he didn't want to blow it, and second, he at this point had no proof.

He would bide his time and watch this lowlife like a hawk. The man opened the stall door and clipped one of the lead lines to the halter, led the horse out and cross-tied her close to the open door to the paddock.

He moved to another stall door and haltered the horse inside. As he led the horse out, his gaze connected with Jake's and in addition to a flash of something in his eyes before he masked it, there was something dark, something evil and it stirred Jake's protective instincts like nothing else he'd ever known. Rage rose up like a beast inside him, wild, rabid, unchained. He fought it with everything he had, managing to wrestle that monster down and remain calm. He nodded once in greeting.

As the man passed with the big buckskin gelding, Alanna said, "Henry, could you work Damsel, too? She's due to be bred and it'll be good for her to get a bit more exercise."

"Yes, ma'am," Henry said.

"Jake, this is Henry Swango. This is Jake McCord. He's training Zorro."

"Better you than me, mister. That's one crazy horse."

Jake forced himself to take the hand Henry offered, but made the handshake brief.

Tamara came into the barn. "Alanna, could I have a few minutes?"

"Clay, maybe we better save this lesson until later."

"Sure," he said, but Jake could tell the teenager was disappointed.

"I could do it," Jake said before he thought better of it. It was uncanny how much Clay reminded him of Matt. That might have been what was motivating him, but he hated to see the kid not get on a horse. There was nothing like riding.

Alanna said, "Are you sure, Jake? You weren't hired to give riding lessons. If my brother…"

"You let me handle that. I'll take over until you get back."

"All right," she said and walked out with Tamara.

Henry moved on after a glance at Clay who scowled and looked away. He headed toward the rear paddock, then paused and looked back at Jake as if he was making sure he either recognized him or didn't. He slung a halter on a hook by the next stall door and leaned inside. "I'm coming for you next, your ladyship, so no point trying to play invisible." Henry chuckled as he continued to the end.

"Let's take her out to the paddock," Jake said, moving up closer to Clay. "You'll want to choke up on the lead rope and take her halter, but just on the edge. You don't want to get your hand wedged in there if she decides to bolt."

"Bolt?"

"Yeah, but…" He indicated the horse.

"Lotus."

"But Lotus looks very docile. Aren't you, girl." The horse nickered softly at him again.

"She likes you."

"She likes you, too." Jake placed Clay's hand on the halter and coiled up on the rope a bit. "You want to walk her to the center of the aisle. Stay just to the front of her forelegs, but to the side of her head."

"Not out in front?"

"You can direct her with the rope, but I want you to stay where you can see if she's reacting negatively to anything. You don't want to be five feet ahead of her and have her spook or rear and yank you on your ass, or worse."

Clay snickered. "No. Ass-yanking doesn't sound like fun."

Jake laughed. "It isn't."

"Says the guy with experience?"

"Hey, everyone has to start somewhere, me included."

He was pretty sure Alanna was avoiding him. After

dropping off those towels a few days ago and his attempts to get her to start to see him less as a stranger and more of a friend, he wanted some more alone time with her. But on this big spread it was hard to accomplish that with all the people who worked here, not to mention Alanna was constantly busy. He felt frustrated and not only in trying to corral Alanna, but his training with Zorro wasn't going well and he couldn't quite figure out why.

Most horses…all right, every horse he'd ever come into contact with, he could bend to his will, show him he was the leader and they would fall into line. Not Zorro. He fought him every step of the way. It had been three days and he still couldn't get close to the animal. He kept moving away every time Jake approached. He'd even spent some time inside the paddock just letting Zorro get used to his presence.

"You think you can tame that stallion?"

"I believe I can."

"And, that's enough?"

He had to focus on the training. He wasn't here for that, but the horse drew him and Jake wanted him to have a better quality of life. Right now he was wary of everyone. Just as Clay was. He was a lot like Zorro. Abused, lost, alone.

"Don't underestimate the power of believing something will happen. I visualize it and keep an open mind. Anything is possible."

Jake should focus more on why he was here and that was to get information about the family. He might have established motive for Alanna; she wanted to actually be in control, not to have to play second fiddle to her father and meddling brother, but he couldn't seem to fully give over to the thought she master-minded her father's kidnapping.

Clay snorted. "Right. That's what adults say to en-courage kids even when there's not even a snowball's chance in hell it will happen."

He wasn't here to help disillusioned teenagers find their way. Jake turned to him and stopped. "Here is fine." Then he took a breath. "You have all you need to get where you want to go. Seriously, believing is powerful." Clay shrugged like he didn't care. Jake hadn't been able to get through to Matt, either. "Drape the rope over her neck," he said, using hand gestures to show how he should do it. "Then hook it around, so it makes one big hoop. You'll use that as your reins."

Henry was on the far end of the paddock working with the three horses on a lunge line. Jake didn't like this development. He was worried Henry would try to recruit one of the impressionable, vulnerable teens. He was more determined to keep tabs on this poten-tially dangerous ranch hand. "I don't need a bridle thing?" Clay asked, his voice a bit wobbly. Jake fo-cused on him again.

"Apparently not with Lotus. Ms. Colton would have bridled her once she got the horse out of the stall."

His expression was wry. "She gave me a horse that babies ride." It was clear Clay was disgusted.

"Not necessarily, but an easy one. Not everything needs to be a battle, especially the first time you learn to ride."

Lotus snorted and shook her mane. Clay jumped away with a startled look.

Jake tried not to laugh. He went over to the kid

and said, "That's a contented snort. She wants you to ride her."

"Don't laugh," Clay said.

Jake nodded, schooling his features. "Let's get you up on her."

Then Alanna's soft voice came from right beside him. "Jake is a professional. He would never laugh."

Caught off guard, Jake turned toward her and caught her eye. The gleam of shared amusement was in the green depths. He must have been concentrating too much. Hardly anyone sneaked up on him. Being this close to her made it hard to think clearly. She shifted her focus to the horse, then to Clay. Pointing at the stirrup, she said, "Hold the pommel with your left hand, left foot in the stirrup, and up you go. Right leg over the back end, one smooth lift as you push up on your left leg."

Jake backed off as Alanna took over. He lingered, watching her patiently and expertly teach Clay to ride, keeping part of his attention on Henry. The surprise and joy on the teen's face obviously fueled Alanna.

So the Colton heiress wasn't as much of a princess as Jake had first thought and she was getting down into the trenches with her staff. Here she was giving her time and resources to this troubled kid. The pull of her was just this side of magnetic. His instincts told him that she couldn't have done anything to her father, but the facts warred with his gut.

Chatting up the staff, he'd only found out the family was private but one effusive stable hand talked about Marceline Colton, Whitney's daughter from her first marriage whom Eldridge adopted and made into a Colton. How she always seemed to be lurking around the stables. He had photos of all the Coltons and he had spied a beautiful, shapely blonde several times, but he hadn't yet been introduced. Then he'd hit pay dirt with Tamara. She had let it slip that Alanna and her father were at odds about the stable. She'd overheard them arguing one day before he'd disappeared. There seemed to be some dispute as to who was in charge. Tamara said Alanna worked hard and knew what she was doing. Her family should let her actually run the stables instead of acting like she was the figurehead.

It made Jake waffle and wonder all over again if Alanna had made the decision to do away with her father and take control of the stables that way. Now it seemed Fowler was blocking her and usurping her authority when he bought the horse Alanna didn't approve in advance. That must have rankled, especially if Alanna had something to do with Eldridge's kidnapping.

With the lesson over, Alanna sent Clay off to dinner. As she headed back to the stable, he came up alongside her.

"You enjoyed that."

She was beaming as they passed into the barn's interior. The sun was waning, getting ready to set. There was a vibrancy about her that added color to her cheeks and lit her from within. And she'd been pretty powerful stuff before.

She reached Lotus's stall and he slid the door open as she led the horse inside. "Was this your brainchild? Colton Valley Ranch Gives Back?" He leaned his back against the side of the stall door as she lifted up the stirrup and hooked it over the saddle horn. She reached for the buckle on the girth and grunted a little as she released the tab.

"Yes, it was. I have always wanted to help the community, get the word out there about how wonderful horses can be for pleasure and work and therapy. Some of the kids are responding beautifully to working at the stables where they hadn't responded in any other capacity."

She pulled the saddle from Lotus's back. Jake pushed off the wall and took it from her. "Like Clay."

He faced her and their fingers brushed again, but Alanna didn't remove her fingers. A whiff of her fragrance among all the other pungent smells of the stall only added to his attraction. The killer was it wasn't some fancy perfume. It was the fresh scent of soap and shampoo. His body soared to life. Like it needed encouragement. Who'd have thought the wafting scent of citrus could give a guy a raging hard-on?

She let go of the saddle and turned back to Lotus. "Exactly like him. He was living mostly on the streets, got caught for shoplifting and instead of juvie, he came here." She unhooked the lead rope and reached for a brush hanging in a basket. Pulling one out, she started to stroke the horse's coat. "I offered him a constructive atmosphere instead of destructive. A place where he could live and get back what it felt like to be safe."

Against his will, memories of Matt surfaced.

She tilted her head and studied him. The look in her eyes was soft and tender, and it did crazy things to his heart. "Did you know someone who lived on the streets? Is that why you have that look on your face?"

She gave Lotus a few more swipes, then dropped

the brush into the bucket. He straightened and followed her out. "I knew someone once," he said.

She headed for the crossover and the tack room. Opening the door, she indicated a saddle rack and he let the pad and blanket drop away into her hands as he slid the saddle in place. She walked over to a blanket bar and set the blanket and pad there.

He was busy neatly adjusting the girth strap, getting it ready for the next time the saddle would be used.

"Making a difference counts," she said. "It feels good to do something for the greater good."

He wondered if that was because there was so much infighting in her family. "What prompted you to take on this project?" She turned to him and opened her mouth.

"Alanna?"

The sound of Fowler's voice sent her gaze to the door. "Here," she called.

He appeared, looking every inch the oil baron. His mouth pinched when he saw Jake. "I need a word with you."

"Me?" she asked, although his gaze was on Jake.

"Yes," he said. "And, you, how goes it with Zorro?"

"It's Jake. Just in case you forgot my name. It's progressing," Jake said.

"See that it continues to progress," he said curtly, then turned to Alanna. "Come on. We don't want to be late for dinner. You know how Whitney gets and it's even worse now Daddy is missing."

"Can't we just talk at dinner?" Her voice was weary and Jake wanted to step in and lessen her burden, but that wasn't why he was here. He had to curb the impulse.

"No. I don't want to discuss this at the house."

"Very well. Thank you, Jake, for your help."

"My pleasure," he said as Fowler's eyes narrowed.

"He can finish up in here," Fowler said, taking Alanna's arm and ushering her out.

She was turning into a paradox for him. She exuded both vulnerability and strength. But she was warming to him. Fowler's interruption was ill timed. His gut told him she was about to say something no one in the Colton family had ever heard from her. He was sure she didn't expose her vulnerability to any of them. That made him feel sad for her and wasn't a good thing in his line of work. Neutrality was what he needed to maintain and he fought against with her.

There was still a wariness about her that had him wondering what it was going to take to win her over completely. Which was insanity. Because winning her over was not the objective here. Solving her problem wasn't the goal he needed to achieve. He was here to get the dirt on her so she could either be eliminated as a suspect or she could be arrested. Once that was accomplished, he would go home and she'd either stay here or end up in jail. So there was no point in winning anything.

As soon as they were out the door Jake slipped to the opening and peered out. They were heading for the Cisco barn. Shutting off the light and closing the door, he shadowed behind them. Fowler's voice carried on the wind.

"I'd rather wait until we got to the stable office to tell you what this is about," he snarled.

"Why all the secrecy?"

"It involves delicate matters and should be discussed in private."

"In other words, I'm going to argue and you don't want everyone to hear."

"Alanna. Wait until we get to the office."

"Okay," she said on a sigh. "But this would be a good time to tell you that I intend to expand the operation. Initiate and open a training center and purchase a string of broodmares and two stallions I have scouted to begin a breeding program for barrel racers."

"For the love of…" He grabbed her arm and all but dragged her the rest of the way. Jake wanted to throttle the man for treating her so roughly, but kept at a safe distance.

Their heels made a clicking sound on the concrete aisle as they headed toward the office and the door closed with a slam behind them.

Jake noticed there was a gap in the top of the office and the beams. He was going to have to climb if he wanted to hear what they were saying. In the dim interior, he found a makeshift ladder that looked like it was used to access the skylights. He set his foot on the first rung and was up into the beams.

"…out of your mind…thinking…not going…"

He heard pieces of the conversation as he carefully made his way over to the office.

"I don't care whether you like it or not, Fowler. I'm in charge of the stables."

"You think you can make this end run because Daddy is absent? He wouldn't approve this."

"I'm sick of hearing that. My name is listed as manager of the stables. I'm the one who practically grew up on a horse's back. They were better companions than half the people I knew. I want to do this my way."

"Alanna. Be reasonable. We have enough turmoil as it is."

"That's just an excuse and you know it. You want to take over everything. I'm not a figurehead, Fowler. I know more about horses, breeding and stock than you do. Zorro was a huge mistake and bringing in a *horse whisperer* isn't going to do a damn bit of good. If you had consulted me in the first place, I would have told you he wasn't worth…"

"Don't you chastise me, sister. That horse has champion bloodlines and will be an asset to the stable."

"You don't like to admit you were wrong."

By the look on Alanna's face, it was clear Fowler sifted out the things he didn't want to discuss and discarded them. "I'll freeze the assets, Alanna."

She pushed a lock of wild long hair behind her ear, her eyes widening. "You wouldn't dare." Her voice was hushed with shock.

He chuckled cynically. "Try me."

She folded her arms over her chest, drawing her composure around her like a queen's cloak, her face masking what she was feeling inside. But she sure was projecting it with her eyes as they snapped when she lifted her chin. "You've made your point."

The tension left Fowler's body and he leaned against the desk, running his hand over his face. "Fine."

"What did you want to order me to do?" she snapped.

"Alanna." His voice held a warning in it, but Alanna didn't heed it. She was deep into her anger and resentment now. He didn't exactly blame her for her reaction. Fowler lived up to his reputation.

"Well, it seems that's your MO," she said through clenched teeth. "Tell me."

"I want to sell off half the stock. I have a list."

"What?" Alanna flinched like the words were blows. "They're not ready."

"You spend too much time training them. It's a money sink and unnecessary."

Her arms dropped and her hands fisted at her sides. "You really do think I'm simply warming those saddles. Don't you? Every cent I spend returns double or triple when I price those horses out." She flung her arm out, pointing to the stables in the distance. "It builds our reputation. Do you think that just happened? No!" She tossed her head. Her blond hair spilling over her shoulders and rippling down her back. "I built it. You have no right to tell me what to do in this respect. At least Daddy would back me on that!"

He lifted a sardonic brow and said slyly, "You're so sure about that?"

"Fowler." Her voice was like steel. "You aren't doing this."

"I am. Get used to it. Daddy isn't here now. Is he?"

She closed her eyes for a moment and said, "No, he isn't." Her breath hitched. "He's gone."

"Sometimes, Alanna, I wonder about you and if your disagreement and passion for the stables made you—"

She advanced on him in a rush and slapped him, her face broadcasting he'd pulled the final straw. The crack of it echoed all the way to the rafters.

Shaking with anger, she said, "Don't you ever accuse me of harming Daddy ever again."

"Fair enough," he drawled, rubbing at the red spot on his cheek. "Don't you ever slap me again, sister." Jake didn't like the menace in his voice.

Fowler started to leave, but realized Alanna wasn't with him. "Aren't you coming?"

"No. I've suddenly lost my appetite," she said, her voice clipped.

"Dinner," he growled. "Whitney—"

"She can go to the devil and so can you, *brother*."

The door shut behind him and she murmured, "I hope you choke on it." Her breath came in short, shallow gasps. Covering her eyes, she burst into tears. Backing against the desk, she sat on the edge and sobbed.

The sound of the raw pain in her voice pissed Jake off and he wanted to take Fowler apart and kick his ass all over Colton Valley Ranch for hurting her. Taking away her power and leaving her ineffectual. She'd been bold enough to make a solid move and tell him her plans for expanding and he'd discounted them without even asking questions. The man was so closed minded it made Jake want to take a shot at opening that mind of his.

But he'd done something to Jake's way of thinking. Just when he was convinced Alanna was innocent, Fowler inserted doubt. He wasn't sure he was the best judge when it came to this woman.

Could it be her disputes with her father, the constant undermining of her skill and authority over the stables, had pushed her too far?

At the sound of shod hooves on the concrete, Jake

jerked out of his thoughts. He moved quickly out of the rafters and back down the ladder. The door to the arena was open and as he watched, Alanna Colton, riding hell-bent for leather, streaked through on a horse that looked like it could run forever, muscled for speed.

Anger and velocity didn't mix well in any vehicle. He took off at a run for his own horse.

Chapter 5

With the wind tearing at her hair and the moon bobbing in the dark, star-filled sky, Alanna pushed her horse Somerset to even greater speed, the landscape covered in shadows. He moved powerfully beneath her, as she bent low over the animal's neck. It was as if she wanted to outrun her pent-up frustrations, her anger and her aching unmet needs.

There was always the sense of betrayal by both her brother and her father in this matter. She was due respect. She'd earned it every step of the way with her blood, sweat and tears.

Tears that now flowed down her cheeks mixed with both sorrow and anger.

The moonlight illuminated the road ahead of her, but she knew this countryside so well as she'd ridden it and played in it since she was a kid.

She'd fought hard all her life for recognition and independence in a family that always seemed to be at odds. She was part of a strange and murky legacy evidenced by the checkered pasts of her father and uncle. It was unnerving to say the least that she'd come from serial killer stock and the rumored information that her father had been a notorious bank robber.

How does someone overcome that kind of a background?

Who could she ever depend on?

Over the whoosh of the wind she heard the pounding of hooves and looked over her shoulder to find a man on a galloping blue roan. Her mouth tightened. All she needed was to spar with sexy-as-hell Jake McCord.

She veered off the road and headed to open ground, spurring Somerset on. But the roan was fast and streaked past her. Jake reached out to her bridle, slowing her horse, starting her to sputter in anger.

She came out of the saddle spitting mad and went toe-to-toe with him. "Who do you think you are?" she shouted. "You had no right!"

"I'm only trying to keep you from breaking your fool neck," he said sounding way too calm. Her irritation escalated. On the heels of Fowler's obvious disrespect when it came to running the stables, Jake got her back up over a simple gallop in the moonlight.

"Who appointed you my guardian?" It wasn't Jake she was angry at, but he did something to her that always made her feel as if she was on the verge of disaster and all it would take would be one wrong move.

Taking a deep breath, she forced herself to concentrate on the anger swirling in her. She had to summon every ounce of determination to hold his gaze. His face was cast in uncompromising lines, his mouth compressed, his expression shuttered. He held her gaze for a moment, then leaned forward and rested his hands on his hips, a strange tension springing up between them that made Alanna feel as if she were about to shatter.

"You're obviously upset and I'm quite aware you don't need a guardian, but you do look like you could use a friend."

Everything stilled in her at the sound of his voice offering her what she had only thought moments ago wasn't possible. Waves of loneliness washed over her. Who could she depend on? Him? She didn't even know him and she still wasn't sure if he wasn't part of a plan Fowler had initiated to influence her.

The expression on his face was so sincere, but she was still so wary, so afraid to give herself over to anyone's care, especially this man who was still a stranger.

"I don't need a friend," she refuted. But that was such a lie. She really did need someone to confide in. She could never talk to anyone in her family and definitely not the servants. Her good friend Samantha was a great choice, but she had a husband and three kids to keep her busy.

"I think you do," he said. "My shoulder is ready and waiting." He offered. He leaned into her space, surrounding her, corralling her. Alanna's heart skipped a beat, and then kicked into overdrive as he dared to get closer, though wariness was not the dominant emotion. It should have been, but it wasn't.

She closed her eyes and wanted nothing more than

to flee again. As much as she wanted someone to confide in, it felt too dangerous. There was nothing easy about leaning on him or in to those oh-so-broad shoulders. That strange sense of desire and anticipation crept along her nerves. If she leaned forward, he would kiss her. She could see the promise in his eyes and felt something wild and reckless and completely foreign to her raise up in answer, pushing her to close the distance, to take the chance.

She took a step back, realizing how close she was to him. "What happened?" he prompted.

What happened? A simple question as loaded as a shotgun that had been primed and pumped. "Jake, please just leave me alone."

His gaze darkened even more and a muscle in his jaw twitched, the charged silence between them growing more electric with every heartbeat. Why did he do this to her whenever he was near? "No can do, not when you left the stables like your tail was on fire." Then he said gruffly, "Let me help."

She folded her arms over her chest and looked away, trying to defuse the building heat. There was something…some underlying intuition that told her he knew exactly how she felt. That he knew the loneliness and the isolation, that he was just as starved for human touch and the kind of understanding that feeds the soul. Oh, God, she wanted to just let go and give him a piece of herself, but she was so terrified she wouldn't get it back or she would be tricked and her heart would be exposed. Better to remain an island. "You can't help. There's no one who can help me. I'm used to taking care of myself."

"Maybe you are, but I'm offering. I don't like seeing you like this. Talk to me."

His masculine scent feathered along her nerve endings, setting off tingling sensations everywhere, and Alanna closed her eyes, struggling against the thick, pulsating warmth that flooded through her. It felt like he was offering a lot more than his attention and sympathy. She couldn't accept because if he showed her any kind of compassion, she wasn't sure she could hold back what she knew would happen and she wasn't sure her heart could handle that right now.

She couldn't trust him even if she wanted to, she didn't have the energy right now to fight off a kitten let alone this sexy, powerful man. Without responding, she reached past him to grab up her horse's reins. His arm shot out and he roughly caught her wrist.

Everything inside her stilled and the anger dissolved into something hotter, fiercer and totally overwhelming. She would have been all right if he hadn't touched her, but this man sent pure adrenaline pumping through her. The same frantic excitement she had experienced when she'd delivered the towels, creating such havoc she could barely think.

"Jake." She turned to him, pleading, "Let me go."

Jake had been watching her with such grim tension around his mouth that he appeared almost angry, the charged silence between them growing more electric with every heartbeat.

Just when Alanna felt she couldn't endure it one moment longer, a tremor shuddered through him and his eyes were suddenly smoky and heavy lidded. He dragged her against him, whispering her name, and then his mouth slammed into hers, and her eyes closed, every nerve in her body primed for the first touch of his lips against hers. Nothing could have prepared her for the chaos that contact created, and Alanna grabbed at the fabric of his shirt as he crushed her against him in an unbreakable hold.

His mouth moved against hers with the kind of thoroughness she'd been aching to experience, and she yielded to his hungry kiss. He made a low sound and silently she tightened her free arm around his waist, a deep poignant feeling unfolding in her chest as she responded to the gentleness, the warmth, the protectiveness of his enveloping embrace. She had never really had a chance, she realized. She'd been attracted and intrigued from the moment she first saw him crossing the arena floor.

Spanning her jaw and inhaling sharply, he molded their bodies together as he roughly caressed her back. He was the one still, solid thing in her wildly reeling world, and Alanna clung to him, her mouth going slack beneath his, the heat and the hardness of his body sapping her strength.

He finally tore his mouth away, his breathing raw and labored. He said nothing, just stared down at her for a long moment, awareness arcing between them like electricity. He watched her, his eyes a dark, bottomless blue, his expression intense. Was he trying to read her? She felt those eyes were reaching right into her soul.

He claimed her mouth again only this time the driving urgency challenged his control, and Alanna's breath caught on a sob, her body responding hotly to his. Roughly banding his arm across the small of her back, he pressed his hips to hers.

Alanna struggled with the nearly uncontrollable desire to let go, to lose herself in the unequaled passion he was offering her, but she couldn't. As much as she wanted to, it was a risk she dared not take because of the circumstances, her uncertainty and her position. And she twisted her head away, fighting for every breath.

"Jake, God, stop," she choked out, her own body turning on her. She clung to him, fighting for one sliver of rationality in the delirium of sensations. "Please, Jake. I can't."

Shuddering violently, he tightened his hold on her, his embrace nearly crushing her. She could feel the conflict within him and she closed her eyes, a heaviness radiating through her. It was cruel to let this go on.

"Alanna, just tell me what's wrong."

The sudden rush of despair was so intense she could barely unlock her jaw to speak, and tears welled in her eyes, then slowly slipped down her cheeks. A sob escaped her as she murmured, "I can't, Jake. I just can't."

She pulled away and grabbed up the reins of her horse and quickly mounted, wheeling him around, forcing Jake to move out of the way of the beast.

For a moment she met his steely gaze with longing, then dug her heels into Somerset's flanks and the horse took off like a shot back into the night.

She raced toward home, tears blurring her eyes, but luckily her mount knew exactly where she was going. She cried even harder when she heard no telltale sound of those hooves pounding behind her. She was a fool to think she could ever live a normal life.

Her background saw to that. Now that she was enmeshed in her father's kidnapping, she wasn't sure how long it would be before Sheriff Watkins would come knocking at her door. Another reason to steer clear of Jake. She didn't want to drag him into this investigation and throw suspicion on a hardworking, innocent man.

She brushed at her tears and tried to calm herself, even as she signaled her horse to slow down into a cantor, then a trot and finally into a walk as she approached the stables. She dismounted outside the barn and the stable boy took the horse's bridle, wishing her a pleasant evening as she thanked him.

Solemnly, she headed for the big, imposing mansion, chaos raging inside her. Struggling for breath against her emotions, reaching for some composure, she schooled her features. It wasn't smart to go into that house without her armor in place.

Taking a deep breath and letting it out, she drew it around her like a cloak.

Held on to it like a lifeline.

The Colton Valley Ranch mansion stood at the end of a half-mile-long front drive that led to an ornate black iron gate, more ornamental than for security purposes as there was open grassland and woods on both sides, Colton Valley Ranch lettered in gold across both gates. Immaculately preserved and painted a pristine white, a graceful horseshoe-shaped double stairway led from the ground level to the upper rooms of the vast house. Alanna, along with Fowler, lived in the left wing. She quietly entered through the back of the house and used the bootjack to remove her muddied riding boots. In her stocking feet, she carefully and silently ghosted into the huge gleaming kitchen, the aroma of head cook Bettina Morely's meal still lingered in the air. Alanna had to curse Fowler for ruining her dinner. Bettina could cook. She went to the fridge, but before she could open it, she heard, "There you are, Miss Alanna. I already fixed a plate for you. We started off with clams, Spanish chorizo, tomato, marigold and parmesan focaccia, then butternut bisque."

Alanna's mouth was already watering. "You're killing me, Mrs. Morely."

She smiled and opened the fridge taking out a covered plate and a small bowl. "The main dish is—"

"Sea scallops, Brussels sprouts, artichokes, carrots, parsnips and bacon. I can smell it in the air."

"And dessert? Any guesses?"

"That's an easy one. The aroma of the apples gives it away. King David cobbler. It's my favorite and I'm sorry I missed dinner."

"I made crème fraîche just for you."

Alanna closed her eyes and made a yum humming noise, her mouth watering for the rich, tangy butterfat–sour cream confection. "You do spoil me."

"How about I fix you up a tray and bring it to your room?"

"Thank you so much, Mrs. Morely. That would be so appreciated. I'll get a quick shower and then be ready to eat."

"Take your time, dear."

All she had to do was make it to the left wing just a hop and a skip from the kitchen and into her suite of rooms without running into anyone. She made it as far as the double doors to her room.

"Alanna. May I have a word with you?" Dammit, she swore under her breath. *Whitney.* The soft breathy voice echoed in the hall. It was amazing how her stepmother's soft voice could carry.

She hoped to at least have a shower before a lecture.

"Yes, of course," Alanna said, plastering a smile on her lips and turning to face her. Her stepmother could be quite unpredictable and often over-the-top.

"Why did you miss dinner?"

Alanna sighed. This woman acted like she was still a child. "I was busy in the stables. I do have work to do there."

"That is apparent." She sniffed delicately, wrinkling her nose.

"I was just on my way to shower."

"I'm sure you got Mrs. Morely to make you up a plate?"

"I did."

"Good, but you know I'd prefer you attend dinner."

Tired and still raw from her encounters with Fowler and Jake, her voice came out flat. "Yes, I'm aware."

"My, you're snippy tonight."

"I'm sorry, Whitney. I'm very tired and would love to shower, eat and go to bed. I've got another full day tomorrow." Unlike her stepmother who floated around the house looking the all-important wife of the prosperous rancher.

"It's important that the family eats together. Especially now that my Dridgey-pooh is missing," Whitney murmured, casting big blue eyes full of tears at her stepdaughter. "I've been feeling just ragged with worry, not knowing what to think. I swear I'm so close to having a spell."

Alanna didn't have the patience to handle Whitney tonight. "We're all so very worried about him. But hopefully the investigation will break and we'll know something soon." She turned and patted her back.

Whitney nodded, dabbing at her eyes with a lace handkerchief. "Yes, I hope you're right."

"I'll see you tomorrow," Alanna managed as she made her escape and slipped into her room.

She went into the bathroom, only turning on a low watt light because she didn't want any more illumination. She stripped off her clothes and turned on the many-jetted spray in the open area.

As the water pummeled her tired muscles, all she could think about was Jake and the way he'd looked out in the moonlight. Her nerves were absolutely raw and throbbing. The memory of his full sensual mouth against hers made her heart hitch, then start to pound.

Lord, she had to make the memories stop. But she didn't know how. Groaning out loud, knowing one thing for sure. She was going to lose it and turn into a basket case if this kept up.

Between Jake and Fowler, she couldn't decide what she feared most. Losing all credibility here on the ranch or losing her sanity in the arms of Jake McCord.

After drying off and toweling her hair, she loosely braided it, then threw on a robe. As she came out into the living area of her suite, she noticed Mrs. Morely had arranged the tray on the coffee table and, bless her, had even lit candles. The woman was so thoughtful.

The aroma made her stomach grumble, but before

she could sit down and dig in there was a knock on her balcony door.

She started and glanced over her shoulder. Her heart stuttered and then almost stopped. Jake Mc-Cord stood there looking more than determined. She closed her eyes, knowing she didn't have the energy to wrangle with him tonight.

She opened her eyes and then got up, drawing her robe tighter around her. She released the lock on the door and opened it.

"Jake."

He gave her a thorough scrutiny from head to toe, his gaze so potent, so heady, that Alanna had to hold on to the doorjamb to steady herself. As if attuned to her reaction, he gave her a small half smile that spoke absolute volumes. He spoke, his voice husky. "I had to make sure you got home safely. I couldn't sleep until I checked." If he didn't stop looking at her like that, she was going to be even more tired in the morning because she wouldn't get a wink.

She should fight off the attraction, but even now, the pull of it was like a vortex.

His face was heavily shadowed by the broad brim of his gray Stetson, but that only emphasized the strength of his jawline coated with the end-of-the-day stubble that looked sexy tough on him. "The offer of my shoulder and ear is freestanding. Anytime."

She tilted her head in exasperation. "You are persistent."

"When I want something," he murmured.

Her heart rolled over, a strange fluttery feeling unfolding in her middle. She wasn't one to beat around the bush or ignore something right in her face. It wasn't only what was troubling her that he was after. She was sure of that, and the thought only made her knees wobblier. "There's something going on between us. We both feel it and it's complicated. I'm not sure how to deal with it. Getting involved with me, Jake, it's not easy."

"Nothing worth having is, but, yeah, there's something all right. I want to kiss you again, but I shouldn't. You're right. It would be complicated."

"Why?"

He bent his head, his hat brim covering his eyes for a moment, and then he looked up. "I'm not exactly the root-burying kind of guy."

That meant he wasn't going to stay and maybe she could deal with that if he could be discreet. What was she thinking? Any man she got involved with would need to have a pedigree, but Alanna cared more about character than she did money and prestige. Her family could be real stuffy about that. But, look at Zane. He *did* marry his administrative assistant. Maybe there was some hope.

Jake was an imposing, sexy as all get-out man, yet even standing here in her robe with absolutely nothing beneath it, she trusted him implicitly not to make any type of move on her unless she made the move on him first and really, could she deny that? No. So at least she was being honest with herself. "I need to ask you a very serious question."

"Shoot."

"Are you softening me up because my brother asked you to?"

He frowned. "What?"

"Are you working for my brother?" She held her

breath. There was something about Jake that was so damned honest that she would believe him if he told her.

His mouth tightened, then he rasped out, "Yes."

Her heart plummeted and she went to slam the door in his face, but the toe of his boot prevented it. "It's not what you think. I'm working for your brother, but I'm here in one capacity—to tame Zorro. That's it. I'm not spying on you or trying to manipulate you in any way for your brother."

"How do I know you're telling the truth?"

"Because, frankly, Alanna, I don't like your brother and, furthermore, I wouldn't cross the street to do any favors for him."

She nodded, then realized it was way past dinner service in the apartment and he wouldn't have a hot meal. Mrs. Morely always prepared more than Alanna could eat.

She took a breath and said, "Have you eaten?"

"No. I was distracted." To punctuate his statement, his stomach grumbled.

"Before I invite you in and very generously share my dinner with you, I'm not going to promise anything."

"Fair enough. I appreciate the invitation and the meal."

She was losing her perspective where Jake was concerned and sharing a meal with him was just that. Nothing more.

Yeah, right.

This was still such a bad idea.

Chapter 6

Alanna got him settled in a chair near the coffee table, trying to ignore how romantic it was with the candlelight. She'd ducked into her bedroom to put on a pair of yoga pants and a loose top, then made a quick trip to the kitchen to get a bowl, plate and another set of silverware for him.

Once she had dished out the food, she sat back and devoured the bisque. They ate for several moments and everything was superb.

"My compliments to the chef," Jake said, scraping his spoon against the bowl before he set it down.

"Mrs. Morely. She's been the cook here as long as I can remember."

"I know this is none of my business—"

"Yet, here you are."

There was a hint of a smile in his eyes as he said, "You were upset. You pounded out of there—"

"Like my tail was on fire." It was more like she was playing with fire and that could get her severely burned.

He leaned forward, setting his forearms on his thighs. "Well, yeah. I don't like seeing you upset," he said in a low, pointed tone. "Does this have something to do with what your brother wanted to talk to you about?"

"I don't make a habit of discussing my family with outsiders," she said hotly.

For the longest time he simply looked at her, his eyes giving nothing away. But she sensed a deep discontentment about him, as if he were enduring some inner struggle. That made her feel like she was dancing on a hot tin roof.

"Doesn't seem like you have anyone to talk to at all. I'm not going to repeat anything you say to me. I'm not that guy."

That statement just struck so true to home that she blinked a couple of times at his astute observation. "Yes, okay, it had something to do with my brother."

He blew out a breath. "He has a reputation so my guess wasn't a stretch. You don't have to tell me what it was about, but all I can say is I expect you stood up to him."

"I tried, but Fowler now has control of the purse strings."

"For the stable? He's trying to squeeze you out?"

Suddenly feeling she had said too much, she looked down, his stare penetrating and quite volatile. "No, he just wants me as a figurehead. He wants to sell off half the stock. Stock that's not ready for auction. He discounts me and my abilities, my skill and worse yet, he's insinuating my daddy feels the same way."

She heard him draw in a deep breath, and then the couch moved. With infinite gentleness, Jake hooked his knuckles under her chin and forced her head up. There was a wealth of support in his eyes as he met her gaze with heart-stopping directness. "That's insulting and closed minded and unfair," he said very quietly. "I've seen you out there and knew this stable by its reputation for well-trained and well-bred stock. Why does he want to mess with that?"

There was so much emotion unfolding inside her that Alanna could barely breathe as she whispered, "Because I think he's spooked by Daddy's kidnapping and it's making him feel insecure. Not that Fowler can't handle Colton Incorporated. That's not what I'm saying. I think he feels he needs to run roughshod over everything to make sure it's running smoothly and efficiently in accordance with Daddy's wishes. Regardless of what people think about Fowler, he cares about Daddy's approval. He would never want to disappoint him."

"To hell with Fowler," Jake said. "What are you going to do about it?"

The temptation to tell Jake everything was intoxicating. "What makes you think I will?"

His mouth quirked and his eyes lit up. "Oh, I'm positive you will."

She wasn't sure she could say it out loud. It was such a monumental move and would shake Fowler and her father to their toes. It was so unexpected from someone who had been so loyal, giving everything to the stables and to her family. It was a bit panic inducing, but she wasn't a Colton for nothing. She had a stronger backbone than her brother Fowler would ever give her credit for.

"Talk to me, Alanna," he murmured. "I'm not asking for anything. I just want you to talk to me." His eyes were dark and smoky just like they had been before he'd kissed her. As if drawn against his will, he cupped her face in his callused hands and softly stroked her cheeks with his thumbs.

Her senses thrown into a mindless muddle by the feeling of his hands on her face, she tried to hold on to her sense of self-preservation and not let her heart get tangled up with his, but that was currently a losing battle. "I have funds of my own. I could open my own stable."

She could see the faintest glimmer of amusement in his eyes. "That would get Fowler's goat and serve the bastard right," he said, his voice deep and heated.

She had a nearly uncontrollable urge to settle into his arms, but even in the daze she was in, she knew it would be a mistake. She knew she had to put some distance between them, but her common sense was at war with her heart and she made no move to separate from him. Having someone on her side, listening to her and supporting her was deeply intoxicating.

"It would be a big step, but it's hard to leave something I've put so much time into."

"I know it's hard, but, Alanna, better to be your own woman than his lackey." His expression altered and the glint in his eyes softened as he slowly caressed her neck. "I saw what he did to you tonight and it was wrong. I saw the pain in your eyes and it tore me up. I want that sass back." His gaze kindled and his voice got husky as he brushed his thumb over her mouth. "You're one hell of a woman."

There was conviction with a whole passel of feeling in his voice that shook the very foundations of everything Alanna had ever experienced with a man. A tight ache started in her throat as she smiled at him. "Do you? Then you'd better get your backside over to your own rooms and get some sleep, cowboy. You're on the clock tomorrow."

He grinned and said, "That so, boss lady?" He eyed the covered dish. "You're sending me away without dessert?"

"Oh, right. That would be cruel when Mrs. Morely makes the best King David cobbler and I have crème fraîche to go with it."

"I don't know exactly what that is, but it sounds delicious. So, you're not that much of a tough taskmaster, then?" He gave her a hangdog look.

She nudged his shoulder and smiled. "Oh, I'm tough," she murmured, "but Mrs. Morely always gives me a generous helping and to keep my hips from spreading, it would be good to share."

He looked up and met her gaze, a glint of humor in his eyes. "Ah, this is all about you."

"Pretty much. Does that mean you don't want any?"

He chuckled and said quickly, "I didn't say that."

She smirked and nodded. "I thought so." She pulled the cover off the cobbler and dished up two good-sized helpings, then dolloped each with a generous blob of crème fraîche. Handing him his portion, she said, "It's a sour cream base combined with butterfat, by the way."

He nodded and dug in and then rolled his eyes, a hum of satisfaction rolling from deep in his chest. She took her own bite as they ate the dessert in silence.

Jake looked up, his expression thoughtful. "If your father was here, would he support you? With branching out?"

She chewed and shrugged, then answered once she'd swallowed. "I think so, but if my daddy was here, I probably wouldn't have to. Fowler would be more focused on Colton Incorporated and I could swing my daddy around to my way of thinking."

His eyes sharpened as if his attention was piqued. "You were at odds regarding the stables?"

She got a little fission of wariness in her stomach, fluttering like butterflies. "Let's say it was a push-and-pull relationship."

"It must be terrible not to know what happened to him" he said, sympathy laced through his deep voice.

"It is," she said, unable to keep the concern and worry out of her voice. There was a lot of turmoil in her family, but she would never wish her father ill will. She wanted this whole thing solved and him back home. "Without a ransom note we are not sure if he was kidnapped or if he's…dead."

He frowned, finishing off the cobbler on his plate. "I hope that's not the case." She scooped out the rest of the cobbler and added the topping, handing him the plate. "It seems Zane was cleared of any suspicion."

"He was."

"Does that throw the spotlight on other family members?"

She stiffened. It felt too much like he was probing and she was reluctant to continue on with this discussion. "Are you asking me if I think someone in this family had something to do with my father's disappearance?"

"Do you?" he said solemnly.

Her eyes narrowed and she couldn't help but wonder if she'd made a mistake. "You ask an awful lot of questions for a ranch hand."

He looked immediately conciliatory. "Just curious about you, about your family. But more about you. Just piecing together the woman instead of the myth."

She relaxed into the cushions and finished off her last bite. It wasn't surprising in the least. Many people wondered about the Coltons. "Ha, yes, I get that."

"Take this Colton Valley Ranch Gives Back," he said, changing the subject and she wondered if it was because the other subject of her family was obviously making her antsy. "That was your brainchild, correct?"

"Yes."

"In the tack room, you were about to tell me why you got interested in troubled teens. I'd really like to hear about that."

"It all stems from my adopted sister, Piper. She was orphaned and my father took her in. I just couldn't help wondering what might have happened to her if she'd been abandoned. Would she have ended up on the street? Would she have become a troubled teen? That made me want to do something to help other kids who might not have the advantage of wealth and family ties."

His voice was very husky and he covered her hand where it lay on her thigh. His hand was so seductively warm and big it swallowed hers. "That's admirable, Alanna."

For some insane reason Alanna found herself fighting tears and she blinked rapidly, trying to hold back the intense feelings that were growing in her.

Turning her hand beneath his, she laced her fingers through his and stood up. "Come on," she said quietly as she pulled him to his feet. "Time to get moving before we get out of hand."

He didn't release his hold on her immediately, and there was something deeply reassuring about that physical link. He gazed at her a moment longer and then let her go, a gleam in his eyes. "Yes'um, boss lady."

With a lighter heart, she grinned at him. "Just as long as you're aware of who's in charge."

He grinned back at her as he settled the gray Stetson on his head and pulled the brim low over his eyes. "I'm quite aware."

She opened the door and he stepped out into the balmy night. "Good night, Jake. Thank you for being so kind."

"It didn't have anything to do with kindness, Alanna. Good night."

She so wanted him to kiss her again, even though she knew it was stupid to want it. "Don't tempt me with that look, Alanna," he growled. Then he turned and she could hear the jingle of his spurs fading as he headed toward the barn. Her knees went totally weak as she braced her back against the doorjamb. She was hot and cold, and she felt as though she could slide right into a pile of goo on the ground.

Closing her eyes, she tipped her head back and

weakly rested it against the frame waiting for her pulse to return to normal.

Then that musical jingle was back and moving fast. She opened her eyes and Jake was standing there in front of her. His blue, Lord, so blue eyes liquid in the ambient light from her suite, his expression taut and filled with a heart-stopping tenderness. He was hatless, his inky hair tousled and soft against his forehead. With infinite gentleness he rested his knuckles against her jaw and slowly smoothed his thumb across her cheek, an irresistible half smile pulling at his mouth. "Damn you, Alanna," he said, his voice low and husky.

Feeling as though her whole body was paralyzed by the magic of his touch, Alanna gazed up at him, her expression soft and misty. "You should have kept walking, cowboy," she whispered unevenly.

He leaned in and her heart sped up as he braced his forearm against the doorjamb above her head, effectively bracketing her body between the wood and all that hard-packed muscle. With his free hand, he very lightly drew his thumb across her bottom lip, his eyes tracking the progress. "I know, boss lady. I know, but you fight dirty."

"So do you, Jake McCord," she said, her hand rising and resting on his hard, broad chest, her fingers aching to touch the tantalizing skin between the open collar of his shirt. He smelled earthy and male, making all her female parts go haywire.

Her pulse erratic, his jaw taut and as though drawn against his will, without saying a word, he jammed his hand into her hair, right at the base of her braid. His fingers tightening, he pulled her head back, a galvanizing charge sizzling between them as her gaze locked with his, and then silently he lowered his head, covered her mouth with a hard, heated kiss. She clutched at his shirt, her fingers slipping against his smooth, exposed skin. His mouth took hers without any charm or grace. Just raw, exciting need.

He hauled in a ragged breath, then murmured against her tingling lips, "I knew you were trouble the minute I laid eyes on you. See you later." And with that he turned and walked away.

All she could do was try to breathe around the fire in her lungs as she touched her thoroughly kissed mouth.

Jake rode away from the big house with a raging hard-on and kicking himself all the way. He'd fallen victim to the woman's allure, her need for comfort was genuine. There was no doubt in his mind. But he was walking a sharp, lethal edge here. Keeping his professional detachment would only get as hard as his erection if he kept getting close to her. But, unfortunately that was part of the job. He would have to skirt that fine line a bit. If only he could stop kissing her, that would be a start. Except the more he kissed her, the more he wanted to continue to kiss her and do other things to that tantalizing body.

The fresh shower smell of her and the musky scent of an aroused woman, stuck with him all the way back to the apartment. He took care of his horse and stopped at the entrance to the barn, running his hand over his face. He noticed movement out of the corner of his eye and just caught the glimpse of a blonde woman sneaking into the apartments.

He started walking, cursing the jingle of his spurs as he stayed on the balls of his feet to minimize the sound. But when he got to the stairs and went up, she was nowhere to be found. Who was she and who had she come to see?

He went up to the third floor and let himself into his quarters. Toeing off his boots, he stripped down to nothing and got in the shower.

He washed his overheated body and then turned the tap to cold only and hissed and gasped as the icy water shocked against his heated skin.

Drying off, he found that even a cold shower couldn't stop his body from responding to the memory of those soft, moist lips and lithe, tantalizing curves of Alanna's body. He could only console himself with the fact that he had managed to glean some information out of her tonight. She'd been jumpy when he'd started asking about her father.

That did not give him an ounce of joy.

Alanna Colton had a very strong motive for kidnapping her father.

Or, he closed his eyes in an attempt to sleep, worse.

Murdering him.

Chapter 7

"You missed dinner last night," Ellen Martin said as she set some bags down on the counter and smiled at the half-filled coffeepot. "Up early?"

Jake returned her smile from the chair at the table. "Got some things on my mind," he said noncommittally as she took out milk, eggs and bacon, setting everything on the counter. She dropped the bag in the trash. Heavy-duty things, he thought. Alanna Colton things, he clarified as he sipped at the hot brew. He had barely slept a wink, his overheated body and imagination keeping him in a frustrated limbo as he contemplated all the reasons he should give up this assignment. In the wee hours of the morning, tired of battling himself, he'd come downstairs and made a pot of coffee. He was still sitting here with not one answer to all the tangled questions.

She had him damn tangled up all right.

"I'll bet you're hungry." She chuckled softly.

"I ate last night, but thanks for the consideration." He fingered the brim of his hat that lay on the table next to his hand. "That said, I am starving right now and would definitely not say no to breakfast."

Feeling boxed in with no avenue to escape, he toyed with the leather of the hat's band. Alanna was so damn tempting. How was he going to keep his hands off her? All she had to do was give him one of those tender looks like she'd been giving him last night and he would cave.

"Jake?"

He dragged his attention back to Ellen. "Sorry?"

"I said it's a good thing, because I'm getting ready to cook it."

Exhaling sharply, he nodded as someone pounded down the stairs and came into view. A teenage girl with the same mahogany-brown hair and hazel eyes as Ellen, her eyes twinkling.

"Mom, can I have pancakes?"

"Did you pick up your room?"

She pulled a rueful face. "It was too heavy, so I didn't bother." She plopped down at the table and smiled, offering her small hand. "Hi, I'm Daisy Martin."

Her smile was infectious and he smiled back, clasping her hand for a quick shake. "Jake McCord."

"Oh, she's got some jokes first thing in the morning," Ellen said without even turning around. She was obviously used to her daughter's shenanigans.

Daisy glanced at him and grinned, a smile most likely perfected to melt her mom's heart. "I'd be willing to negotiate for some fluffy, syrupy, buttery goodness."

"You having a good time laying on that Daisy charm, young lady?" She reached up to a cupboard and pulled out a mixing bowl and Daisy's eyes lit up. "Now, is your room done?"

"Yes'um."

"Vacuumed and dusted?"

She licked her lips in anticipation, "So dust-free, Mr. Clean would be giving me a thumbs-up."

Ellen turned from the counter and narrowed her eyes as she started setting mugs on the table. "Your laundry's gathered up?"

"Big pile right in front of the washing machine just pining to be washed, folded and squeaky clean." Daisy gave her a guileless smile.

Ellen set her hands on her hips, her mouth twitching. "Bed made?"

"With hospital corners. You could bounce a quarter off it."

Jake chuckled and Ellen gave him a don't-encourage-her look.

"Well, that's too bad. You know we strip our linens on Saturday."

Daisy groaned. "Ah, come on, Mom. I forgot. Can't I get breakfast first? I'm just aching for pancakes," she said with a dramatic flair to her voice.

She shook her head. "Go ahead and strip your bed. I'm sure you didn't hear your sheets aching to be squeaky clean, too."

"Very funny," Daisy muttered. Her tone registering her disappointment.

"You'll thank me when you have fresh, clean bedding when you go to sleep tonight. I'll get those pan-cakes going."

Daisy sighed dramatically as only teenagers can do. "She beats me and makes me do awful things," she whispered to him.

"Do you deserve it?" he whispered back, and Ellen laughed.

"I'm going," Daisy groused, getting no sympathy.

Ellen still chuckling looked over at him. "You want eggs, bacon and toast or are you aching for pan-cakes?" she said with the same drama.

Jake chuckled as a deep voice from the right said, "Both for me." Clay Ford settled in the next seat over and Jake noticed how the kid's eyes followed Daisy as she climbed the stairs. She gave Clay a bold smile and direct look as she disappeared out of view. A straight-out invitation if he'd ever seen one. The feel-ing between these two was mutual. He remembered how he'd been a walking hormone when he'd been sixteen. He wondered how much restraint bad boy Clay would have around Ellen's daughter.

"Hmm, that's quite a bit of food," Ellen said.

"I'm a growing boy," he said, giving her a disarm-ing smile. She smiled back and poured a steaming cup of coffee into the mug in front of him. She went back to the counter, grabbing up and then setting two creamers on either end of the table. There was already sugar in the lazy Susan in the middle. But Clay ig-nored the sugar and went for the creamer.

"How about you, Jake?"

He glanced at Clay, grinning. "I'll take both, too."

Voices drifted down from above and there were footsteps on the stairs as other men entered the kitchen. Dylan Harlow settled in a chair at the head of the table and Mike Jensen took a seat across from Clay. Ellen brought the coffeepot, filling Dylan's and Mike's mugs.

Henry Swango came in as she was refilling Jake's cup and his eyes went over her in an insolent way as he sat next to Clay and shoved his mug across the table for her to fill. "Stuff in this kitchen always looks so tasty good," he drawled, his eyes going over her again.

Clay's shoulders stiffened when Henry Swango leaned over into Clay's personal space and said with a surly tone, "Hey, kid." Clay nodded. Tension radiated off him. Henry completely avoided Jake's eyes and didn't even bother to greet him. There was something menacing about the guy and the fact that he may be the man who killed Tim Preston made Jake's blood boil.

That brought back the memories of Tim's pretty wife and the tears on her face, the shell-shocked look of a woman who had lost everything, still round and heavy with their unborn child. He'd never forget the look in her eyes. Every man on that task force would have been ecstatic to see the man who'd killed Tim behind bars.

Before Jake had come downstairs, he'd called headquarters, but his boss had been adamant. Getting information on the family was his number one priority and going after Henry would blow his cover. He was ordered to lay low until the Colton operation was over, then they could look harder at Henry. He'd argued that Henry could be a potential cop killer. But when his boss asked for something concrete, Jake didn't have anything to give him. They would run him through the system and see what popped, but in the meantime, his attention needed to be on Alanna.

That didn't sit well with Jake. While he was pussy-footing around with his covert operation, a murderer and drug dealer could slip through his fingers. As a cop, that rankled and only added to his disillusionment.

Daisy came back downstairs and settled between Clay and Jake along with several other hands who joined them at the long table. Ellen was soon busy cooking and serving them all, but he noticed Henry touch her arm and her draw away from him several times.

Henry, obviously feeling Jake's scrutiny, turned his head and gave him a level, hostile look behind those shifty ice-blue eyes of his. He said nothing, his gaze flicking away.

The conversation revolved around bar visits and the local ladies, but everyone, except Henry, kept it from spilling over into offensive.

"Let's keep it clean," Jake murmured, aware Daisy was looking a bit uncomfortable.

Henry smirked and said, "Who died and made you sheriff?"

"I second it," Ellen said firmly, giving Henry a distasteful look and Jake a grateful one.

Setting his hands on the table, Dylan pushed up from his chair and stood up. "I guess we should get to work, boys, before we have the foreman in here after us."

There was the sound of scraping chairs and men started leaving the table. Clay stood up and Jake went to pick up his own plate and cup. Ellen waved him off.

"I've got it."

Henry was near the sink, washing his hands when Ellen came over with an armful of dishes. He sidled close to her and said something too soft for Jake to hear, but whatever the man said made her stiffen and give a shocked, menacing look.

Jake walked over with his dishes anyway and pushed his way between them. "Why don't you keep your lewd comments to yourself," Jake snarled between clenched teeth.

Henry's expression narrowed and everything in his tough face told Jake this was no regular cowhand. "Why don't you mind your own business, sheriff?"

"No, I agree, Henry. Breakfast is over. Beat it," Ellen said, setting the dishes in the sink.

Henry stared across the space at him, bitterness etched into his face. He wanted to slam the man's face into a wall and Henry looked like he'd be happy to return that favor. He backed away then with a disgusted look, grabbed up his hat off the side of the chair, jammed it on his head and left, a defiant smirk across his weak mouth.

"Thank you," she said softly. "It wasn't necessary to come to my rescue, but appreciated. I can handle Henry."

Jake tugged at his hat and nodded. "My pleasure."

He headed out of the apartments and toward the corral where Zorro was housed. The black stallion wasn't out and Jake entered the barn and walked to his stall. He was inside, his back hoof raised and his head lowered.

He was still asleep. Jake grabbed a lunge line and

went to unlatch the stall door when he heard what sounded like angry muffled voices.

He listened intently and discovered the voices were coming from the loft above him. Jake hung the lunge back on the hook and went to the stairs. He climbed up to find Clay boxed into a corner by Henry. "You are as dense as a box of rocks. I'm offering you something good here. Don't turn your nose up at it," Henry said.

"What's going on?" Jake took a step forward and Henry moved back off Clay.

"Nothing, just teaching the kid how to stack hay." He thrust out his chin, his stance telling Jake he was pissed about being interrupted and even more ticked off that it was Jake.

"That right, Clay?" Jake stared at him, the muscles in his face taut.

Henry glared at Clay, his face rigid, then swung his gaze to Jake. Clenching his fist, Jake was sure he wanted to bury it in his face.

Clay swallowed, his expression telling Jake he was intimidated but rebellious. He looked at Henry and then back at Jake. "Yeah. That's all."

Jake folded his arms, a small smile appearing. "Well, aren't you the Good Samaritan?"

Henry held up his hands, a look of anger and frustration on his face. "I see I'm not wanted and I have plenty of stuff to do," he said, backing up, distaste on his face. "Just think about what I said, kid." He formed his hand into the semblance of a gun, leveled it at Clay and pretended to shoot it, his index finger mimicking a trigger and his low *"Pow"* still audible to Jake. "Later."

Henry left the loft and Jake turned back to Clay.

"Are you sure Mr. Swango is nothing more than a good friend and mentor to you?"

His face tightening, his eyes shuttering, Clay set his hands on his hips. "I have bales to stack and now thanks to you, I'm on my own." Clay turned away.

"I'll stay and help," Jake offered.

Clay gave him a dubious look and shrugged. "Suit yourself."

"You can stack," Jake said.

Clay huffed a skeptical laugh. "These weigh upward of eighty pounds each, old man." Clay smirked. "You sure you don't want the easy job?"

"Who you calling 'old man.' I'm thirty-four."

"Double my age and besides, your eyes tell me you've seen things. They look old."

Jake blinked a couple of times. Out of the mouths of babes. "I never take the easy way out." Jake walked to the open loft door, pulling his gloves out of his back pocket and slipping them on. It was still warm, at least ninety degrees, his back was already sweating. He grabbed the first bale.

Clay shook his head and walked over to where Henry had started the stack. "Let's go."

After thirty bales Jake was feeling the pull and burn across his shoulders and in his arms. His breathing was a little faster from the constant movement. He wasn't used to this type of labor. He trained horses, but the Rangers had people who took care of them. He'd pulled double duty every so often, but it had been a long time.

"Feeling the burn?" Clay said, wiping his brow and grabbing two bottles of water. He threw one to Jake and downed his own from a stash he had.

Jake caught it and pulled off one of his gloves with his teeth and unscrewed the top, his throat working as he drained the bottle. He put his hands on his hips, trying to ease the biting tension in his shoulders.

Pulling the glove back on, he said, "So how did you end up in a community program."

"Court mandated," Clay snapped.

"I guessed that much," Jake said with a small smile. "I mean what did you do to get yourself jammed up?"

"Shoplifting," Clay said, his face hardening.

Jake hauled another square over to Clay. "What? Video games, electronics?"

"Food," he said, grabbing the bale Jake handed him and shoving it onto the stack, setting it in tight with his knee.

He reached for another bale, the ache in his shoulders turning hot and sharp as guilt stabbed him hard in the gut. The kid reminded him so much of Matt, who had also been tagged for shoplifting when he'd been Clay's age. A year later he was dead from a drug overdose. Pain stabbed even harder and he took a breath as he pulled the bale off the pulley and shot it toward Clay.

"That's tough," he said, his voice gruff. Sweat blinded him and he swiped the back of his gloved hand across his brow.

Clay shrugged. "My mom wasn't the most reliable person."

"And your dad?" His tone softened.

A look of resentment and annoyance on his face, he said, his eyes bruised, "Didn't know him. Split a long time ago."

Their old man hadn't split, but had tried to run both

their lives. Jake had heeded the call to law enforcement like their dad, but Matt had resisted and rebelled. There had been a time he thought Matt would buckle under, but he'd run away from home instead and that's when their dad had lost his influence on him and the street had taken over. Matt had a dad, but the pressure from him had sent Matt into the streets to discover who he was. Along the way he got so lost, and then his dad had lost a son and Jake a brother. Maybe if Jake had tried harder to get through, Matt would be alive.

"Even tougher."

"Yeah, I'm a hard-luck case." Clay smoothed his palms over the gloves on his hands with more force than necessary. His chin lifted and the pain in his eyes was replaced with challenge. "I don't need your help."

"That so?" Jake set his hands on his hips. "Well, I'm offering it whether you need it or not."

"Right." He slung the bale and this time he settled it in place with a little more force than necessary, his smile just a little nasty.

"You sound skeptical."

"Just drop it," Clay said, his voice flat. "I'm here because I was ordered here. End of discussion."

Handing him another bale, slightly out of breath from the exertion, Jake said, "Doesn't mean you can't use it as an opportunity to change your life around."

Clay grabbed another bale, his eyes dark and haunted. "What would you know about that?"

"Only that you are the one who's in charge. I get the feeling you like this ranching stuff."

Clay shrugged without answering, taking the next bale.

"The cowboy way is an honest, hardworking living. With what you're doing here, you could get a job on a spread." He'd loved ranching and horse whispering. But now he was an undercover Texas Ranger. He'd lied to Alanna about not spying on her, but that was permissible. So why did he feel so much like he was betraying an innocent woman? This was an investigation based on her likelihood of being involved with her father's kidnapping. But there was a draw to the simplicity of living the ranching life. He was worn-out, burned-out, sick of always bashing his head against a brick wall. He'd made mistakes and maybe it was best to give it up. Get out. But that was wrong. He was the best of the best in Texas. A Ranger. He'd worked hard to get where he was. He was just tired. The feeling would pass.

Jake's cell rang and he pulled it out of his back pocket. "McCord." The voice belonged to Sheriff Troy Watkins who was responsible for investigating Eldridge Colton's disappearance. "We have a witness who's come forward with information regarding Alanna Colton and we want you to be on hand when we question her. Can you head over to my office?"

"I can be there in about half an hour."

"See you then."

"You've got to go," Clay said. "I can handle the rest."

"No, I can finish. We're almost done."

They worked for about ten minutes and when the last bale was stacked Jake headed for the stairs and the lower barn. He had to grab a quick shower, then drive over to town.

"Jake?"

"Yeah," he said, pausing.

"Thanks for sticking around."

"Sure. No problem. It's none of my concern, but if you get into a tight spot regarding Henry, you should bring that up with Alanna."

"I'll think about it," Clay said, looking away. As he went down the stairs and headed for his apartment, he had hope Clay was open to turning his life around.

He hadn't been able to save Matt, but maybe he could help Clay.

"I'm telling you. That's what I heard with my own two ears."

Jake eyed the woman, her unkempt appearance and stringy blond hair not engendering confidence in what she was saying. "You heard Alanna Colton, the heiress?" He tapped her picture again, the one of her all dolled up for a charity function, in a scarlet-red dress, showing just a hint of her tantalizing cleavage and baring her creamy shoulders. She had on emerald earrings and a necklace that probably cost more than his salary, her lips painted a siren red, her makeup making her eyes appear a smoky, sultry green. Her hair was piled on top of her head, with a ringlet of soft blond curls snaking around the delicate column of her throat.

"Yeah, that's her."

"And, she threatened her father?"

"Yeah, that's what I said." The woman rolled her eyes, her tone belligerent. "Are you hearing me? I said she told her father if he didn't butt out of the stable business, he'd be sorry. Can I go now?"

"No," Jake said as he rose and exited the interrogation room.

"What do you think?" Troy Watkins said just moments later as Jake leaned against the door.

There was something about her that didn't ring true and he didn't like what she had to say. Didn't make it a lie, but Jake wasn't one to take anyone at their word. "Did you check out this woman's background?"

"Ella Wilson is a waitress for the place where Alanna and her father often ate in Dallas. Meddlesome Butterfly. She could have easily overheard them. She was working that day. Charlie checked it out."

Deputy Sheriff Charlie Kidwell, nodded his head. He was in his midthirties with blond hair and blue eyes. He pulled out a notebook and flipped it open. "I sure did, Ranger McCord. Her manager said she was on the lunch-to-dinner shift that day."

"Did he confirm Alanna and her father were dining there?"

"There's a charge on Miss Colton's credit card for lunch that day. She was there and the manager confirmed it by looking at a picture of her on my phone."

Jake didn't want Alanna to be guilty, thinking he should really recuse himself from the case, but the thought of leaving her and Clay alone with Henry Swango working there stuck in his craw. He might be struggling with his conflict of interest where she was concerned, but he wasn't willing to abandon them. If Alanna was guilty, he would do his duty no matter how much it hurt. He'd done that in the past when he'd taken his brother in for a DWI. He often wondered if that jail time had set him on his path to drugs and ruin. If he had pulled strings or gotten the charges reduced, maybe Matt would be alive.

Second-guessing himself wasn't helping, but his

instincts had been shattered the day Tim Preston had been gunned down and breathed his last breath. Trusting in himself and his abilities put him on shaky ground right now. Really, HQ should have put a different Ranger on this case and left him with his horses.

"You should bring her in for questioning," Jake said, rubbing the back of his neck. He saw no way around it.

The sheriff nodded. "I'll go get her myself, but we can't have her see you."

"I'll be in the observation room."

He nodded.

Jake waited, pacing back and forth, for Alanna to show up. Once the door to the interrogation room opened and the sheriff ushered a pale-faced Alanna in, he was driving himself crazy wondering about her guilt or innocence.

"Have a seat, Miss Colton."

"What is this about, Sheriff? I've answered all the questions you had about my father's disappearance." She might be under a lot of stress, but the woman could hold her own. Her voice was strong and her gaze direct.

"New information has come to light."

"Oh, God. Have you found him? Is he—"

The anguish in her voice made his gut clench. Either she was a good actress or she was totally sincere.

"No, we haven't found him. This is in regard to your lunch at Meddlesome Butterfly."

He named the date and she frowned. "Yes, I was there."

"A witness has come forward who says you threatened your father." He looked down at the file in his hand. "The waitress serving you that day reported to us that you said, 'If you don't butt out of the stable business, you'll be sorry.'"

"I never said that to him because he wasn't there that day. I was having lunch with a horse dealer. He's bald like my dad, so she must have gotten them mixed up. I can assure you, he'll back up my story."

The sheriff pulled out his pad and pen. "His name and where we can contact him."

"His name is Jeremy Bellows." She pulled out her cell phone and tapped the screen then read off a number. "I'm sure he'll clear this up."

"Let's hope so, Miss Colton."

Alanna's lips thinned. "I didn't have anything to do with my father's disappearance," she said, anger in her voice, her eyes flashing. "I would never hurt him."

Jake immediately pulled out his cell and tapped in the number.

"Heritage Ranch," a female voice said.

"Hello, I'd like to speak to Mr. Bellows."

"I'm sorry, Mr. Bellows is unavailable. Can I take a message?"

"Yes, tell him it's urgent I speak to him."

She took his name and number and he hung up. The sheriff entered the small observation room, but Jake couldn't take his eyes off Alanna. "I just called. He's not available," Jake muttered.

"I think she's stalling for time."

"You think she's guilty of kidnapping? That she's holding her father somewhere?" Jake dragged his eyes away from Alanna to Sheriff Watkins.

"Maybe she just did away with him. There was blood at the scene."

"She can't weigh more than a buck ten soaking wet," he said, gesturing to Alanna who sat at the table with a composed look on her face.

The sheriff shifted, the leather of his holster creaking. He sighed. "Maybe she had help. Her dad was pretty frail and in ill health. Maybe this hump Bellows is in cahoots with her."

Jake took one last look at Alanna. "Keep me posted. I've got to get back to the ranch. I've already been gone too long. Give me a head start."

"Will do."

Until they got ahold of the man she claimed she was having lunch with the day she allegedly threatened her father, there was no way to refute what she had said or prove her innocence. The truth of the matter was this was damaging information for her, and the sheriff's office would have no choice but to put her right at the top of the suspect list, which meant he should really back off her.

He was already in too deep and compromising himself further would jeopardize both his career and his sanity.

If the witness's testimony held up and Alanna had lied about threatening her father, this would make her the prime suspect—make her look guilty as hell.

And if she was…he would arrest her himself.

Chapter 8

Alanna sat in her car for a few minutes after the sheriff released her. Her heart still pounded at the accusation. How could that waitress mistake a simple conversation about the purchase of a string of barrel racer stock for Alanna threatening her father?

Panic and adrenaline rushing through her, she rubbed at her temple.

It was true Mr. Bellows looked a little like Eldridge Colton. In fact, she had thought that when she'd first seen him. She barely knew the man, but he was now instrumental in clearing her of this allegation.

The feeling of being, once again, completely alone in a situation washed over her. Really, there was something so basic about relying on the people you loved. But when she thought about how this made her look guilty, she couldn't help but wonder who might be behind it.

Then she remembered Jake and how he'd comforted her last night and the way that had settled right into her bones and heart. He was a third party, someone outside her family's influence and he made her knees weak.

Was that smart?

No.

So not smart, but it was an irrefutable fact. Of course, he could have an ulterior motive. She couldn't be sure he wasn't after her name recognition, favors, her money. All of the above. It just didn't *feel* like that, though.

No, Jake made her feel things she'd never felt before. Things that made her feel safe and oh so good.

Safe. That was an alien concept.

She leaned her head back against the headrest and closed her eyes. Mr. Bellows would clear her. There was nothing to worry about. She'd had lunch with him at Meddlesome Butterfly. Plenty of people saw them.

But that waitress had said she'd threatened her father.

How many people in the restaurant thought Mr. Bellows was her father? She had picked up the check because it was a business meeting she had requested. She wanted to keep it on the QT. Her plans for the stables hung in the balance.

She started the car and drove out of the sheriff's office and headed directly to Hugh Barrington.

Once seated at his desk, her father's attorney steepled his fingers together, looking thoughtful. "This sounds like it could be a problem," he said, his gaze going laser sharp. "I'm not a criminal attorney, Alanna, but I can refer you to a very good one here in Dallas."

"That would be something, Hugh," she said, her voice tight.

He leaned forward and grabbed a pitcher of clear liquid from a tray and poured a glass. Getting up he came around the desk and put it into her hands. "There's still no word on Eldridge?"

She accepted the glass. "This isn't gin, is it?"

He shook his head. "Water, but I do have something a bit stronger if you'd like."

She took a sip, the cool liquid soothing her parched throat. "No. I'd better not. I'm distraught and driving." He clasped his hand against her shoulder and gave it a squeeze. "No. Nothing on my father. I'm so very worried about him." She pressed a hand to her chest.

"I understand. But at this point, all we can do is wait. There does seem to be some indication of foul play as your family hasn't received a ransom note."

A few minutes later in her car, she mulled over what Hugh had said as she drove back to Colton Valley Ranch. She couldn't agree with him more. She swallowed, a shiver going down her spine, her stomach so tied up in knots. What was going on? With her father? With this whole mess?

Was he dead?

She entered the gates, pressing everything back, and drove up to the house, parking her car in the massive garage. She headed straight back to the barns and the arena. As she entered, Tamara was working the horses. She immediately dismounted when she saw Alanna.

"Thank God. I was so worried when the sheriff said you needed to come with him. You're not under arrest, are you?"

"Not yet."

"That's ominous."

"It's terrible and I'm not really sure what to do or think at this point."

"Do you want me to take over here? Why don't you do something peaceful this afternoon? You never take enough time off, Alanna. Really. Get Mrs. Morely to fix you up a basket and go have some downtime at the creek. The bluebells will be blooming this time of year." Tamara got a sly gleam in her eyes. "And sunflowers. Be a shame to miss that." She nudged her. "It would do you good. I can handle anything that comes up here."

The creek was a very peaceful place and it was true. She hadn't had a day off in a very long time. She did have to work out what she was going to do about Fowler threatening to sell her stock before it was ready and also figure out what she was going to do if he continued to treat her like she was nothing more than a figurehead. That wasn't going to suit her at all. Quite frankly, she deserved the respect he was withholding.

"All right."

"Of course." Tamara smiled. "I'm so glad you're going to take some time for yourself. Please don't give it another thought."

A half an hour later, she was on the back of Somerset with Mrs. Morely's basket hooked on to her saddle. She'd changed into a pair of jeans and a lacy white top layered with a denim jacket. On her feet she'd indulged herself with a pair of brown cowgirl boots tooled with flowers on them. A straw hat on her head, sunglasses breaking the glare.

She followed the road for about half a mile, then veered off. The narrow trail to the creek was overgrown with small trees, scrub and bushes, grass sparse on the hard-packed dirt. With barbed-wire fences marking the boundaries, Alanna skirted a dead tree, Somerset confidently navigating the rough track, the branches of bushes scraping against her legs. She pulled Somerset up and removed her jacket due to the heat of the day.

She loved this part of the ranch—loved the vastness, the spectacular vistas, the untouched beauty of it. With the necessary evil of the fence lines, this area was just as it had been a hundred years before, and she was always overwhelmed by it.

There was a gap along the west fence, and Alanna stopped and shielded her eyes as she stared out at the view.

It was breathtaking, her family's property. The rises, the thick forest of oak, hickory, tupelo and sweet gum trees rooted deep in the fertile, sandy loam. And the distinctive green of the massive pines that towered over her, swaying gently in the early fall breeze. There was no place like it in the entire world. And there was a sense of unfettered freedom here she'd never experienced anywhere else. Shifting her gaze, she followed the line of the treetops, the sound of birdsong thick in the air, the wind whipping loose hair across her face. It was as if this space allowed her to take a full breath, to expand her lungs to their total capacity, to shed all her constraints.

Even if the effect was temporary.

She continued down the narrow, winding trail as

it disintegrated into more of a path. When she heard the sound of rushing water, Somerset picked up his pace. Soon the wide creek came into view and she gave her horse his head as he picked his way down the gentle slope to the water. The recent abundance of rain had left the creek full and the waters tumbling around the rocks. She leaned on the saddle horn and breathed deep.

The scent of fresh air and water was a boon to her soul. Nudging Somerset away from the edge of the fast-moving water, she found a firmer place to dismount. Once her boots hit the ground, she reached for the saddlebags and the picnic basket. She unpacked a tarp, then spread a blanket over it, setting the food down.

Folding down onto the soft fabric, she dug into the basket, realizing with dismay she must have left the thermos of lemonade near her horse's stall. Darn it. She was going to have to go thirsty.

"Forget something?"

Her head jerked up at the deep sound of Jake's voice. She shaded her eyes as he came toward her carrying the missing thermos, leading his pretty roan Valentine by the reins. She watched him, a familiar warmth starting in her middle. He was so damn good to look at. He dropped the reins, and set his hand on his belt buckle holding up a pair of nice fitting jeans over his lean hips and thick thighs, all in all an impressive lower half. The upper half was just as mouth-watering with his Western plaid shirt stretched across a taut chest and covering very broad shoulders. His

Stetson shadowed his eyes, the sun glinting off the stubble of his unshaven jaw.

He looked all kinds of cowboy sexy, approachable and...safe.

His eyes went over her in a heated, lazy way that was purely Jake. "Nice boots," he drawled, his tone warm and intimate.

"Nice play."

His brows rose, a glint of humor in his eyes. "Oh, yeah? In what way?"

He went to his knees beside her and set the thermos in her hands. "Bringing me my thermos. You wouldn't be trying to butter me up, hmm?"

He grinned for real, sat back on his heels, his big hands resting on his thighs. "Why would I do that?"

She tilted her head, feeling oddly flustered. She'd never had this...teasing kind of relationship with a man. She'd been much too closed up and suspicious. Jake seemed to break down all those barriers. "Habit?"

Laughter in his eyes, he braced his hand against the blanket and leaned close, gazing directly into her eyes. "What kind of habit?"

She gave him a cheeky smile, nudging his shoulder. "Horning in on my meals."

He nudged her right back. "Not by design. But it's a good thing you learned to share when you were in kindergarten."

She made a face at him. "I wasn't all that nice in kindergarten."

He nodded his head wisely. "Spoiled?"

The devil glinted in his eyes, something exciting drifting through her. "A tad, and tough, too. Liked to get my way." This time she smacked his arm and he captured her hand in his, laughing. She felt the contact all the way through her. Jake took a breath. She knew exactly what he was experiencing because she was experiencing it, too—that hot rush, the debilitating weakness, making her senses swim.

"You're still going to share. It's good for the soul," he coaxed, his voice gruff as he rubbed his thumb against her palm.

"Well, you did ride *all* the way out here to bring me my lemonade."

Grinning, he looked like a desperado with his dark stubble. "Attagirl, not so tough or spoiled now, huh?"

"Not with a charming cowboy worming his way into my affections," she murmured as he let go of her hand.

His glinting eyes narrowed. "You're pushing it, Alanna."

She reached for the basket and lifted the lid, then dropped it. "It occurs to me, if you really want to get your hands on more of Mrs. Morely's cooking, you could probably bat your pretty blue eyes and say 'ma'am' in that aw-shucks, I'm-not-a-threat-to-your-heart way and she'd melt like sugar in the rain."

He growled and picked her up into his arms and she squealed. "How about I go and dunk you in the river, smart mouth?"

"Creek." She laughed so hard, she could barely speak. "It's a creek, and no." She tried to kick free, but he held her hard, the strength of him astonishing and breathtaking.

"You're not helping yourself here, Colton." Amusement was ripe in his voice. "Creek, river. I bet the water's just as cold."

"Please, Jake," she pleaded, her voice breaking from laughter and exertion. "I'm sure Mrs. Morely would feed you even if you weren't so darn charming."

He stopped and looked down at her, his voice getting softer as he looked into her eyes and she got so lost in the blue depths of his. "You just want to save your fancy boots."

"Naw, I could probably make a whole new pair out of the leather from getting your goat."

He captured her gaze then, the expression in his eyes softening, growing warmer until those amused glints were like honey, a little more intimate—the look you gave someone you really liked down deep.

"You're a really sassy brat, Colton," he said, his voice deep and husky.

"Everything I learned, I learned in kindergarten," she said, her voice hushed as he let her go and she slid down his hard-muscled body.

"How about this?" he said before he lowered his head. Cupping her jaw to protect her from his heavy stubble, he brushed her mouth with the softest, slowest kiss. Alanna's breath caught and her pulse stumbled. Alanna molded herself against him, holding the back of his head. His lips moving against hers, he spoke, his voice very low, very raspy.

"I think we might have to do some quick two-stepping here, darlin'," he said, his tone soft. She started to pull away, but he held her secure. "I might need a minute. My knees are a mite weak."

That made her smile and, my God, could this man be any damn cuter. "That's a pretty good line."

She felt him grin, and he gave her hair a tug. "Well, hell, I was trying to impress you with my cowboy charm."

She smiled again, "Oh, *that's* what that was?" Feeling oddly vulnerable, and fighting her attraction to him was a double whammy.

He chuckled. "I think we'd better eat before we do something we'll both regret."

Her throat suddenly tight. She wasn't sure she'd regret it, but his suggestion made good sense. Unable to answer at the moment, she hung on to him, her body deconstructing like every molecule had melted. He turned his head and shifted his hold, a shudder coursing through him. It was as if they were both paralyzed, unable to move, unable to separate.

Alanna felt him gather his control, his whole body tensing. He gripped her arm and pulled it from around his neck, clasping her by the wrist. His face going tight, he turned and headed back to the blanket.

She cleared her throat when they were seated and she said, her voice soft, "No, I didn't learn that lesson until I met you. You're a good teacher."

They sat in silence, eating the fried chicken, potato salad, corn on the cob and baked beans while sharing the lemonade between them, the breeze ruffling through the oak leaves and sighing through the pine needles.

They were just above the creek and she enjoyed the view. Shortening her sight, she took in the brown-eyed Susan clustered in the field across the rushing water, along with daisies and a clump of sunflowers. Then to her left as far as she could see were bluebells bobbing in the sunlight and mingling with the grasses. They were the same deep blue as Jake's striking eyes.

It would have been perfect if Alanna hadn't started thinking about her morning and getting all tied up in knots. Not to mention this thing with Jake that they both wanted to take to a different level, but were just managing to keep from disaster.

After they had cleaned up their food, she understood he hadn't come out here to deliver her lemonade. He'd come out here to make sure she was okay and she didn't want that to mean something, but it did.

"Why don't you tell me why the sheriff hauled you off this morning and why you came back looking all sorts of spooked?" He leaned forward, resting his arms across his knees, staring off across the valley, his tone quiet. "You in trouble?"

Her insides clenched, Alanna toyed with a loose thread on the edge of the blanket. She shrugged. "That remains to be seen?"

There was a very tense stillness and he responded, resignation in his voice. "I think we established last night that you weren't an island and I had this shoulder right here, ready and able to handle a little leaning."

She felt totally emptied out. She had needed a reality check, and this whole you-threatened-your-father was as real as it got. But now she was trapped by someone else's agenda.

In spite of how rotten she was feeling, she craved that shoulder and everything that went with it. "I really appreciate that, Jake. I do, but I prefer to handle this on my own," she said, her voice uneven.

His mouth tightened and he nodded. She poured some lemonade. Her throat suddenly parched.

"I think your idea about just cutting ties and opening up your own place works. Do it your way without either your brother's or father's influence, constantly undermining you and looking over your shoulder with the second-guessing."

She had the cup halfway to her mouth, and she abruptly brought it back down, lemonade sloshing over the edge. She stared at him, her heart starting to pound. She held his gaze for a moment, caught so off guard that she couldn't even think. "What?"

"Go out on your own. You must have the funds. Open your own stables. Do it your way and show them how tough you are."

She looked at him, trying to recover her equilibrium. "I said that when I was angry." She wasn't sure why his question made her feel exposed and guilty— or ineffectual.

He gave her a humorless smile. "Maybe you should. I bet that would be a kick in the pants."

He had his back braced against a tree, one knee up, his forearm draped over it. His hat was low over his eyes and she got that outlaw vibe again.

She shrugged. "We've always worked together."

"Have you? Sounds to me like they have no respect for you and don't appreciate you to boot. Make them sit up and take notice."

"It's bad timing."

He snorted. "That's just an excuse."

She was backpedaling so fast inside, she was making herself dizzy. "It would be another terrible upheaval. With my father gone—"

"Alanna, Fowler *is* taking over...has *already* taken over. Do you want to fight him?"

"It's part of my legacy." She heard her father's words from when she'd been very little. He had told her all about how he'd built up everything for his children, that she was special. When he'd put her in charge of the stables, she'd been so happy to have his approval, to really feel like this was family. She'd always had this unnamed fear deep inside. She was a Colton and they stuck together.

"Why can't that change? Why can't you make your own legacy?"

How had this happened? How had he just gotten her to examine something she'd never even contemplated? She had been bold and vocal, but she'd been shot down so many times, she'd become grounded, weighed down with a sense of duty, with feelings of accountability, with uncertainty. She'd lost something in the process and that gripped her.

Shaken, she couldn't figure out when that had happened. When she'd stopped asserting herself, fighting for what she believed in. She looked up at him with a jolt of realization. Jake was watching her, an odd contemplative look in his eyes.

She stared at him, suddenly dangerously close to tears. This dark-haired man with the killer grin and the sexy eyes just blew her to smithereens and her world had shifted on its axis.

He chucked her under the chin as if his comments hadn't just sent her into a tailspin. "Just think about it, sweetheart." He rose. "It's getting late and we should get back."

She was tense the whole way back thinking once again she couldn't seem to trust anyone in her family. She glanced over at Jake, afraid to even allow the warm feelings he invoked in her to really get a chance to settle. The temptation was incredibly intense.

As they road into the stable area, she saw Fowler and Marceline talking near the arena. That didn't bode well. As soon as Fowler saw Jake, his face went thunderous. Before Jake could even dismount, her brother was yelling.

"Why aren't you doing your job?" he growled loudly.

Jake finished dismounting, slipping the reins over Valentine's head before he turned toward Fowler and answered him, "Mr. Colton, it takes time to undo the kind of abuse that stallion has endured. You have to be more patient." Jake's voice was firm, but calm.

Anger flashing in Fowler's eyes, he shouted, "Then get on with it. I want to breed that damn horse."

Alanna dismounted and wedged herself between Jake and Fowler. "You are expecting miracles!"

"Stay out of this," he said, shoving her out of the way. "I know you don't approve. You've made that abundantly clear."

Jake reacted by catching her arm. "What the hell? That's no way to treat your sister."

Marceline watched everything with glittering eyes and a smirk on her face.

"Look, she's been against Zorro from day one and she's not too fond of your methods. Thinks you're a fake."

"She's already told me that to my face."

"I have no doubt she did. Alanna pulls no punches. But that horse has excellent bloodlines." He looked at Alanna with a raised brow. "Alanna agrees."

She sighed. "It's true. I agree. His bloodlines are excellent, but don't get your hopes up."

Jake's expression fell at her words as if he was hurt she didn't believe in him. "Jake—"

"Don't worry, Mr. Colton. I'll fix him for you so you can breed him. I am confident about that." He gave her a glance as if to say he didn't care whether she believed it or not.

Marceline turned with a bored look on her face now that everything had died down and Alanna wasn't in the hot seat.

"Wait just one second," Alanna said, grabbing her arm and dragging her out of earshot.

Marceline jerked out of her grasp. "Let go of me. What do you want?"

"Did you pay someone to lie for you about me threatening Dad?" she hissed.

She burst out laughing and folded her arms over her chest. "No, you ninny. I didn't. You do have an imagination, Alanna. I had nothing to do with that. What could I possibly gain by hiring someone?"

"The fact that you could be guilty and you're trying to deflect attention onto me. That's enough motive for me!"

Marceline sniffed, dismissing Alanna with a toss of her head. Flouncing off, her parting shot to Alanna came out cold and nasty. "Maybe, *sister*, you didn't like Dad meddling in your stable business. Maybe *you* were the one to bump him off."

She turned to find Jake staring at her. Fowler gave his sister a glaring look and walked away.

She hadn't killed her father! Everything hinged on Mr. Bellows backing her up. She was back to square one. Who could she trust?

Chapter 9

She stood there looking so very alone and he couldn't stand it. He grabbed the reins of his horse and hers. "Come on," he said and headed toward the arena. Looking over his shoulder to ensure she was following, he led the horses inside, making for Somerset's stall.

He hadn't fully gained Alanna's trust. She was still skeptical about what he did for a living. If she was a kidnapper/murderer, he wanted her to be all in so he could get every bit of information out of her.

"I can handle this on my own."

Apparently she could handle everything on her own. She shut him down and he had bubkes. He tied Valentine and pulled the big horse inside, then removed the saddlebags, draped them over his shoulder and snagged the picnic basket. His shoulders protested, anger churning in his gut.

He set everything just outside the stall and removed Valentine's bridle, hooking it over his shoulder, then stripped the saddle off his back along with the blanket.

"Why don't you brush him down?" Jake said, and she snapped out of her thoughts, but she sidled past him and went into the stall.

In the tack room, he swore low. He was a seasoned Ranger and had heard plenty of perps confess they were innocent. He never took them at their word, so why did he believe Alanna was innocent of any foul play in the disappearance of her father?

He set the saddle on the peg and draped the horse blanket on the appropriate rack. He had come close to losing it in that meadow down by the river. He'd never been so caught up in the kind of teasing banter that came so easily between them.

He cleaned the bit and tidied up the bridle before hanging that up, as well.

She almost made him forget why he was there and that wasn't an easy feat. But he had a job to do and he couldn't forget Alanna didn't know he was a Texas Ranger undercover to spy on her. With a knot in his gut the size of Texas, the tension that had been building from the moment he met her settled between his sore shoulder blades. Resting his hands on his hips, he wearily tipped his head back, a sleepless night and manual labor all piling up on him. When she found out who he really was, she would feel so betrayed. Getting in any deeper with her was only going to make it worse on her and definitely on him.

Distance would be the best thing here and now. No matter how hard it was to do that, he had to keep his perspective. He wasn't worth a plug nickel if he couldn't do his job. The job he was sent there to do. Walking that fine line with her was making everything blur for him.

Every time he got near her, he found it even more difficult to let her go. He had no choice. He was tasked with getting close to her. It was up to him to keep from crossing over that line.

He rubbed his hand over his face, his shoulders tight with an achy throbbing.

He straightened and left the tack room and when he reached the stall he looked into the gloom. He saw her brush at her cheeks. Then with her arms folded tightly in front of her, she leaned against the stall wall. He wanted to walk out of there, call his boss and tell him he was compromised. But that would leave her vulnerable to Henry and her family. He had to stick it out and find out what was going on. He had to get her to open up to him. A sudden ache jamming up his throat, he said, "Hey, slacker."

When she jumped away from the wall and faced him, she tried to smile, the worry in her eyes evident in the dim light. "You're a slave driver, McCord."

"I might be." He looked away, trying to handle the sudden thickness in his chest. This woman was getting good at turning him inside out. Finally managing to get a shaky breath past the lump in his throat, he looked at her, aware of how she had drawn her self-protective armor around herself, aware of the shadow of loneliness in her eyes.

That stripped him to the quick, and he went into the stall and hauled her out, "Come here," he whispered gruffly.

With a choked sound she came into his arms, and he gathered her up in a tight embrace, pressing her face into the curve of his neck. She took a deep breath, and then she pressed her face tighter against him as she slid her arm around his waist. Feeling her tremble against him, he pressed a kiss to her temple, then slid his fingers along her scalp, cradling her head in a firm grip. The heavy silk weight of her hair tangled around his fingers, the loose fall like satin down her back, and Jake closed his eyes and hugged her hard, a swell of emotion making his chest tight.

She took another shaky breath, and he smoothed one hand across her hips and up her back, molding her tightly against him. Easing in a tight breath of his own, he brushed his fingers over her face, his voice gruff and uneven. "I'm sorry you have to go through this."

He shifted, bracing them against the wall.

"Can't you sweet-talk Somerset into brushing himself?"

This was the opening he needed. "Why is it you don't respect what I do?"

Her expression startled, she stared at him, wariness filling her eyes. He hated that he had to do this, but he had to gain her trust fully. This may backfire, but he had to take the risk.

"I don't think you're exactly a fake. Just that you can't work miracles. There's no magic in the world, Jake. It's all hard work—"

"And protecting your back. Right? It's hard for you to trust anyone or anything. That would make you much too vulnerable. Well, you want to know why I'm so good with horses? You want to know why people hire me? Want to understand what it is I do?"

She stepped away, and his stomach dropped like a rock when he saw the distressed expression in her eyes.

"I build a bridge of trust, Alanna. I build, reinforce it and follow through. That's the magic."

"I trust in myself and my family."

He held her gaze for a moment longer, then looked down and toed the side of the stall, his voice quiet and very subdued when he continued. "Is that so? You're like Zorro. Maybe that's why I can't seem to get through to him, either."

She looked away and swallowed. "I know what I'm doing." She stared at him, her eyes dark and fixed, and then she abruptly turned her head, her expression starkly contained. Jake watched her for a moment; then looked down as he exhaled.

"Okay, Alanna. I get it. None of my business." She tucked her hands into her pockets, her face averted, but Jake saw the glimmer of tears in her eyes. He looked away, experiencing a feeling that was a mix of guilt and anger. Pulling into herself wasn't going to get the job done. It was clear she was closing down. His anger only grew. "I better get back to work," he said grimly. He untied Valentine and started walking toward the big double doors. He waited for her to call out his name, get him to stop, but she didn't.

Two steps forward, one step back.

He tried to get close to Zorro all afternoon, but the horse was too spooked. Frustrated on both fronts, he headed back to the apartments, the pain from his shoulders now driving a spike into his neck.

He ate without comment, the conversation flowed around him. Ellen, her eyes concerned, leaned down and said softly, "Are you all right?"

"I'm fine. Just beat," he responded, forcing a smile.

"Feeling the effects of those bales now, huh?" Clay said with a smirk.

Henry laughed, but Jake ignored him and went upstairs, Ellen's anxious eyes following him. Feeling like a complete failure, he entered the apartment and headed for the bathroom. He turned on the water and got it as hot as he could stand it, then stepped in. He quickly soaped himself, groaning at the pain of his sore muscles, and then he let the water beat down on him, using the heat and the pounding of the water to ease the tension. With the pain across his shoulders, he couldn't help thinking of Clay and with Clay came memories flooding him. Memories of Matt and how he'd so thoroughly failed his brother. His dad had been wrong. Matt wasn't ever going to come around, because he didn't want to be part of the family legacy of protecting and serving. He'd just gotten that this afternoon as he'd challenged Alanna to go out on her own. It was a stark realization.

Matt wanted his independence. Wanted to be his own man, but his dad had drilled it into Matt's head that anything short of becoming a cop or going into the military was unacceptable. Even as Matt wanted to break away, the guilt had consumed him. To combat that, he'd turned to ways to cope with the mental anguish.

Bracing both hands on the wall of the shower stall, Jake bent his head and violently pushed away his brother's ghost, focusing on the hammering spray and the heat. Only to have Preston's ghost manifest. Another terrible failure at the cost of a young life, one that had affected him deeply. Preston's wife and his child were living with his failure, as well. He fisted his hands, even the flexing of his fingers causing more pain, but it was nothing compared with the guilt and pain churning like a volatile mix in his gut.

With Henry walking around, his freedom only added to Jake's turmoil. Damn, he was tired. So bone-weary exhausted. He craved a simpler existence, one where he didn't have such a heavy responsibility on his shoulders, one where life and death didn't come with the territory. But even now he battled against his old man's influence. If he wasn't a cop, he wasn't anything. How would his dad handle it if he quit the Rangers? The elite of law enforcement in the state of Texas, hell, around the world. It was out of the question.

This job was going to kill him one way or the other.

He knew all about honor and duty, but Alanna was in a different position here.

She could make a new life for herself.

Unless she went away for murder.

The water turning tepid, he got out, the room full of steam. He made a cursory effort to dry himself, then pulled on a clean pair of jeans, not bothering to do up the snap. Avoiding his reflection in the fogged mirror, he reached for the can of shaving foam, his mood somber. He sometimes wondered if he would ever get out of his own way.

A knocked sounded loudly in the room and he wanted nothing more than to get some sleep. He opened the front door and Alanna stood there.

"Ellen said you were in pain, something about too much hay stacking. I don't think Fowler hired you to stack hay."

She walked into his living room without an invitation, but not before she galvanized him with the heated look she gave his bare chest. He absently rubbed at a droplet of water. He flipped the door closed.

"Why don't you come in."

"I brought something that will help."

"Alanna, you don't have to—"

"I want to. Take these," she ordered, walking into the kitchen and pouring water into a glass.

He threw the pills back and took the glass out of her hand, not about to look a gift horse in the mouth.

"Now let me rub some of this ointment into your back."

"It's not necessary."

"Are you going to do it yourself?"

He huffed out a breath, too weary to fight with her. She sat down in the armchair and patted the ottoman.

"Come on, Jake. Stop being stubborn."

"Me? Stubborn. The guy with all the cowboy charm." He sat down. Closing his eyes, he braced himself for her touch. It was certainly not impersonal when she set her slick, warm palms against his shoulders. When she kneaded, he let out a soft groan it felt so good. She worked his lats, then curved her arm under his and really dug deep.

He was gasping with the exquisite release of tension when she said, "The sheriff brought me in for questioning. There's a witness in Dallas who is accusing me of threatening my father."

He was so shocked that she was opening up to him,

finally, he tried not to show it. "Did you?" he asked softly without any inflection in his voice.

"It's true that I've wanted control of the stables for some time and it's true I have voiced that wish many times to him, but not once did I threaten him. My pride isn't more important than my father's life. I guarantee you that." Her voice wobbled with a heavy rush of emotion. "I never would…"

Her kneading changed to something softer, more of a caress. "You believe me. Don't you, Jake?"

He was torn about committing himself here. Trying to stay neutral was his only hope in getting out of this with his sanity intact. "Just tell me everything," he said, and she did. Everything that had happened in the sheriff's office, and then how she'd gone to their family lawyer, Hugh Barrington, and got a referral for a good defense attorney.

"The attorney is smart, but if you're innocent, this should be easily cleared up with Mr. Bellows's support of your account of the story. Did you call him?"

"No, to be honest. I thought it would make me look guilty or like I was trying to get him to change his story. I thought it best to let the sheriff make the inquiry."

Was she telling him to throw him off her scent or was it the truth? She was absolutely right. It would have been suspect and made Bellows's statement suspect. "That's the way an innocent woman would think. Anything else come to mind?"

"No. It was horrible. The blood on the floor and windowsill. The room was trashed like he'd had to fight someone off. Whitney blamed Josie right away.

She's my cousin who had come here to search for something of her father's."

"Matthew Colton."

"Yes, the serial killer," she said bitterly. "The police dragged the Lone Star Lake for Eldridge's body and we waited for a ransom demand, but nothing ever came. Everyone was accusing everyone else. Some of them even thought Whitney had Eldridge killed. Planning to wait for the body to surface and then claim his fortune.

We can't read his will until we have a body, so we really don't know his wishes or who would stand to gain the most from his death. Blame fell on Fowler and he was cleared. Josie was also cleared and during the time she was here, she fell in love with our foreman Tanner. He left with her. Then Zane was cleared. The only one of us who doesn't have an alibi is Marceline. She wasn't in the house when Eldridge disappeared and she hates him. She's made no bones about it."

Then it occurred to him. The information the witness had was pretty personal and not something that was outside the family's knowledge. "If you weren't having lunch with your father that day and the waitress is lying, how did she know about the private information? About you wanting control of the stables?" The heat from her body was almost drugging. Alanna drew a deep breath. "It would have to come from someone who knows you well. Fowler?"

"No, he was cleared." He could feel the tenseness through her hands, her whole body was on edge. "I wouldn't be surprised if it's Whitney or Marceline. Could one of them be trying to frame me?"

"Sounds like without an alibi Marceline is the prime suspect and maybe she's trying to deflect attention."

He leaned into her magic hands, wanting those hands all over him. "That's possible. She won't budge about where she was that night."

"You confronted her when we got back. That's what you two were arguing about."

"Yes," she whispered, placing a soft kiss against the back of his neck.

He stilled, his body going on red-hot alert as he grew hard against the zipper of his jeans. "Alanna..." he murmured.

"Jake. I'm trying to trust you. But this is new to me."

She stood and went to the kitchen, wiping her hands on a towel. Unable to stand the way she looked, that aching look in her eyes, he closed the space between them. She looked up at him and met his gaze, her voice husky when she whispered, "I feel so close to you."

Jake drew an unsteady breath and angled her head back, making a low, indistinguishable sound as he covered her mouth in a kiss that was raw with regret, governed by the need to comfort and reassure. Alanna went still. Then, with a soft exhalation, she clutched at him and yielded to his deep, comforting kiss. Jake slid his hand along her jaw, his calloused fingers snagging in the long silky strands of her hair as he altered the angle of her head. She moved against him, and Jake shuddered and tightened his hold, a fever of want slashing at him. Torn, concerned this was the best and worst thing that could happen between them.

Dragging his mouth away, he trailed a string of kisses down her neck, then caught her head again and gave her another hot, wet kiss. His breathing ragged, he tightened his hold on her face and drew back, holding her against his chest. He held her like that, his hand cupping the back of her neck, until his breathing evened out, and then he started backing toward the bedroom.

She was trembling by the time they made it to the bed, and he paused and drew her into a fierce embrace. Roughly pressing his face against the curve of her neck, he held on to her like she was his lifeline to sanity.

Trying to get a grip on the wild clamor rising up inside him, he realized he had to stop this. But she chose that moment to cup him, kneading him through his jeans. He gritted his teeth and tipped his own head back, groaning at the pleasure of having her hand on him. Somehow he got her out of her clothes and his off without letting her go. Somehow he managed to tear open the small foil packet and sheath himself.

He was beyond control when he lifted her onto the bed, then followed her down, dragging her beneath him. He felt as if his heart would explode, as if his lungs would seize up if he didn't get inside her, if he didn't get as close to her as he could possibly get. She made a small desperate sound and drew up her knees, urging him forward with urgent hands, and Jake clenched his jaw and closed his eyes, burying himself deep inside her. Damn, so deep. So tight and deep.

He locked his arms around her, a shudder coursing through him, and he ground his teeth together, the sensory onslaught nearly ripping him apart. It wasn't the sex, it was the physical connection, as if being inside her fused them into one united whole. Braced against the mind-shattering sensation, Jake remained rigid in her arms, waiting for the heated, electrifying rush to ease. Releasing a breath, he braced his weight on his forearms, his heart trapped in his chest as he covered her mouth in a hot, desperate kiss.

Alanna sobbed into his mouth, her hands clutching at him, and she lifted her hips, rolling her pelvis hard against him. Jake roughly slid his hand under her head and locked his other arm around her buttocks, working his mouth hungrily against hers as he lifted her higher, then rolled his hips against hers. Alanna made a choked sound, and Jake drank it in, his mind blurring when Alanna countered his thrust, her body moving convulsively beneath his. Aware of how desperately she needed this kind of comfort, Jake dragged his mouth away and gritted his teeth, a fine sheen of sweat dampening his skin as he moved against her, trying to give her everything she needed, trying to give her the pleasure that would make her come apart in his arms.

She made another wild sound, and her counter-thrusts turned desperate and erratic, and Jake tightened his hold. His senses rocked into overdrive, he roughly buried his face against her neck and thrust into her, fighting to go the distance.

Alanna arched stiffly beneath him, and Jake's face contorted with an agony of pleasure as her body convulsed around him, pulling, pulling at him. Then, with a ragged groan, he went rigid in her arms and let go, emptying himself deep inside her. Holding on to her with convulsive strength, her face wet against his neck.

Feeling as if he'd been turned inside out, he pressed his mouth against her temple and closed his eyes, his pulse choppy and erratic, the feelings in his chest almost too much to handle. Man, she filled him up— made him feel indestructible.

He drew a deep, shaky breath and pressed another kiss to her beautiful mouth, his touch slow and comforting as he softly stroked his hand across her breasts and taut nipples. She wrapped her arms around his neck as he buried his face in her throat, and he marveled at the feel of her legs wrapped around his waist.

He lifted his head and took her mouth again, taking great care to do it thoroughly. He released a soft sigh, and she slid her free hand up his torso, finally cupping the back of his head. He deepened the kiss, and Alanna yielded full to his questing tongue. Jake slid his arm under her, holding her with infinite care, then drawing away and gazing down at her as he caressed her bottom lip with his thumb. He traced the contours of her face and gave her another quick kiss. He withdrew from her and she arched her back, her breath caught. He rolled to his back and off the bed, taking care of the protection.

Then was right back in it, snuggling her body up against his. He drew her long, muscled leg between his. Cradling her hips against his, he ran his hand up her naked back, then kissed her one more time. "Stay with me," he murmured, his tone husky.

She went still in his arms, and then she turned her face against his and tightened her arms around his waist. "Oh, God, yes," she whispered, looking up with such a fragile look in her eyes, his heart tightened. He had never seen her like this before.

It was almost as if some inner defense had been stripped away, leaving her exposed. He wasn't sure how she would handle that exposure. After all, Alanna Colton had spent her whole life keeping her guard up. He didn't know how she would react if someone ever brought it down. A someone who was here under false pretenses, working her over to solve a crime, betraying her even as he was making love to her. A first-class heel.

He didn't need one more ghost to haunt him. He worried he'd gone too far here, but how he'd wanted her and not just for a night.

He closed his eyes, his heart throbbing. He'd give up his next breath if he could avoid hurting her.

But he knew that would be impossible.

Chapter 10

She stirred against him, then shifted her head. "Are you all right, Jake?"

She asked him this while both of them were wading into the deep end. "Right as rain," he murmured and that wasn't a lie. Having her, holding her, set him on top of the world, even with the threat of heartache and pain, but that would come. He stayed in the here and now. "Why do you ask?"

"I didn't like the way you looked when you left the barn this afternoon. I felt like I had...let you down. Maybe even let myself down. There have always been people around me to push me, pull me, challenge me and break me down. But...never one I trusted to simply walk away and let me decide. You using some of that horse whispering on me?"

Staring into the darkness, he let his hand rest on

the swell of her hip, giving her a small, prompting squeeze. "No. I'm trying to understand you, Alanna. Gaining your trust comes with the territory."

She lightly ran her fingertips along his collarbone. Her gaze averted, she continued to stroke his collarbone and Jake waited, sensing her struggle. Her hair was draped around her face, and she lifted it. Jake waited for her to answer, knowing this was critical.

"Something is happening between us. I think it's not all one-sided and it's addictive and scary."

"You'd be pretty accurate there. Would one of those people you're speaking about be your brother?"

"We have a strange mixture of people in my family and the dynamics have always been volatile, but Fowler is complicated. He cares, but he's also like a bull in a china shop, all rough display and throwing his weight around. He can't help being a bull."

"Your family has taught you to be tough. To put on armor to face the outside world. In your circumstances, that's not a bad lesson. It's good to be strong, but, Alanna," he said quietly, "too much of a good thing leads to imbalance. Sometimes you just need to lean and that doesn't make you weak or ineffectual."

Alanna rose up on one elbow and looked down at him, her hair creating a waterfall of golden sunlight around her shoulders. She stared at him, the faint light from outside washing across her face and revealing the hesitancy in her expression. A glimmer of alarm appeared in her eyes. "It doesn't? What does it make me?"

He met her eyes. "It makes you human." Her face softened, her eyes going tender, she pressed her face hard against his jaw, placing a kiss there and his arms tightened around her.

He was a fool. He wanted her to trust him, but it had nothing to do with his mission objective or his job. It had to do with something he couldn't control deep inside him. He wanted her to see beyond her fear, see him deep down and know he couldn't hurt her. Not really. His job aside—a necessary evil— there was something honest about what they shared.

Her face still pressed against him, she murmured, "What motivated you to rehabilitate horses, to work with them?"

He stared up at her for a moment, then shifted his focus. Avoiding her gaze, he painstakingly hooked his thumb under a thick swatch of hair and drew it back, tucking it fully behind her. "Other than my natural tendency?"

She felt so good against him. "Don't do that. Don't make this about something you can't define. I want to know."

For some reason Jake felt as if he'd just been let out of a dark, tight space, and he closed his eyes and hugged her hard, feeling as if he could take his first deep breath in days. "This is about the things we never talk about, the things that mean something deep down. About opening up and laying it all out?"

"Yes. It works both ways."

Screwing up his courage, he took the step that he knew could change everything. "My brother."

She gazed at him, her eyes wide, hearing the pain and uncertainty, and then she looked away. "Tell me, Jake. I want to know you. Not on the surface, but deep down where you hold all your secrets."

"Opening up a Pandora's box." He couldn't tell her everything. He had to hold back on her. He didn't want to, but he still had a job to do. A cover to protect.

"Maybe, but I'm prepared to handle what comes out."

He took a breath. He never talked about Matt with anyone, not even his old man; his mom had been dead for ten years from cancer. Discussing Matt was such a sore subject, a wound that had never healed for either one of them.

"My brother died alone from a drug overdose. He was sixteen. The pressure he was under changed him from an easygoing kid to a worn-out teenager."

"Why?"

"My father's expectations. It was his way or the highway."

"I know all about that. I understand it. He just wanted to escape."

"Actually, he wanted independence. He didn't want to be in our old man's pocket. He didn't want him calling the shots and telling him how to run his life. It would have, like the drugs, killed him. He had to get out—had to make it on his own. But the internal battle was too much."

She held his gaze for a moment, then bent her head and started rubbing her thumb back and forth across his collarbone again, her touch not quite steady. She swallowed, then took a deep, unsteady breath. "I'm so sorry, Jake. I truly am. Maybe, I ought to think about what you suggested today."

"Go out on your own?"

"Yes."

He pressed a kiss against her brow, then hugged

her again. His chest expanding with a deep, uneven breath. "I think you're strong, smart and so damn beautiful. Only do it if it makes sense to you," he said gruffly.

Cupping her hand against the angle of his jaw, a solemn, reflective expression appeared. She stared off into the darkness, inhaled and spoke, gently caressing him. "I will. I'm not sure I could handle being treated like I don't matter."

His throat suddenly closed up on him, and he tightened his hold on her, hugging her head against the curve of his shoulder. He had to wait for the spasm to ease, and then he said, his voice husky with emotion. "You matter, Alanna."

Her head came up, and she stared at him, a look of wonder on her face. "I do, huh?"

A warped smile appearing, he tucked some loose hair behind her ear. "Yeah," he said, his voice lighter. "Very much." She stared at him, and Jake ran his thumb down her cheek, a tight feeling unfolding in his chest. "What more—"

She pressed her fingers against his mouth and he tried his hardest to maintain the trace of a smile. "You talk too much, McCord," she whispered.

The tightness in his chest expanding, he shifted his gaze to her mouth as she drew her thumb along his lower lip.

"Is that so," he muttered.

She shifted her thumb to the fullest part of his mouth, her expression as soft as her touch. "Yeah, that's so," she said.

He met her gaze, something painful happening around his heart when he saw the glimmer of moisture in her eyes. Sliding his hand along her jaw until his fingers were buried in her hair, he drew her head down. He took her mouth in a soft, comforting kiss. Wrapping his fingers around the back of her head, he held her still as he softly, slowly brushed his mouth back and forth across hers, tormenting her, tormenting himself. "So beautiful," he whispered unevenly against her mouth. "So, so damn beautiful."

Releasing her pent-up breath in a rush, Alanna slid her arms around his neck and moved on top of him. Closing his eyes against the onslaught of sensation, Jake turned his face against her and wrapped her in a hard, enveloping embrace, wondering how in hell he would ever manage without her. Grasping a handful of hair, he clenched his jaw and turned his head against hers, something raw and wild breaking loose inside him. Inhaling raggedly, he clutched her against him. A tremor coursed through her, and she drew her knees up and pulled out of his hold, her hair cascading around her face as she rose above him. Realizing what was happening, realizing what she intended, he snatched her hand away. She twisted her wrist free, reached for protection and sheathed him. Then drew his hand to her mouth placing a hot, wet kiss against his palm. Lacing her fingers through his, she caught his other hand and repeated the hot, erotic caress, then forced his hands down by his head. Another tremor shuddered through her and she rose up, lowered her weight fully on him, taking him deep inside her. Deep, deep inside her.

Breaking out in a cold sweat, Jake clenched his jaw against the sharp, electrifying surge of feeling, his shoulders coming off the bed as she moved once, twice against him. His heartbeat a frenzy in his chest, his pulse thick and heavy, he tightened his fingers against the pillow.

"Alanna…darlin'. Ah… God. I can't…you've gotta stop, babe."

Bending over him, she stroked the palms of his hands with her thumbs, her breasts grazing his chest. "No," she whispered brokenly. "No." Another shudder coursed through her, and she tightened her hold on his hands, her breath catching as she flexed her hips, her hot, wet tightness gripping him, stroking him, drawing him closer and closer.

An agony of sensation shot through him, and he rolled his head again, the cords of his neck taut, and he sucked in a breath through clenched teeth. God, he wanted to let go, wanted to ride out the hard, swelling need.

Then she moved against him, taking him ever deeper inside her, and he went under, the fever claiming him. He groaned and flexed beneath her, driving inside her. He lost it.

Wisps of a dream receded when Jake roused from sleep, half aware of a heavy weight on his arm. He shifted, a jolt of pain shooting through his shoulder, and he drowsily wet his lips and opened his eyes. The room was still dark and Alanna was sound asleep, her head resting in the hollow of his shoulder, but he guessed it was early morning. He waited for the mental fog to clear a little, and then he carefully drew her head onto his chest and flexed his hand against the tingling sensation. After scrubbing his face to rid himself of the last vestiges of sleep, he tucked his head and brushed a soft lingering kiss against her forehead, smiling a little when she made a soft sound and turned her face toward his warmth. If only things could be that simple.

Brushing back the wisps of hair clinging to her face, he kissed her again, then cautiously rolled his throbbing shoulder. Easing the tightness, he leaned forward and stuffed two pillows behind his shoulders, settling himself into a more comfortable position before resting his still-tingling arm along her hip. He stared into the darkness, thinking about what had happened last night. He had received something from her that he had never expected. An emotional gift. And he wouldn't be sorry about her deep, abiding trust in him.

It filled him up at the same time as it hollowed him out.

He liked the way Alanna dealt with almost everything in her life from a strong base of operations. What she had given him was tangible. But what left his gut in a knot was he bet she'd never lost it the way she had. Had never gone over the edge. He recognized something in her that pinged off something in him. It shook his foundations.

Releasing a heavy sigh, he gazed at her, his expression solemn. Even in the faint light from outside, he could see the shadows under her eyes, and he wondered if she'd had as little sleep during the past few days as he had. It was pretty obvious he'd shaken up her world outside of her missing father.

A small, wry smile appeared. Of course he'd given himself a good shake in the process. He lightly brushed his thumb along her cheekbone, then tucked a loose piece of hair behind her ear. Remembering that galvanizing instant when she had taken him deep inside her, Jake tipped his head back and closed his eyes, fighting the urge to draw her up against him. He waited for the thick, heavy surge to ease a little, then took a deep, steadying breath and glanced at the clock on the bedside table. Four o'clock.

Maybe it was time to stack a few thousand bales.

She stirred when he gently maneuvered away from her, and he leaned over and brushed a light kiss against her temple. "We better get you back to your room," he whispered gruffly. He lifted her hair off her face, then sighed deeply when she wrapped her arms around his neck and hummed softly against his throat.

"You smell good," she mumbled.

Her hand traveled down his body, heading south, and he grabbed her wrist, laughing. "Oh, no you don't. We don't want a roomful of cowboys watching as you trot your beautiful butt down those stairs."

She raised her head. "You're trying to protect my reputation." Her mouth hitched up in a teasing grin, her sleepy eyes glinting. "That is so darn sweet."

He threaded his fingers through her hair and gave it a little tug. "Don't be sassy in the morning."

She gave him a full-on smile and it made him want to let go of her wrist and find out where she had been going with her hand. "I'm buck naked and we've just bared our souls. I don't think I have much else going for me."

Instead, he slapped her on her shapely backside and got out of bed. "Oh, I beg to differ on that front, lady. You've got plenty going for you."

She jumped at his playful slap and rubbed her butt.

"I think I like waking up in your arms, cowboy. I think I like that a lot." Her eyes went over him in a slow, heated slide.

He set his hands on his waist and grinned. "Now you're dealing your blows beneath the belt," he growled.

She waggled her brows. "I happen to enjoy what you've got below the belt, McCord."

He shook his head, his heart squeezing. "Sassy. So damn sassy."

She giggled and it sounded so lighthearted.

"Get dressed before I do forget about your reputation and haul you back into this bed." The sensual threat hovered between them for a moment, and then she sighed.

As he rounded the bed toward the bathroom, she stood up, grumbling, "Promises, promises."

He changed direction and grabbed her around the waist and hauled her against him. She gasped as his mouth came down on hers, then groaned. They spent another fifteen minutes kissing the stuffing out of each other.

He pulled away and grinned, gave her another quick kiss, then turned her around and gave her a push toward the bathroom. "You can go first."

He watched her bend to pick up her discarded clothing and cross to the bathroom door, appreciating the rear view, appreciating the lazy, loose-hipped way she moved. He wondered what she would look like pregnant.

Caught square in the gut by that random thought, he clenched his jaw and turned back to the bed, wishing he could punch someone. He knew what was building in him and it was moonbeams and fairy tales if he thought there was any way he was going long term with Alanna, no matter how he felt about her. She was right. There was no magic, only hard, cold reality.

He knew all about that from experience.

Fully dressed, they crossed the stable area with no one but the horses seeing their progress. Up the back road to the quiet and dark house, they climbed the stairs to the back patio, skirting the pool to her suite of rooms. "How did you know which room was mine the other day?"

"I didn't. I took my chances. I knew you were housed in the left wing. I'm just lucky I didn't knock on Fowler's door."

She laughed at that, finding it extremely funny. "You would have had some 'splaining to do," she said, wiping her eyes.

They stopped outside the door. "I had a good time, Jake. I will admit rubbing ointment into your shoulders was just a ruse to get inside to talk to you."

Hooking his thumbs in the front pockets of his jeans, Jake watched her, his expression light. "Sassy and underhanded."

"Guilty." The longing on her face made his heart trip a little.

"Come here, sweetheart," he whispered.

She didn't hesitate and went right into his arms. He shifted, widening his stance, when she slipped her arms around his waist and turned her face against him. Resting his jaw against her head as he began slowly massaging the small of her back, Alanna tightened her arms around him and Jake could detect a light quivering in her, as though she had been braced for pain that hadn't materialized. Shifting his hold, he cradled her head firmly against him and brushed a gentling kiss against her temple, his expression unsettled.

He didn't know what in hell was going to happen to them. And if he'd realized anything during the past few days, it was that he wasn't sure what kind of future they had, if any. He suspected when she found out about why he was there and who he really was, that would be it.

Was he a fool to hope for a different outcome?

Would she see he was just doing his job and everything he'd said and done had been out of a genuine and real respect for her and who she was? Or would she cut him loose, her anger and betrayal too much for her to overcome?

He gave her a reassuring hug and pressed his mouth against her hair. He shifted his hold and turned slightly, keeping her against him for a few more minutes.

Alanna exhaled heavily and reluctantly eased back in his embrace. Hooking his knuckles under her chin, Jake lifted her face and made her look at him, the heavy feeling in his gut intensified when he saw her give him a sweet smile. "You are something. You know that, Jake?"

He held her gaze for a moment, then tightened his hold on her jaw and brushed a soft kiss against her mouth.

"Yeah, and life's a bitch, isn't it?" he whispered huskily.

Alanna gave a shaky laugh and stared up at him,

the look in her green eyes warm and intimate. "You just figuring that out, huh?"

He held her gaze, the corner of his mouth lifting a little. "Quick, aren't I."

"So very," she said as she eased out of his arms and opened the door, slipping inside. She stood there for a moment staring at him. She touched the glass and he raised his hand and pressed it firmly to the pane.

She blew him a kiss and disappeared inside.

Something stirred in him, something that was a direct result of Alanna Colton and her courage and determination. Maybe he should reassess his life? Maybe if he took a look at what he was doing, he would discover it wasn't something he wanted to continue to do? Maybe he'd been hooked too long ago to know what it was he was getting himself into. Maybe, just maybe, as a result, he could change his life.

His gut clenched with the thought and how it would affect his dad, but maybe it was way past time to have a talk with him about Matt, about how Jake felt about everything now.

He entered the apartment and the sound of a coffee grinder broke the stillness, shattering his thoughts. Ellen smiled at him. "Up early again. Went for a little walk? It's breathtaking when the sun comes up. The sky has such a way with its good-morning colors."

"Yeah."

"Oh, if you're going up. Would you mind telling Dylan that Buck was by? He wants him to help out on the cattle ranch today. They're going to be short-handed."

"No problem." He headed up the stairs and stopped on the second floor. Walking down the hall toward

Dylan's suite, his boot kicked something metallic on the floor just outside his door and it jingled as it re-settled after getting punted. He bent down and picked it up.

It was a wire bracelet with *Marceline* in diamond-filled gold lettering.

As he stood there, absorbing that information, Henry Swango came out of his room and Jake tucked the bracelet in his side pocket and knocked on Dylan's door. Henry gave him a hostile look as he turned and headed for the stairs.

Dylan pulled the door open as Henry disappeared from view.

"Hey, Jake."

"Hey, Buck wants you to head over to the cattle ranch after breakfast. They're shorthanded today."

"Oh, okay. Thanks for the info."

"Sure." As Dylan went to go back in his room, Jake pulled out the bracelet. "Dylan, do you know Marceline Colton?"

Dylan laughed and shook his head. "No. Like a wealthy Colton would ever give me the time of day."

"Yeah, right," Jake agreed. "See you around."

If she wasn't hooking up with Dylan, that meant she was here—he glanced at Henry's door—to speak with Henry? Maybe Marceline's hands weren't quite clean. Maybe she had hired Henry to do away with her father. She had no alibi and she hated him. She was one of the prime suspects. He couldn't help but wonder if this had anything to do with Alanna and how it might tie into this witness allegation.

After all, Alanna seemed to be sure Marceline might be trying to frame her. She also pointed fingers at her stepmother, Whitney, but it wasn't her bracelet that was found outside a suspected felon's door.

His cop instincts heightened, he stepped over to Henry's door. But at that moment he heard voices on the stairs and decided to leave it for now. He headed for his own room to shower and change. He had work to do today. Worry gnawing at him, he entered his room.

If he did this by the book, he would get probable cause to search Henry's apartment and turn that into the form of a warrant. At this point, he had nothing but his own suspicions to go by and the orders from his boss to let this go for now. He decided quietly snooping around was a good use of his time. Maybe he would get lucky and find something in Henry's room he could bring to Alanna's attention and at least get the man thrown off the ranch.

But if Henry endangered Alanna or any innocent civilian on this ranch, all bets were freaking off. He'd blow his cover in a heartbeat and collar the lowlife before he let him harm anyone.

And if he threatened Alanna, he'd kill the bastard outright.

Chapter 11

Alanna strolled down Main Street in the heart of the district. The narrow tree-lined route favored by pedestrians was also home to sidewalk restaurants, basement nightclubs and retail stores, but Alanna was here for a purpose, not to shop. She adjusted her dark sunglasses, her hair tucked under a brown Stetson as she cut through Pegasus Plaza framed by the Magnolia Hotel, Iron Cactus Restaurant, Adolphus Tower and the Kirby Building onto Commerce and walked to a high-rise overlooking the JFK Memorial Plaza.

She entered the building, stopped at the front desk and smiled at the receptionist. "Daisy Martin to see Rebecca Stratton."

The woman gave her a bright smile and consulted her computer as Daisy, aka Alanna, signed in. "She's expecting you. Go right on up."

Alanna headed for the elevator and went to the correct floor. As the doors opened a large sign in metallic letters read Rebecca Stratton & Associates. She made her way to the door with Rebecca's name engraved in gold, then gave a cursory knock and entered at the request. A woman in her late forties with deep red hair and a still-trim figure in a dove-gray suit rose when she saw Alanna, her eyes widening.

Alanna closed the door and smiled.

Rebecca's voice a sultry alto, she said with a quirk of her brow, "I wasn't expecting you. Are you my ten o'clock?"

"Yes. Sorry for the secrecy and the alias, but I want to make inquiries and the Colton name makes everyone sit up and take notice."

Rebecca came around the desk as Alanna experienced a rush of adrenaline and the thought: Was she really going to do this? At this point, she was just going to look. There wasn't a commitment. She took off the hat and sunglasses. "Well, you are being so dramatic about it, it's making my day. I feel like I'm in a spy novel." She hugged Alanna then indicated a seat.

Becca watched her with an indulgent maternal look, then gave her a feral smile. "Don't tell me you want to sell Colton Valley Ranch?"

"Ha!" Alanna's stomach jumped and the knot that had been there ever since she made the decision to come into Dallas and talk to her father's real estate agent and friend about changing her life and taking a chance…on herself. "No. I couldn't even if I wanted to."

"I'm so heartbroken over Eldridge. He is one of

my dearest friends and quite the character. Has there been any news?"

"He's very fond of you, too, Becca, and no. He's still missing."

Rebecca stared at her for a moment, her expression intent. She sat back, the panoramic view of the city behind her through the large windows. "What can I do for you?"

Alanna looked away, trying not to let her throat cramp up. It took a minute, and then she answered, her voice as strong as she wanted it to be. "I want to look into midsize properties that have either stables already on the property or lend themselves to building stables."

"Oh my God, you're going out on your own? Good for you! I take it Fowler has been throwing his weight around now that he's completely in charge?"

She couldn't keep the surprise from her face. "Yes, and nothing is going to change and I'm tired of being second-guessed and discounted."

Rebecca had a deep, throaty laugh. "My dear, I've known that boy since he was in diapers. He's a damn tyrant." She reached out across the desk and opened her hand. "Let's talk about your price limit and the location."

Alanna never hesitated. Jake was right. It was time for her to make a stand. She would make sure she had a backup plan before she made her ultimatum. But if Fowler didn't listen to her and give her the respect she was due, she would walk. She leaned forward, a smile sliding across her face as Rebecca's eyes lit up and she placed her hand in Rebecca's.

An hour and a half later with her hat and sunglasses in place she was once again traveling down Commerce Street. In the distance the early lunch crowd was milling about and all of a sudden Alanna saw a bald head bob in the crowd and her heart skipped a beat. She froze on the sidewalk, staring at the place where she'd seen him.

There was something endearingly familiar about the man's short, skinny frame. Could it be?

She surged forward as the man faded into the crowd. She hurried and passed the place where she'd seen him. Stopping to catch her breath and search Pegasus Plaza, she whipped around looking for that shiny pate.

She saw him again, but he ducked past a planter and she lost sight of him. Taking off again, she raced across the plaza and made a sharp turn around the planter, almost running over a woman with a baby in a stroller. She apologized quickly, searching again as the man exited the plaza onto Main Street, disappearing around the corner of the building.

Her mouth dry and her heart pounding, she sprinted and came around the corner at a fast run only to run right into him as he was searching his pockets. He caught her against him and they stumbled around in a little off-kilter dance until they caught their balance.

She looked up into his face, her breath caught in her throat only to discover it wasn't her father. Deep disappointment washed through her, fighting to contain the nearly unbearable ache in her throat and her chest.

It wasn't her father, but an elderly man who stared down at her with a kind, fatherly smile on his face.

"You all right there, miss?"

"Yes," she said as he let her go, stepping back and swallowing against the awful feeling of distress. She shivered and cupped her hands on her upper arms, trying to hold everything in. "I'm so sorry."

"That's quite all right," he said, then started walking away from her down the street.

She'd held all the fear and worry at bay, sure that something would turn up, but it had been too long since her father had gone missing and it was unlikely…without the ransom note… Oh, God, she felt the tears and the grief rising in her as she went in the opposite direction. When she reached her car, she climbed inside and pressed her head to the steering wheel, working hard to keep the dread and the reality at bay.

He wasn't dead. He couldn't be.

But if that was the case, where was he? Why hadn't they been contacted?

What the hell had happened to her father?

It was then that she acknowledged how much she loved him, regardless of the rumors of his background, regardless of how he treated her like a little girl when she was a grown woman. He was her dad and she was worried sick and she wanted him back.

She hit the steering wheel several times, the tears starting to fall in silent tracks down her face.

She wanted him back, now!

Hard on the heels of grief for her father came the one sure fact that twisted her up even tighter.

Would Jake stay? Would he brave her family and her status and her wealth to remain with her? Would he deal with her family for the rest of his life? Could she hold on to what they had, or as a Colton heiress would that mean she'd have everything but the one thing she wanted?

Love.

And she could so love him. It would be so damn easy. He pushed her out of her comfort zone, he made her think, grounded her. Oh, God, she caught her breath on a soft sob. He grounded her.

Yet, she could only think about what the risk was to her heart. Had to assess that to remain sane. Last night was so beautiful. His dark gaze filled with need, his hand sliding up between her legs, and all she could do was watch his face—so striking, his hair so silky beneath her fingers, his eyes so deep set, so thickly lashed, so intensely focused on her.

She was on the verge of giving him everything... all her secrets, all her heart. And that was the risk, wasn't it?

She was already sliding, had really moved over the halfway mark and was going downhill fast.

She had no idea if he would stay and that was the biggest risk yet.

Could she ask him?

Could she go so far out on that ledge to risk a terrible, terrible fall?

It was after lunch when Alanna finally showed up at the arena, and it only took one look at her face to know something serious had happened. She tried to pull off that she was just fine, but there was something about her that made Jake's gaze narrow. She met his glance when she first came in, and the hollowness in her eyes made his gut clench. It was heartache he saw—deep, gut-wrenching heartache. That glimpse dazed him, and as he stood on the concrete walkway, his hand resting on the low wall, he felt like someone had just clipped his legs out from under him.

Without thinking, he went after her. Grabbing her arm from behind, he hauled her into an empty stall and into the corner where no one could see them, then caught her by the back of the head and she wrapped her arms around his neck. After getting rid of her hat and tossing it aside, he wrapped her in a tight embrace. He didn't say anything; he just held her tightly. It took a while, but finally the rigidness left her body, and she drew a deep, wobbling breath and loosened her arms around him slightly.

He pressed a kiss against her neck, then snuggled her closer to his warmth. He knew better than to ask her what was wrong. Alanna was like a horse that was green and real jumpy—he didn't want to do anything that would make her pull back. Resting his jaw against her head, he rubbed his hand against her firmly muscled hips.

She murmured, "You've got being a good guy down pat."

"Doesn't make me a hero, darlin'."

She gave a shaky laugh and slid her bare hands into the back pockets of his jeans. "Oh, yes, it does, McCord."

He mimicked her hold, then leaned back and grinned at her. "If you say so, boss lady, but why do I always have these wicked, wicked thoughts in my head."

She watched him, giving him a slightly scandalized look. "Okay, so you're a hero with delicious layers," she responded drily. "I'll give you that."

He brought his head up, his tone soft, he asked, "Do you want to talk about it?"

"Not now," she whispered. "I've got to get to work. You go. Finish what you were doing. I'll be all right."

He was reluctant to let go of her, but this wasn't about him. This was about her and what she had to do to really, fully lean on him. He couldn't push that or pressure that.

He went back to the horse he was saddling and got the gelding ready, marveling at the well-behaved animal. Tamara took him, and Alanna walked onto the arena floor. She gave him a warm, tender look tempered with something that looked haunted and bruised, he retreated before he hauled her back to that empty stall.

Patience. He had to have that with her. Wait for her. That was one of the easiest things he'd ever done with horses. Have that staying power.

He closed his eyes, then opened them and prowled out of the arena.

He wasn't playing with her heart; he was certain about that. When this was all over, it wouldn't be up to him to decide what would happen between them.

It would totally be up to her.

Whether it was seconds or days, that...*that* would be the longest wait of all.

Jake went to Zorro's stall and when he got some flak from the stallion, he clipped on a lead line and murmured to him, praising him as he asked him to move back and forth until he settled down. He went outside to the paddock, removed the lead line and replaced it with a lunge as Zorro came easy into the corral.

A couple of hands were at the fence and he noticed one of them was Henry. Clay stood a few feet away, also watching, but not interacting with Henry.

"Hey, horse whisperer," Henry said. "Why aren't you riding that stallion yet?"

The guy standing next to him huffed a laugh, but Clay just watched with an intentness that Jake recognized as an openness to learning. That made him smile. Maybe he had gotten to Clay.

"Come on," he said in a soft, even tone. "Around the ring a few times—let's see how we're doing today."

He let out the lunge line, standing in the center of the ring and working him along the fence. To his credit and Jake's keen eye, he didn't balk, which was promising. If anything, he seemed almost eager. That was a positive sign, too.

Even though he really needed to focus on the stallion and be fully present in working the horse, his mind couldn't seem to get off what was going on with Alanna. What had happened to put that look on her face?

This woman was doing more to him than he should let her. Trying to put everything in perspective was what he needed. He rounded along the far end of the paddock…only to discover Alanna leaning against the fence as they came around the other side.

Well, he hadn't minded the other audience, but Alanna was heavily on his mind right now.

He smiled at her as he worked Zorro closer to where she stood.

He moved Zorro off the fence slightly, and nodded to Alanna as they passed. She gave him a pointed look, saying his attention should be on the horse.

All of them were still watching as he brought the horse around the ring one more time, his glossy black coat catching the sun and showing its shine.

He started to slow the horse, figuring he'd had enough time on the lunge. He wanted to work with touch and see if he could get the horse to move without the lunge. Show him that the herd leader was this two-footed, determined man.

There was a sudden popping noise and Zorro reared his head back. Jake, too lost in his thoughts to react quickly enough, was a split second too late.

The horse sidled and shoved him hard into the fence where his head bounced off the top slat, momentarily stunning him.

"Jake!" Alanna called, but he couldn't get his bearing fast enough. Then there was another pop and the horse's sudden lunge snapped the lead tight in his grip, yanking him forward, off his feet. He landed hard on his knees and hands, then went sprawling in the dirt as Zorro took off. Had he not let go, he'd have been dragged face-first.

From the corner of his eye, he saw Clay clear the fence in one high hurtle and quickly, instinctively, lift his hand to warn him off even as he was scrambling to his feet. Jake took off after Zorro, who was stampeding toward the end of the ring and the stable gate.

He didn't have time to look to see what had set the horse off, but he suspected Henry had done something to spook him on purpose.

"Please, don't jump," he murmured. Then he saw

Clay standing his ground while Zorro pounded straight for him, with only the gate between them.

"Move!" Jake shouted, knowing that yelling right now was not a good idea, but having no choice. He was running full-out behind the horse, with no hope of catching him. It was like watching a train wreck about to happen and being helpless to stop it.

Jake had never liked that feeling.

Clay moved, but toward Zorro, not away. He didn't run, but moved steadily toward the gate, his hands raised, palms out, not waving them around, but holding them steady.

At the last possible second, Zorro seemed to falter and pull up just slightly. Even in his panic, he didn't see Clay as a threat.

"Good boy, Zorro, that's the way," Jake called out, keeping his voice as calm as he could. He slowed as he came up along the fence beside him, keeping well clear of his hind legs.

Clay stopped on the other side of the gate, hands still up as Zorro dug in and tried to slow down, balking now as the gate drew closer.

Jake held his breath as the horse slowed even more, trotting a few steps. Slowed sufficiently, he trotted past the stable gate, then danced sideways a bit into the center of the ring, spooked still and more than a little confused by what had happened.

Clay had already eased toward the horse, talking to him as he drew closer. "Whoa there. Good boy," Clay said, doing all the right things, approaching the horse slowly, using a calm, steady tone, talking continuously, gauging his reaction so he wouldn't bolt again. Jake couldn't be prouder of him. The kid had either been doing some studying, interacting with Zorro, or both.

"Careful," Alanna called out as she caught up. He calmed a bit more and turned to look at Jake. He ambled closer, head down, eyes not as wild and he nudged Jake.

Alanna stood a good ten yards away and her eyes widened and he could hear her audible gasp. Zorro was still breathing heavily through his nose, but his ears were twitching toward Clay, no longer pinned back, and he was clearly listening to what the kid was saying.

"Jake," Alanna said, her voice tinged with anger. "I want to talk to you."

"In a minute," he said, "I can't let this training session end on a bad note."

"Jake—"

"Give me a few minutes, Alanna."

She narrowed her eyes and turned and marched back to the fence, slipped through the slats. Clay gave Jake a look that said he wouldn't want to be in his shoes.

"Good job, Clay." Jake gripped his shoulder and squeezed. "Good instincts." He picked up the lead line as he felt the trickle of blood slip down his temple. He ignored it, sending the horse into another circle. When Clay tried to retreat, Jake took his hand and set it on the lunge line.

Clay sucked in a breath and a huge grin split his face as he focused his attention on the horse. After a few times around, Jake was totally aware of Alanna's hot gaze burning the back of his neck. He led the horse over to the water and Zorro drank heavily, snorted in the way that said, *Okay, you might be a pretty tough herd leader, but no bad feelings.*

He unclipped the lunge and ducked through the slats with Clay right behind him.

"See you around," Clay said, glancing a little ways away at Alanna. Jake nodded.

"Thanks for the quick thinking."

Clay leaned over. "I can't prove it, but I think Henry was the one who made those noises. I'm not sure how."

"Yeah," he said as he met Henry's eyes and the gleam of satisfaction in them. He laughed, hit the guy standing next to him on the arm. They walked away, laughing.

As Clay walked away, Alanna grabbed Jake's arm and pulled him toward the arena. Once inside the dim interior, she dragged him through the doorway, catching the door with her heel. Grasping his shoulder, she forced him down into a chair, her tone firm when she said, "Sit down."

She went behind her desk and pulled out a white first aid kit and opened it. She walked over to him, her flat gaze unreadable. Taking out some gauze pads and a brown bottle, she walked back to him and bent over him, the scent of her full of horses, sweat and all woman. She pressed the pad to the open end of the bottle and tipped it.

"Are you seeing double? Do you have a headache? Do I need to take you to the hospital?"

"No, no, and um, no."

She gave him a sharp look and he added quietly, "Ma'am."

"Don't be cute with me right now, Jake," she said,

and he'd only heard that tone once when she'd told him not to argue with her when he'd first gotten there.

"Got it. No cowboy charm."

She dabbed at his temple and he hissed in a breath at the cut's sting. She grabbed his chin when he pulled away and held him steady. "Don't be a baby."

He winced again, but she cleaned it thoroughly, then pressed a bandage to it. "It doesn't need stitches," she snapped.

He nodded.

She paced away and folded her arms over her chest, her back rigid. "You should probably get back to work."

She looked pissed. She acted pissed, but her voice gave her away. He rose and came up behind her, turning her, but she didn't unfold her arms or give him an inch.

"I'm all right," he murmured, trying to pull her into his arms. "He didn't hurt me that bad."

But she wasn't having any of it. She fought out of his embrace and put the desk between them. "What about the next time?" she hissed. He looked into her eyes. What he saw there was what he suspected. He just hadn't expected her concern to hit him so hard. Raw fear for his safety radiated. This was intimate fear, the kind a woman had for a man she cared about more than she wanted to let on.

That one small realization touched him like little else had. He waited for the feeling to ease, then said, "Alanna, don't overreact." His voice was gruff.

It was the worst thing he could have said. Her eyes flashed even hotter and she shook her head. "Don't tell me how to feel, Jake. Don't."

His entire world shifted to some new position, rotating on a completely different axis, with an orbit that was no longer his own to navigate. It should have scared him more. He went around the desk and her look warned him off, but he kept going.

He wished this damn assignment was over. He wished she didn't have dragons he couldn't slay right now. He jerked her against him, tightening his arms when she stayed stiff and unresponsive.

Then she abruptly turned her face against his neck and released her arms, slipping them around his waist and he felt her chest expand with a shudder against him. "He could have killed you," she said with less heat.

Affected by her emotional struggle, Jake drew her deeper into his embrace and rested his cheek against the top of her head. "I'm all right," he said huskily. "I know what I'm doing."

She tried to pull away, but he held her. She mumbled into his throat, "I have had enough of this. That stallion goes and I'll tell Fowler to his face."

"No. Zorro was deliberately spooked to make me look bad. When this gets back to Fowler, he might fire me."

She stared at him and gave him one of her dry looks. "No, he wants that stallion tamed too badly and he said you were the best, so, Jake, trust your instincts." She chewed on her lip. "I did hear the popping noises. What do you think caused them?"

"I don't know, but if I find out…" He bent down and gave her a soft, lingering kiss. She gave herself up to it, but then pushed at his chest.

"You'd better get back to work, but please be careful."

He backed away from her and exited the office. Be careful? He was already doing the most reckless thing on the planet.

He was falling for the heiress, a *suspect* no less, one who broke the princess mold into tiny pieces and shattered him to smithereens.

He'd already blasted way past careful.

Chapter 12

All through the next week, Jake backed off. He didn't push her, he didn't try to get her talking, and he never asked her why she had that bruised, haunted look in her eyes. And he didn't ask her why he kept seeing traces of the fear that had surfaced after he'd gotten caught between Zorro and the fence.

He guessed she was wrestling with deep-seated emotions, and he knew she was more vulnerable than she'd ever allowed herself to be. It was just a gut feeling. It was as if she was stranded on a high, narrow ledge. No matter what he did or said, it didn't matter a damn unless she let go and took that first step. He didn't care how big a step it was, or how she took it. He just knew nothing would change unless she did.

There were times when he felt as if he was an inch away from going crazy, and then there were times when she'd seemed so damned fragile that he would get her alone somewhere and just hold her. And every time he did it, she would huddle in his arms, almost as if he was a lifeline.

At night, she didn't want comforting or gentleness. There was a kind of wildness in her, an urgency, and she pushed him to the limit, pushed him until he finally lost it. And then the fire in her would consume him, and he would need her so damn bad and be so desperate to get inside her that there was no room for patience, for gentleness, for comfort.

He'd never had such powerful climaxes. And he'd never been so emptied afterward. Or so hollow. He had never, ever used a woman to satisfy his own needs, but he felt as if he was using her now, and it bothered the hell out of him. He probably would have had it out with her, except afterward, when they lay spent and trembling in each other's arms, she seemed to need him more than ever. She would hold on to him, her whole body trembling, and even in her sleep, she stayed close.

There were so many times when he came close to asking her what was wrong, but he didn't. He needed her to take that first step by herself. She had to let go of whatever handhold she was hanging on to and come to him. She had to; it wouldn't be worth anything if he forced her into it.

In the meantime, there was still no return call from Jeremy Bellows and as the time passed, he worried more about how the investigation would go. There wasn't a whole lot of evidence to link her to her father's disappearance, but circumstantial evidence could be used to try to build a case against her.

He had tried several times, but the woman on the other end of the phone kept putting him off. Finally, the sheriff went out to his home and there was no answer. At his office, his receptionist indicated that he was away and wouldn't be back for a while. She said she'd be happy to contact them when he returned.

It was a few days after Zorro had bolted and Jake got an opportunity to pick the lock to Henry's room. He realized anything he found in there couldn't be used in court, but he hoped to find some clue that would at least confirm Henry was a drug dealer. He let himself in just after dinner when Dylan and Henry were busy playing poker downstairs. He moved through the darkened apartment methodically, but found nothing until he reached the bedroom. There on the nightstand was a small bag of balloons. Jake realized Henry had blown up two of them and then popped them when he'd been training Zorro. That bastard had wanted Jake to get hurt. It made him wonder if Henry had somehow recognized him. He did after all chase the perp that night Tim was murdered.

But, no, if Henry knew he was a Ranger, wouldn't he have hightailed it out of here? Unless he was just biding his time until Jake was finished his job with Zorro.

Later that night when Alanna came to him, nothing seemed to change in their lovemaking. Maybe she was considering this an affair and didn't want to take their relationship to the next level. He wanted more and he shouldn't. Really, he was here to do a job, but her cooperation would make it an easier task.

It was later when he woke up alone in bed that he expected to find her gone, but she wasn't. She stood at the balcony, her arms folded tightly in front of her, his oversize shirt covering her delectable body. He wished he knew how to reach her, but sometimes problems, deep-seated ones, had to be worked out alone.

Resting his shoulder against the door frame, he said huskily, "You okay, darlin'?"

Her stiffening indicated she hadn't heard him enter the room. She turned and said, "I just couldn't sleep."

He closed the distance between them. "It's okay. Whatever you're thinking about, I won't try to pry it out of you," he whispered softly.

For a moment she dropped her guard and the knot in his gut eased. She nodded. Not wanting to push her any further, he closed the distance, giving her a reassuring smile as he framed her face with his hands. He held her gaze for a moment, then lifted her face and gave her a slow, comforting kiss. He heard her breath catch, and she gripped his wrists. Moving his mouth gently over hers, breathing in the clean scent of her, he drew her deeper in his embrace. Then he turned her toward the bedroom. Without letting her go, they negotiated the doorway.

He pulled the T-shirt over her and stripped his jeans off, then slid into the bed beside her. When she started to stroke him, he snagged her wrist and brought her hand to his mouth where he kissed her palm, then set her hand against his chest.

"Let me just hold you," he murmured. He needed it as much as she did.

After a week had passed, Alanna still couldn't get out of her head the terrible image of Zorro almost crushing Jake against the rails. She woke often with a headache, a dull throb that plagued her every movement. She had resisted going to his apartment. She needed to figure something out before she saw him again.

These feelings were so invasive. When she stepped out to the patio she walked past the pool to where Mrs. Morely was serving up eggs, bacon, ham and assorted fruit. She sat down thinking if she ate something it would go away.

She suspected the headache was caused by stress, worrying about Zorro hurting someone…and…that run-in with the man she thought had been her dad had rattled her quite a bit. More than she'd initially thought. It brought home to her that she might never see him again.

Her adopted sister, Piper, took in Alanna's face, her eyes sharpening.

"You all right?"

She'd always gotten along most with Piper. Adopted at seven, she had grown from that timid little daughter of a maid into the beautiful woman she was now.

Marceline entered the patio and dished up some fruit and sat down across from Piper who said, "Good morning."

Marceline gave her a tight smile and started to eat her fruit.

"Alanna?"

"I'm fine, Piper. Just a headache."

"The way you traipse around in the muck, mire and manure it's no wonder." Marceline's perfectly painted mouth drew into a tight line. "I get a whiff of you at the end of the day and frankly…ewww, Alanna."

Piper gave her a rolled-eye glance and Marceline sniffed. "Brownnosing it again, Piper? I'm sure you have to compensate for your…dubious breeding. After all, blood always tells, doesn't it?" Marceline preached primly, lifting her chin and sniffing.

"Oh, Marceline, you do go on. Even the same tune gets old after a while," Piper responded with the same kind of uppity-nosed sniff.

"I wouldn't need to beat a dead horse if you really fit in here, Piper. After all, you aren't a Colton."

"And neither are you, Marceline," Alanna said quietly.

Her gaze returned to Alanna and she could see the jealousy in her stepsister's eyes. "You're just as adopted as Piper is. Although, at least Piper doesn't rub your nose in it every damn day. Colton blood does run through my veins." Her voice rose and a sharp stab to her head had her rubbing at her temples.

"At least my mother married a Colton. We'll never see eye to eye on breeding, Alanna. I'd say it skipped a generation with you." She rose and went back into the house, slamming the door.

Piper gave her a half smile and they bumped fists under the table. "Feel better, Alanna, and have a good day."

The clouds on the western horizon were still undercoated with slate gray, while the upper eastern strata were burnished with orange and gold and deep, deep coral. Soft purple wisps trailed out behind those clouds like the wake of a boat, painting the sky with slashes of color. On most mornings like this, she felt that if she could take a deep enough breath, she would be able to absorb all the colors and hues, all the open-sky beauty. But today the magic didn't work for her, and she turned and started walking down the trail that led to the arena. The long grass along the path was wet with dew and the boughs on the pine trees shed a heavenly fragrance along with beads of water. Alanna noticed a cluster of bluebells near the edge of the barn as she accepted the reins of her horse.

Somerset trailed behind her as obedient as a well-behaved child. He snorted, but otherwise made no comment until they got closer to the arena. Then Zorro let out a welcoming nicker and Somerset whinnied back.

Well that was something new.

She thought about those flowers, a funny feeling unfolding in her chest. So exquisite, so delicate and, for all their fragility, they somehow survived. She wondered if they would survive transplanting. That startling thought made her heart skip a bit, not wanting to consider the reason.

She'd heard back from Becca and that only reminded her how she'd chased after that man who she'd thought had been Eldridge. She hadn't said anything to anyone, feeling much too raw.

The morning was totally off. The first horse she mounted was a two-year-old colt who had the bloodline and look of a champion, but who had a stubborn streak. He bucked when she saddled him, he bucked when she mounted him, and then he refused to follow direction at all. She called it quits and had Tamara shadow with a more obedient horse while she continued to ride him, and she didn't give up until he finally bent to her will. Even so, it was a fight to the finish, and she was drenched in sweat when she finally got off him. He was lathered up, but he was totally docile until she got off him, then he had the nerve to bite her in the ass. She wanted to punch him.

The next horse, one who was close to being fully trained, simply sidestepped her attempt to mount and she took a dirt dive, headfirst.

Swearing under her breath, she pushed herself to her feet and dusted the worst of the dirt off her chaps, wanting to punch him, too. She looked up and found Jake hanging on the side wall, his elbows bracing his wide, muscled chest, a smile tugging at the corner of his mouth, and she could tell by the look on his face that he hadn't missed one minute of her little horse show. "The saddle is there, right between his shoulder blades, boss lady," he said, a gleam in his eyes. "It's the first time I've ever seen anyone do a perfect ten into the dirt."

"Can it, McCord."

The glint intensified. "You've got dirt on your chin."

She gave him a bad-tempered scowl and wiped her face, then snatched her hat off the arena floor. "Keep it up and you're going to have something on your face. Like maybe my open hand."

He grinned and tipped his chin at the horse, who stood quietly beside her. "Want me to give you a leg up?"

"Yeah? You'd do that for me? Why don't you come over here and I'll use my leg to give you a swift kick? Now beat it. I don't need anything more from the peanut gallery."

Resting his chin on his folded arms, he stared at her, his blue eyes twinkling like sapphires. "How about you show me where you got bit and I'll soothe it for you?"

"How about I show you some bales that need stacking, cowboy?"

"In the loft?" He continued to stare at her, a warm sensual gleam appearing in his eyes. Alanna could feel the sexual heat from ten feet away.

Determined not to give him the satisfaction of making her smile, she stared at him, gave an exasperated sigh and spoke, her tone very dry. "Get your mind out of the gutter, McCord."

He grinned in response, his eyes alight with that same sensual glint. "You were the one who brought up making hay...not me." He chuckled.

He started walking backward toward the arena doors, his spurs jingling and the view giving her sudden improper thoughts. Damn that sexy walk and damn that gorgeous man.

He kept his gaze fixed on her. "Where you're concerned, beautiful, getting my mind anywhere is an impossibility." Then he smiled that slow, bad boy smile of his. "And, boss lady," he said, his voice low and husky and loaded with intimacy.

She could feel the heat of that sultry tone right down to her toes, and her knees felt suddenly weak. "What?"

His eyes held hers, that same sensual look still there. "Just so you know..." She waited, wondering just what this tease would be all about. He smiled, the laugh lines deepening. "If you're still all dirty when you're done here, come see me. I'll wash yours if you wash mine."

All she could do was let out a rush of heated breath as he disappeared out of the arena.

By late afternoon, the headache was intensifying, and she found she couldn't concentrate, which wasn't a good thing around horses as was evidenced every time she came into contact with Jake.

Taking into account the mood she was in, she didn't even get on her last two mounts of the day, but left them in the capable hands of Tamara.

Instead she left the arena looking for Jake. She found him back with Zorro, only this time he was just finished with the lunging. She approached cautiously and Jake didn't notice her. He was too busy coaxing Zorro.

She had watched him yesterday and it was amazing what he'd already accomplished with a stallion she believed was a lost cause. Then he set the horse free and filled the water bucket. Every time after training he'd done that, but Zorro had wheeled and trotted away. But this time, Zorro was watching Jake, his ears pricked forward, his eyes still full of fire, but tempered. Each time Jake talked, Zorro moved toward him, the magic of his voice whispering on the wind, reaching the ears of the stallion and working a miracle.

He swished the water and his deep, melodic voice said, "I know what you want. Come on, boy. I've got your ticket." His voice was quiet, reassuring, soothing. Zorro stretched out his neck in the direction of the basin that Jake held.

He took a step, then another as Zorro took a step. More people gathered at the fence and a low murmur mingled with the soft sound of Jake's voice.

"Come on, pretty boy, strong boy, you independent son of a gun."

Another step. Then two more, as if his fear and his dominance weren't needed there. As if he started to realize Jake was safe, a leader. She urged him on and that sign was on everyone's face as they silently encouraged the horse toward Jake.

It was a step toward building trust.

The stallion took another step toward the bucket, and Jake tipped it toward him, letting him see inside, talking to him, coaxing him forward. He pricked his ears, smelling the water, and they all waited with bated breath, urging him to take that final step. Jake crouched and scooped up water in both hands, his voice filled with confidence.

After an agony of waiting, Zorro snorted, dipped down and took a quick drink, then jerked his head up and shied back. Jake scooped up more water and extended his hands and kept talking to him. It took another bout of coaxing in soft tones, and Alanna had almost given up hope. Then the stallion took that critical step forward, dropped his head and drank from Jake's outstretched hands, then deeply from the basin.

Alanna's throat closed up completely, and her jaw ached. It was so wrenching to watch, the bridging of all the hours of work he'd done to get Zorro to drink water out of his hands. She expected Zorro to wheel away as soon as he drank his fill, but he didn't. Continuing to talk to him, Jake very slowly lowered the empty basin and reached out his free hand. Alanna tensed, expecting the horse to bolt, but the stallion tossed his head and took a single step backward. Jake kept crooning to him and took a step toward him, his hand outstretched. The horse watched, his ears flicking at the soft sound of Jake's deep voice.

Then it happened as a reaction shivered down her spine. Zorro closed the scant space between them, and Jake slid his hand up the side of his face and over his neck.

Suddenly blinded by feelings she couldn't even face, Alanna soundlessly backed away from the fence and walked briskly away.

It was as if Jake had reached inside her and touched something that was raw and tender and hurting. Something she was having a hard time dealing with.

She headed back to the arena and started tidying up. Tamara tried to help, but Alanna insisted she go. When the whole place was empty, Alanna was heading back to the house when her cell phone rang.

"Miss Colton, this is Sheriff Watkins." His voice was flat over the line. "Could you come to my office now." It wasn't really a question and she knew it. He was just giving her the courtesy of couching it as such.

Her stomach dropped and she said, softly, unable to tamp down the hope that this had to do with Eldridge. "Of course. Is this about—"

"I'm sorry," he said, and softened his voice into conciliatory regret. "There's no news about your father, but this does have to do with him. I'll see you in thirty minutes."

"Make that forty-five," she said. "I'm just leaving the arena and I need to shower."

"Yes, ma'am. Forty-five it is."

She wanted to confide in Jake in the worst way, but the thought of it intensified the throbbing in her head and it occurred to her that if he was making progress with Zorro, his job would be done there. He would then leave. What good would it be for her to make a habit of telling him anything?

Arriving on time to the sheriff's office, he ushered her to an interrogation room and she settled at the small table.

He sat down and faced her, his eyes grave. "We haven't heard from this Jeremy Bellows you claim you had lunch with. In fact, his assistant doesn't have any record of him having lunch with you on the day in question. How do you explain that?"

"I wanted discretion. I contacted him directly and asked him to keep it between us until I was ready to propose my plan."

"Isn't that convenient?" he said, staring at her without any inflection in his voice.

She stiffened and leaned her elbows on the table. "It's the truth."

"We questioned the patrons of Meddlesome Butterfly and all we could get was more corroboration that it was your father you were dining with. Why don't you just own up to your threat, Miss Colton, and save both of us this charade?"

"I didn't threaten my father. I had lunch with a dealer to buy a string of barrel racers because I'm planning to expand the stables."

"Did your father know about these plans?"

"No. He did not."

He leaned forward, his tone menacing. "Did you harm your father?"

"No!" she snapped, then sucked in a breath, her headache almost blinding. "I would never hurt him. I had nothing to do with his disappearance. I don't know why you haven't heard from Mr. Bellows, but I can't tell you any other information because I don't have it. That witness is mistaken or she's lying."

"Why would she do that?"

"I don't believe that's my job to find out, Sheriff. I think it's yours. I'm leaving now unless you're going to arrest me."

"No, not at this time."

She got up from the table and said, "The next time you drag me in here and accuse me of threatening my father, I can assure you I will consider that harassment. I will be bringing my lawyer."

By the time she made it home, her head was thick and throbbing. She closed the door behind her as she entered the foyer. "Miss, the family is all assembled for dinner."

"Tell them I'm not well and am lying down, would you please, Mr. Manfred?"

Their aging butler gave her a smile and nodded. "Very good, miss. I will let them know."

She made her way to the left wing and her room. Rolling her shoulders to ease the tension, she stripped down to her panties, donned a stretchy pink tank top and climbed into bed.

The next thing she knew, someone was pulling the comforter up around her and she worked at clearing the gray tendrils from her mind. Feeling as if she was wading through quicksand, she turned over.

Jake was sitting on the bed beside her, his hand on her shoulder, gazing down at her. "Hey there, darlin'," he murmured.

Alanna scooted away from him coming fully awake.

"What are you doing here?" she asked.

He stood up releasing a heavy sigh and stuck his hands in his back pockets. "Checking on you. Wondering what is going on with you. You came back from town looking all spooked and upset," he said, his voice very quiet. "I was hoping to see you last night. You can tell me anything, Alanna."

"What happened in town is my business," she said, unable to get the memory of the way he'd coaxed Zorro just this past afternoon out of her mind. She wasn't a horse he could tame.

He turned and stared out the window. "I see."

When she made no response, he turned, staring at her. She sat with her legs drawn up, her arms locked around them, her forehead resting on her knees. He watched her a moment, then spoke, his voice still quiet.

"How about we get this out in the open," he said.

"Don't push me, Jake, I'm not in the mood."

"Someone needs to push you, Alanna. You can't hide for the rest of your—"

"I don't respect what you do. This isn't going to work for me. Let's just leave it at that."

The lies tumbled out of her mouth and she wanted to take them back immediately. But she felt so closed off.

"Okay, Alanna. We'll leave it at that. Do you want me to leave?"

It would be so much easier for her if he would, but she couldn't bring herself to deny him his livelihood and something so basic in her rebelled at him going anywhere. "No. Stay until you finish the job."

"Right. The one you don't respect. See you around, Alanna."

She closed her eyes as she heard his footsteps retreat. Then she lay back down, a hole so black and empty opening up in her.

Chapter 13

Jake stood at the foot of the bed with his suitcase open two days later. He'd tried to go about his business like Alanna hadn't shoved a lie in his face to get distance. Didn't she know all she had to do was ask him to back off?

His throat thick, he went to the dresser. This assignment was over. Without Alanna's trust, there was no way to get close to any information from her or the family. He might as well get the hell out of there and stop torturing himself with something that was never going to happen anyway. He'd call his boss and let him know.

He was fooling himself.

He didn't feel good leaving Zorro's training unfinished. He'd been able to garner the horse's trust, but he still needed to work with him some more. But that was now a moot point. Fowler would have to find someone else to handle his stallion.

Just as he got everything into his case and was zipping it up, his cell rang. "Hello," he answered.

"McCord, is that you?" his boss said gruffly.

"Yes, sir, it's me."

"I owe you an apology."

"Why is that?" Jake said, not much caring.

"Henry Swango. I finally got a report on him. We've been shorthanded, and, well, he's one seriously bad hombre."

Suddenly all Jake's energy focused into a ball of dread in his gut. "What are you saying?"

"Henry is suspected of several murders in Dallas. He is a drug distributor and according to the local cops, he's apparently laying low after a brutal murder. Unfortunately, they have nothing on him to hold him."

"What do you want me to do?"

"Watch him closely, but don't blow your cover. You observe anything illegal or he's a threat to the Coltons or their employees, you collar him and haul him off their property and blow your cover and tell them who Henry really is."

"I think he was responsible for Ranger Tim Preston's murder. But I have no proof except the sound of his voice and this slight limp I remember from the perp I chased after Tim was gunned down."

"I'd like this son of a bitch. You know that, so keep your eyes peeled and watch your back."

"Roger that."

He sighed as he unpacked his bag. He wasn't going anywhere now that it was confirmed Henry was as dangerous as Jake thought he was.

The next day, he did his usual training with Zorro, then headed for the tack room to put everything away. As he opened the door he discovered Clay and Daisy in a lip-lock. The kid had her up against the wall, his hands on her rib cage under her shirt.

"Clay! Daisy!"

They jumped apart and Jake said, "Daisy, get back to your chores."

Her face flaming red, she threw a look at Clay and rushed out the door. Clay went to go past him and he caught him by the collar and hauled him back.

"What the hell are you thinking?"

"This isn't any of your business. You're not my dad or my counselor."

"Don't think that makes a difference, and I'm making it my business."

Clay snorted. "Oh, man, now I gotta get a lecture about safe sex."

Jake ran his hand over his face. "Damn, boy, you haven't got the good sense God gave you." He set his hands on his hips and shook his head. "Clay, there is a right way and a very wrong way to treat someone like Daisy."

"You mean a good girl?"

"I mean a lady and she falls into that category, yes."

He shuffled his feet. "She's pretty and sweet. I like the way she smells."

"Yeah, that's where it begins. Don't manhandle her for God's sake and no more kissing in the tack room or any other room."

"Right, Jake. Got it."

"Do you?"

Clay nodded as he slipped out the door.

He turned after he finished hanging up the bridle and Alanna was standing in the doorway. It was the first time he'd seen her since she'd told him how she felt two days ago.

"That was good advice," she said.

He nodded and sidled past her. He felt her staring at him as he walked away, but he was adamant the ball was in her court. Except his palms were sweaty and he'd thought about how good she looked.

This wasn't going to get him anywhere. He threw himself into hard labor for the rest of the morning. At noon, Buck Tressler tracked Jake down while he was cleaning tack.

"McCord, Fowler wants to see you. He said to go up to the house."

"All right," Jake said and finished his task. As he climbed the path to the house, he couldn't help looking in the direction of the left wing.

Fowler along with most of his family was sitting on the patio, including Alanna. Jake recognized them all. Eldridge did have an eclectic mix of children, seven in all. When Fowler saw him, he motioned him over and said, "How is it going with Zorro?"

"He's coming along great. I'm planning on getting a saddle on him this week and seeing how that goes."

"It's about time you had some progress on him. See that it continues."

Alanna glanced at him several times and he tried to remain neutral and keep his eyes off her, but it was damn hard.

Piper Colton said, "Why don't you stay and have something to eat… Jake, is it?"

"Yes, ma'am. I wouldn't want to intrude."

"You wouldn't be. You work hard for us. Fix yourself a plate and enjoy."

"Thank you. I'll just wash up."

Fowler gave Piper a sour look, but after a quelling look from Alanna, he didn't say anything.

Jake didn't really care. He knew he was a fool, but he wanted to be close to Alanna. Then he saw Marceline studying him and he averted his eyes. He still had her bracelet. He wanted to confront her about where he'd found it, but he'd never gotten an opportunity to speak with her alone.

It was going to have to wait. Inside in the kitchen, he soaped his hands and washed them in hot water under the tap. After drying them, he headed back outside. Zane and his pretty wife, Mirabella, had finished eating, which left an empty spot next to Alanna. He grabbed a plate and filled it with the delicious fare and settled next to her.

"Can't get enough of Mrs. Morely's cooking, can you?"

Jake grinned and turned to her. She seemed tentative as if she was worried she'd say the wrong thing.

He wanted her to be at ease. He didn't like the pinched worry of her face or the dark circles under her eyes. He missed her in his bed and in his arms. "The woman can cook like a dream. You won't see me turning down anything prepared by her hands."

She smiled, but it didn't go as far as her eyes, and she stared at him with an odd kind of sorrow. The silence stretched between them as the conversation from her siblings flowed around them. Just for an instant he thought she was going to say something. He wanted to bridge the gap, but it was up to her. She had caused the rift. She would have to be the one who mended it.

"Jake—"

Whitney burst onto the patio, her face contorted, tears streaming down her face and her fists clenched. "Why do I have to hear from some gossip in town that someone came forward and said you—" Whitney jabbed her finger at Alanna "—threatened your father!"

Alanna rose in alarm at the shrill tone to Whitney's voice. Her face drained of color.

She held out her hands and opened her mouth, but Whitney wasn't going to be deterred. She fended her off and took a step back. Her voice caught on a sob.

Everyone was staring at Alanna. "I can explain," she said, but Whitney was now crying in earnest.

"I can't believe this," she wept, fat tears trailing down her cheeks. "You killed your own father!"

Other than Whitney's theatrical sobs, there was utter silence on the patio. "I didn't kill him," Alanna said, her voice constricted.

"Of course not. I can't believe you would ever do such a thing." She turned as Reid slipped his arm around her shoulders.

"Come on, Mom. Let's get you some tea and get you calmed down. Alanna wouldn't hurt a fly," he said, giving her a bolstering look.

She squeezed his arm as he ushered his still-sobbing mother into the house. She looked at Jake, her lip quivering. "If you'll excuse me," she said before turning and disappearing around the side of the house.

He wanted to go to her in the worst way, but he had to force himself to finish his lunch.

Marceline turned to him and said, "Lucky you.

Dinner and a show," she said with disdain. She got up and left the patio.

That left Fowler and Thomas, or T.C. as he was most widely known. They were discussing what sounded like business. Jake tried not to wolf his food, but as soon as he finished, he got up and said, jamming his hat on his head, "I'll get back to work. Good day to you."

Fowler ignored him, but T.C. nodded and so did Piper.

He went down the path, but doubled back and slipped around the pool to Alanna's door. He knocked and no one came. He tried the handle and the door opened. He went inside and heard the shower running. He was torn. Was she in there crying her eyes out or was she really just getting clean?

Just as he was going to go in, Alanna came out of the bathroom. She gasped at the sight of him. For a moment she stood there, her eyes caught by his, looking so miserable all he could do was open his arms.

With a soft cry, she went into them. As they closed around her, she buried her face in his throat.

Despite all they had been through, she felt exquisitely good and right in his arms. Experiencing a sharp clenching pain in his chest, he tried not to think, tried to give her some reassurance. She sure as hell needed some now.

It took a while, but he finally felt her relax, and he eased his hold on her. When he withdrew, she exhaled unevenly and looked up at him, the pain in her expression stark.

"I didn't mean what I said. In fact, I was completely

blown away by what you did with Zorro, I have to admit I was wrong. You're not a fake or fraud. You're very good at what you do and I'm sorry if I hurt you."

She softly brushed her mouth against his, the warmth and moistness of the kiss making his breathing erratic. She licked his bottom lip slowly—very slowly.

"I'm not going to ask, Alanna. If you want to talk to me. Talk. Otherwise, I'll just say, 'apology accepted.' But we both know talking about what happened to you that day you went into Dallas will only help."

"You are such a smartypants, but I'd rather talk… later," she said, maneuvering him toward her big, king bed. She pushed him down, then walked over to close her bedroom door as he tucked his hands behind his head, then she was back, folding down onto him and the bed.

Opening his mouth beneath hers, Jake raised his head just enough to deepen the kiss, resolutely keeping his hands beneath his head. He wondered just how far she was prepared to take this little bit of seduction. She changed the angle of her head, perfecting the seal of her mouth against his, and then she smoothed her hand down his chest, undoing the snaps on his shirt with little flicks of her thumb. Holding his head immobile with her other hand, she deepened the kiss and pulled his shirt out of his waistband, then lightly dragged her thumbnail across his nipple. Jake jerked, her touch sending a sharp current of sensation through him, and his heart went into overdrive when she lightly rolled the hardened nub under her fingers.

He wanted to grab her and drag her on top of him,

but her seduction was too sweet, too new, too arousing to let go. With a wild flurry of excitement building in him, Jake tightened his muscles against her tormenting touch, yielding his mouth to hers as she deepened the kiss. He groaned and jackknifed when she trailed her fingernail down the hard ridge of his erection beneath the fly, and the dual sensations made him groan again.

His breathing turned heavy, and it took every ounce of control he had to remain still beneath her lightly exploring hands and mouth. She stroked the full length of his hard, thick arousal again, and Jake sucked in a ragged breath and released a guttural sound against her mouth when she trailed her nails between his legs and down the sensitive base.

Working her mouth slowly against his, she shifted slightly, then used both hands to undo his belt. Jake lifted his hips off the mattress, and she pulled the belt free of the loops and dropped it on the floor, then slid her long fingers beneath his waistband. Her intimate touch electrified him, and he lifted his head and drew her tongue deeply into his mouth, the pulsating hardness in his groin nearly exploding as she carefully drew his zipper down. With the same slow care, she freed him, and Jake abruptly ceased to breathe. Unable to remain passive one second longer, he caught her by the back of the head and ground his mouth hungrily against hers, heat searing through him as she lightly smoothed her thumb over the moist, slick tip of his arousal.

Grasping her face between his hands, Jake gazed at her, his breathing labored. Her eyes dark and heavy lidded, her full sensual mouth swollen from the urgency of his kiss, he couldn't get enough.

His hands circling her neck, he stroked the line of her jaw with his thumbs, her pulse frantic beneath the heels of his hands. He wanted her naked and on top of him, he wanted to be buried so deep inside her that he would become part of her, and he wanted to let go of the heat that had him hard and erect. But this was as far as he could go.

"Condoms, babe," he pleaded.

He heard her fumble in the nightstand drawer and the glorious sound of a foil packet. He looked up at her, completely at her mercy.

"Alanna," he murmured fiercely.

She stood and dropped the towel and he took in her high, full breasts tipped with hard pink nubs, the exquisite line of her rib cage, the flare of her hips and the sweet V of her thighs.

She leaned down and moved her hand over his torso, his teeth clenching and sucking air when she took his hard, pulsating flesh in her hand, stroking him again. His face contorted at the sharp, intense pleasure that ripped through him. Alanna cupped him in both hands her eyes dilating, her pulse quickening, and Jake rose up on one elbow and caught her behind the head, pulling her toward him. She resisted.

Moistening her lips, she held his gaze for an instant longer, then looked down. His heart hammering like a wild thing in his chest, Jake watched her stroke him, firm and deliberate. He watched as she put the condom in place and rolled it down, her touch soft and unsteady. The instant she had the protection in place, he caught her by the back of the neck and rolled, carrying her beneath him. Urgently finding her mouth with his, he drew up her knees and roughly settled himself in the cradle of her thighs. A low groan escaped as he entered her, his awareness shattering into a sunburst of sensation. Then he slipped into a space where there was nothing except him and Alanna—and driving urgency.

It took Jake a long time to come down after the earthshaking climax. And it took him a long time before he could relax his urgent hold on her. But finally he was able to collect enough strength to ease back a little. The first two things that filtered through his consciousness were how fiercely Alanna was holding on to him, and that she was trembling. Shifting his hold on her, he lifted her hair out of the way, then protectively cradled her face against his chest, his hand cupped at the base of her spine. He brushed a kiss against her hair, then rubbed his thumb along her heated skin.

"I'll be right back. We should really talk," he said. He went into the bathroom and took care of the rubber and was back in bed. As soon as the mattress dipped she snuggled into him. He wanted to just hold her.

"Can we talk later, Jake? I'm too emotionally raw right now after what Whitney said to function normally."

"All right, but I guess, it's really up to you. If you don't want to talk about anything, I get it."

"No, I'll tell you. I want to. I think you can help me." Moments later, she went slack and her breathing evened out. He reached down and pulled the comforter over them. His throat suddenly tight, he gathered her damp hair and pulled it free, then tightened his arm around her back. Taking a deep breath, he rested his head against hers, wishing he knew how to say all the things that needed to be said. Wishing his hands weren't tied by him being a Texas Ranger...

He jerked awake and rolled to look at the clock to see it was really late. His stomach growled, but Alanna was curled against him still asleep.

He slipped out of bed and used the bathroom, then dragged on his jeans and left the room. The house was dark and he could hear murmurs from what was probably the living room.

He grabbed some chicken out of the fridge and then heard the sound of the front door opening. He went to the front window and saw Marceline get into her car. This was an odd time of night for her to go out. His gut told him to follow her.

He streaked back to Alanna's room and grabbed up his shirt and boots. Wait. He needed a car. That's when he saw Alanna's keys on her bedside table. He snatched them up and rushed out of the room and the front door.

Hitting the automatic door lock, he found her car and jumped inside and was soon tailing Marceline.

He followed her for a few miles when she turned off and headed toward the lake. He continued to follow her, keeping the lights off. Thankfully, the moon was bright enough that he could see.

She pulled up into a parking spot adjacent to a small boat slip and got out. He slowed and waited for her to hurry to the dock and the boat that was bobbing softly against the swells of the lapping water.

As soon as she disappeared inside, Jake noted the second car. He parked Alanna's car out of sight, then soundlessly shut the door. He carefully moved toward the boat, alert for any movement. Once he got close enough he heard voices. Then he saw her.

It was Ella Wilson.

The waitress who had accused Alanna of threatening her father. Obviously this was some kind of conspiracy.

What the hell? Had Alanna been right? Had Marceline set her up? Alanna did need someone to lean on if these were the types of things her family member did. Talk about a dysfunctional family.

"You need to stick to your story," Marceline said in a strident voice.

Ella's voice was strained. "It's only a matter of time before the sheriff finds out I have a record in New York, then it's all over."

Marceline grabbed her wrist, but Ella broke free. "You just have to sit tight," she hissed. "What's so hard about that?"

"I'm not going back in the joint. I'm out of here." Jake went for cover as Ella climbed off the boat and marched to her car. The sound of the engine loud in the night. Her red taillights disappeared into the distance.

He came out of hiding once Marceline hit the dock. She jerked and cried out, her hand going to her heart.

"You hired this woman to make a false accusation about your sister? That is low and underhanded, Marceline."

"You followed me? Who do you think you are?"

He blocked her path and she made a soft, angry sound. "Get out of my way."

"Not until you answer me. Now tell me. Did you frame your sister?"

"No. I wanted to get to the bottom of this, make the witness tell the truth. Someone paid her to lie."

He didn't believe a word she was saying.

"I can see you've fallen under Alanna's spell," she sneered. "That's so noble of you to protect her."

"I think you've been a busy woman." He pulled out the bracelet and even in the dim lighting, he could see she blanched. "I found this on the second floor of the apartments. How did it get there?"

She snatched it out of his hand and sidestepped him. "I don't know. It was probably stolen by some-one with sticky fingers," she said pointedly.

Before she could take another step, Jake grabbed her by her arm and hauled her around. "Are you mixed up with something involving Henry Swango?" he said, his voice a harsh rasp, showing he meant business.

"I do not consort with the hired hands, Jake. I don't answer to you."

She shook him off and rushed to her car. Her wheels churned up gravel and dirt as she left. He waited a few minutes and went back to the house and was soon easing back into bed with Alanna.

He lay there caressing the bare expanse of her back, enjoying the weight and the heat of her, mull-ing over the information he'd gleaned tonight. It was Marceline who'd hired Ella to lie, so the accusation against Alanna was bogus, which dropped her way down the suspect list in his book. But his work wasn't done there. He had to keep an eye on Marceline and

Henry. Whatever plan they hatched was probably not on the up-and-up.

There was no way he was leaving Colton Valley Ranch until he knew Alanna was safe.

Chapter 14

Alanna woke at dawn, tucked into the curve of Jake's body, his arm secure around her waist, his breath warm against her neck, and she let her eyes drift shut, loving the feel of waking up in his arms. She could get used to this every day.

She bit her lip. It was time she faced some facts. She'd looked at herself the last few days and she hadn't liked what she saw. She'd been so afraid of taking a step closer to Jake, she'd driven him away.

In the past she'd had boyfriends, but they hadn't been anything like Jake and they hadn't run in his circles. She'd been with some playboys when she'd been younger, bankers, Wall Street types and big oil. None of them suited her as much as this solid man did.

She was in love with him.

That was the bottom line. That's what she was

running from. Not sure what she was going to do about it at this point, she smiled when his arm tightened around her. All she knew was she wanted him to stay in her life even after the training of Zorro was complete.

"What time is it?"

"Five forty-five," she said.

"Damn, I'd better get going," he rasped.

She looked up at him and smiled. "We should really talk, Jake."

He pulled her closer to him. "Yeah, I know."

"Becca, my real estate agent, has some properties for me to look at and I was wondering if you'd like to do that…today…with me."

"It's my day off." His voice gave her no clues about what that meant. Did he want to cool it? No, that couldn't be, not after last night, not the way Jake comforted her after her stepmother had made such a terrible accusation, not after the way he'd made love to her.

She propped herself up on his chest and said, her voice as light as she could make it under the circumstances, "Oh, did you have plans?"

"Yeah," he said. "With you looking at properties." He had that desperado look this morning. His dark hair tousled, that stubble lining his face and giving an edge to his dangerous good looks. He looked like he was ready to strap on his shooting iron and go rob a train.

"You are such a tease," she laughed, nipping at his bottom lip, loving the warm glimmer in his eyes.

"I'm glad to be back to this place with you, Alanna." His voice grew hoarse and she was so darn mad at herself for treating him like she had. She stretched up and kissed him, loving the way his mouth went soft and lax beneath hers. He cleared his throat. "We can take my truck if you like."

She pushed away from his seductive heat, reluctantly. "As long as you're not one of those men who can't take a little direction."

His mouth hitched up and the light that came into his sexy blue eyes made her whole body weak. "Oh, babe, I can take plenty of directions," he deliberately drawled. "I think I proved that last night when you were directing all over me."

"Jake," she said softly, and he dragged her against him. She breathed deeply of his scent and kissed his neck as he hugged her tight.

He gave her one more quick squeeze and rolled out of bed.

"Okay, I'll get cleaned up and meet you over at the apartments," she said as he offered his hand to help her off the mattress.

"That's a deal."

She donned her robe and walked him to the door. He stood there in the light, waiting for her. She went to him and wrapped her arms around his waist, the pensive quality in his eyes making her heart beat a little harder. What if he didn't feel the same way about taking their relationship public or about getting involved in her crazy, drama-filled family? She wasn't sure he wanted to handle all this, but she was sure of one thing. He was solid and down-to-earth, kind and gentle, made love to her with a passion she'd never known before and she'd be a fool to let him go because of her own insecurities. If she didn't give him her trust, this man who had given her every reason to trust him, who could she ever trust?

He tipped up her face and stared down into her eyes for a few minutes. Swiping his thumb along her cheekbone, he sighed. Slipping his hand into her hair, his fingers tightened and he covered her mouth with a warm, firm kiss that went all the way down to her toes. The man did know how to plant one on her.

"Thirty minutes?"

"Make it twenty," she murmured. "I can't wait that long."

He smiled and there it was again, that shadow in his eyes. Her heart lurched and she had to prepare herself for him to back out. That was only fair as she would be asking a lot of him. With her father missing, the media coverage of their lives was even more intense. With a new man in her life, one that was a ranch hand, there would be talk and speculation. Fowler would hate it and she could imagine how Marceline would turn up her nose, but she didn't give a damn about any of that. Jake was worth it.

As she was waiting for him, she saw Clay coming out of the apartments and she waved to him, but he didn't see her. She took in his face and her heart lurched. Was that a…black eye? Without hesitation, she headed toward him just as Jake came out the door.

"Clay?"

He looked up, startled, and the eye seemed worse up close. "What happened to you?" She stepped forward with concern, but he stepped back.

"Wasn't watching where I was going," he said with a self-deprecating smile, avoiding her eyes. Jamming his hat on his head, he turned away. "I'd better get to them stalls. They aren't going to clean themselves."

She gave Jake a worried look and they walked toward the underground garage and his truck.

"Do you think he's telling the truth?"

"I don't know," Jake said, the brim of his hat offsetting his striking features. "Clay keeps to himself." But she could tell. Jake was worried, too.

"Unless he needs advice about women." She'd never forget the advice that Jake had given Clay. How his words had settled deep inside her like blood, bone and muscle. Intricate and necessary. He would make such an amazing father. Her stomach jolted at the thought.

Jake chuckled. "I was just trying to steer him in the right direction and he was the one who asked."

"Did I say there was anything wrong with your advice?"

"No."

Now that they were alone and this was going to get real, Alanna's mouth got dry. The first tentacle of fear uncurled in her belly. She wasn't quite ready. She wasn't sure if she'd ever be. She didn't know how to let go of the fear. She didn't know how to get from the place where she was and cross over to the other side.

They entered the garage and the light dimmed as they walked side by side. When she felt him slip his hand around hers like he knew she was wrestling with herself, she melted.

She gave him a glance and he said, "Talk to me, Alanna. That's all it takes. We don't have to make any heavy-duty decisions. We don't have to make any plans if that scares you. It's just that my job here is almost done."

"I know, and when it is, well, what will you do after that?" He opened the door for her and she slipped into the passenger seat. Closing it firmly he walked around the front and she watched him move. She liked so much about him...just about everything.

He got behind the wheel and stuck the keys in the ignition. His eyes unreadable, he said, "What I'm trained to do." He smiled.

She nodded. He should train horses. He was a master at it and she'd let her bias show. For that she was heartily sorry.

He navigated out of the garage. She had her tablet with the directions and all the properties listed. There were three in this area and three others that were about an hour away. Her heart twisted thinking about being that far away from her family and Colton Valley Ranch Stables that she'd built up from a few horses and barns into a fully functioning training and breeding facility with a stellar reputation in Texas horse circles.

He followed the back road out of the ranch and onto the highway. "Alanna, I need to talk to you about what happened last night while you were asleep." He tightened his big hands on the wheel.

From the subdued tone of his voice and the solemn look in his eyes, what he had to say wasn't going to be good. "What?"

Jake clenched his jaw and stared straight ahead. "I followed your sister Marceline."

"What? Why?"

"You told me that she might be responsible for this whole witness thing. I had a gut instinct."

"And I was right? She set me up?"

"She was meeting with Ella Wilson at the lake. I confronted Marceline and she denied everything. She told me she was trying to get the witness to give up the person who hired her. But it was too late, babe. I'd already heard her trying to convince Ella to stick it out. I'm sorry."

A jolt of adrenaline and anger swept through her with pure, energizing force, and she was suddenly so furious she couldn't see straight. "Don't be," she said. "We've always had a terrible relationship. Maybe part of the blame has to go to me. I wasn't ever close to Marceline."

"She's jealous of you?"

Maybe. Who could say? Marceline had never opened up to her about how she really felt. There were a lot of trust issues in their family and everyone, including Alanna, had learned to live with them. It was hard to break out of that mold. "I guess, or maybe it's because I have a father and she lost hers." Flustered and sad over what Marceline had felt the need to do to a family member, her hands twisted in her lap. "She never let Eldridge in and I don't know if that's because she was just scared of losing another dad."

Jake reached out and covered her agitated hands, his warm and soothing. "You have a big heart to be able to see that after what she's done to you. Alanna, that could have gone badly for you if your alibi didn't come through."

She blew out a relieved breath and laced her fingers through his. "Yes, I guess it could have. But now, I should be in the clear, right?"

"I'd say so." He tightened his fingers. A feeling of anxiety clutched at her. He then said, with more of that solemnness in his voice, "There's something else I need to mention to you and I don't know what it means."

"Just tell me."

He glanced at her. "I found Marceline's bracelet on the second floor of the apartments. There are only two hands on the second floor. Dylan Harlow and Henry Swango."

She frowned. "Why is that alarming?"

She could feel the tension in him and her apprehension turned to dread. If Jake was worried, she had to heed that warning. He wouldn't mention it unless it was significant. "Dylan says he doesn't have a relationship with your sister."

Alanna laughed without mirth. "I can't see her giving Henry the time of day."

Jake nodded his agreement. "Maybe not, but she was doing something shady by hiring that witness. Could she have hired Henry to do away with your dad?" This time his look was intense.

Alanna closed her eyes. "Oh, God. I don't know, but she did hate him so much. Jake, it's heartbreaking, but it could be true."

"I think Henry's a bad guy. I've had my problems with him. Those popping noises that day with Zorro. It was Henry bursting balloons in his pockets to spook Zorro."

"How do you know that?"

"You don't want to know. But, I would suggest you let him go."

Firing someone was a delicate matter, but if Henry was a threat to the ranch, he would be gone in an instant. "Are you sure about this?"

He flexed his jaw. "Yes."

"I'll look into it. I wouldn't want to fire a man without being sure about the facts. It's not that I don't trust you. I just have to cover myself in case of lawsuits, that type of thing."

"I understand. But the sooner the better. I don't like the idea that he's around impressionable kids who are trying to get their lives back on track."

She'd taken on this project because she saw the need and wanted to be a part of helping those kids see there was something other than a life of crime. A normal life filled with ambition and hard work that would give them a sense of pride and accomplishment. If Henry Swango was on her property to subvert her efforts, he would most definitely get the boot. "No. That wouldn't be healthy for them at all."

"Speaking of that. I was wondering. Now that Zorro is doing so much better, I'd like to help you with the kids, if you're interested."

She turned to look at him, a smile breaking across her lips. The first one since they'd started having this heavy-duty discussion. "Yes. I would love that. Thank you, Jake, so much. Clay has responded to you really well. It feels like you're getting through to him."

"You think? That means a great deal to me, Alanna."

"Because of your brother," she said, touching his arm.

He nodded, emotion thick in his eyes. "Yes. Because of that."

They pulled into the driveway of the first property. Becca waved to them and Alanna waved back.

They spent the morning looking at all the properties and when Jake was checking out one of the barn's lofts, Becca said, "This one seems like quite the keeper," she said, and Alanna blushed.

"Stop. He's a valued ranch hand and knows what's what. Since I have to keep this secret from my family, especially Fowler, I couldn't very well ask his advice."

"Sure," Becca said. "Just a ranch hand. The way he looks at you? I'm a happily married woman for twenty-five glorious years and I know when a man finds a woman irresistible. And, the way he supports you, thoughtfully answers and asks questions. Touches you gently on the small of the back. I'd say he's got it bad."

All the way back to the ranch, Alanna couldn't help thinking about what Becca had said. But something held her back from telling Jake right now how she really felt. She knew she had to take the first step for it to be meaningful, but her insecurities piled up on her.

"Would you be interested in a ride before dinner?" he said when they emerged from the garage.

"I would love that. We could ride around the lake. It's beautiful this time of year."

Suddenly two tussling forms emerged from the barn. Alanna looked at Jake, but he'd already took off at a run. Several people were milling around watching and, to her shock, Clay punched Mike right in the face. Mike gave as good as he got and then they ended up on the ground.

Jake reached the struggling teens and grabbed Clay only to get an elbow in the face. Dylan jumped into the fray and managed to get ahold of Mike's arm. He hauled the kid off and Clay got in one last good punch before Jake made him back off.

"Take your hands off me," Clay said, his lip bloodied, his cheekbone and his jaw were red and swollen. His already black-and-blue eye was puffing up.

Jake held up his hands as Clay backed up. Daring Jake to touch him again.

"My office," Alanna said as Dylan brought along a docile Mike, but Clay's face was contorted and sullen. He looked like he wanted to be anywhere but there.

Jake said, "You heard her, Clay. Move."

Clay bent down and picked up his hat. Something sick and torn coming into his eyes. Eyes that were now full of despair.

They went into the arena. Tamara was working a horse and she watched them as they passed. "Hold Clay out here until I talk to Mike. This is so unlike him."

She went inside and Dylan set Mike into the chair across from her desk. With a firm voice she said, "Mike, what happened?"

"He didn't like the way I was hanging the bridles. He started pushing me, then it got intense when I told him to back off."

"Has he ever acted hostile to you before?"

"No, never. I thought we were friends. Then he gets in my face and, well, I had to push back."

"You know fighting is grounds for termination of the program, Mike."

"I know, but please, Miss Alanna." He looked at her, his face solemn. Then his eyes filled up, and his mouth started to tremble. "Don't send me back," he whispered, knuckling his eyes. "I like it here. I like the work. I don't want to go back there."

She set her hand on his shoulder, struggling against an awful pressure in her chest. "All right, Mike, calm down," she said softly. "I will think about this and let you know what I decide to do after I talk to Clay. Violence is never a good response, but I understand you have to defend yourself. The usual recourse in these situations is that both boys have to be released from the program."

"Mike's a good kid, Miss Colton," Dylan said, his voice thick. "I will vouch for him if need be."

Mike gave Dylan a grateful look and Alanna's heart contracted some more.

She nodded. "Go ahead and take him back to his room and get him cleaned up."

"Yes, ma'am."

Mike rose with hope on his face. "It'll never happen again. I'd rather have the stuffin' kicked outta me than have to leave. I'm real sorry, Miss Alanna."

"I know you are, Mike." She smiled. "Go with Dylan now."

After Mike left, Jake ushered a rebellious Clay into the office. "Clay, did you start hassling Mike?"

"He wasn't doing the bridles right," Clay said, his eyes downcast, his shoulders slumped. He looked like he was going to the gallows and that bothered Alanna more than Mike's teary plea to stay. It was as if Clay had somehow given up. He had been so full of promise and now he seemed defeated. What had happened to him to cause this?

She crouched down in front of him and lifted his chin so that his eyes met hers. "So instead of showing him, you punched him."

Instead of the anger she expected all she could see was desperation. "That's right. You sending me back to juvie?"

"Do you want to go back there?"

He shrugged and looked down. "It's where I belong. All this is bullshit, anyway."

"Did something happen with Daisy?" Jake said.

Clay shook his head. He didn't say anything for the longest time. Finally, he said, "No." His voice shook. "You were right, Jake. She's a lady and I should steer clear of her. Just send me back."

She gave Jake a stricken look. Jake was studying Clay as if he couldn't believe what he was hearing. He was in obvious distress. He cared deeply about the boy and it was so closely tied to Matt. Her heart ached for both of them.

She reached out and squeezed Jake's forearm. If anyone could get Clay to talk about why he was acting like this, it was Jake. "Clay, could you please wait outside?"

He rose and with a start she realized he was almost the same height as Jake. The lines of his young face were strong, his features attractive. He was dusty and bloody, his mouth tight in a mutinous line. But when he looked at her, there was a plea for help there, too. Something so scared, like a little boy alone. Her heart clenched in her chest.

She ached to help him, but if he wouldn't tell them what was wrong, how could she?

"I can't believe he's acting like this."

"He's scared of something, Jake. I'm not sure what, but take him back to his apartment. Give him first aid. Try to see if you can get him to talk about it. I'll wait here."

He left and Alanna sat down behind her desk. What had driven this boy to do something drastic enough to get him thrown off a ranch he clearly loved? She could only pray Jake would get through to him.

Jake walked with Clay who looked like his world had just come to an end. All he could do was think about Matt and it hurt to look at him. If Alanna decided to send him back to Dallas, back to juvie, Clay would have lost his second chance at making something of himself. Jake was disillusioned, wondering if Matt had tried harder, believed more, dreamed bigger, he wouldn't have succumbed to the drugs that had killed him. He'd failed with Matt. He wasn't going to fail with Clay.

Once inside the apartment, Mike was sitting with Dylan on the couch and he was nodding. He looked up when Jake and Clay came in. Mike's mouth tightened, but when Jake expected him to look daggers, he just looked sad. This was definitely a kid that had gotten caught up in the system. He worried if the two of them went back they would be lost.

"Hey, Mike," Dylan said, exchanging a knowing look with Jake. "Let's go get some lemonade downstairs."

"Can we play some cards?" Mike asked.

"Yeah, sure."

As Mike passed Clay, he stopped and extended his hand. "Hey, Clay, no hard feelings."

Clay shook his hand, looking stricken. "I'm sorry I got you into this, Mike."

Dylan clasped Mike on the back of the neck and they went out the door.

"That was a step in the right direction."

Clay didn't respond. He looked like he was re-signed to his fate.

"Let's get you cleaned up." He headed for the bath-room and Clay didn't move. "Come on," he said, using the same kind of voice he used on anxious horses.

Finally, Clay set his hat down on the coffee table and entered the bathroom. Jake pushed him down to the commode.

"So, you like being locked up better than working with horses and the wide-open spaces." He opened the medicine cabinet and pulled out gauze pads and an-tiseptic. He doused a pad and pressed it to Clay's lip.

Clay hissed in pain, a sick desperation lighting his eyes. "It's where I belong." He blinked rapidly and Jake felt that desperation all the way to the pit of his stomach.

"No, it isn't. We talked about this. You have an opportunity here that no amount of time in juvie is going to give you. Alanna went out on a limb for you. She believed in you."

"I guess she has bad judgment."

"No, she doesn't and neither do I. Tell me what happened, Clay. We're here to help you."

"You can't help me. It's best that I go."

"Best for whom? Look, I overheard Henry intimi-dating you. Does this have anything to do with him? Tell me what's wrong and we can go from there."

Clay turned away and stopped talking. Jake washed away the blood and then got ice for his bruises. Clay stoically resisted all of Jake's probing and Jake left the apartment feeling raw.

Alanna and now Clay. He was getting more than he'd bargained for with this assignment. It was clear it was coming to a close. His boss would probably pull him out as soon as Alanna's alibi stuck.

He had to resign himself to what he knew he'd been denying. He had to either tell Alanna who he really was and lose her or walk away and lose her anyway. Either way he lost.

He was so ripped up inside, already feeling the edges of that hollowness return. When he'd gotten there, he'd been burned-out, heading for either a line-of-duty death or a desk job or worse yet, getting fired. They had already relegated him out of active cases. This job was supposed to be a cakewalk.

Somehow with Alanna, Zorro and Clay, he had found his footing, his calling.

He had to wonder if this job that had caused him so much grief didn't fit anymore.

Chapter 15

A nighttime stillness had settled outside, and a breeze rustled through the leaves on the old oak tree just beyond Jake's open window, filling the room with a soft, whispering sound. Alanna draped her legs over the backs of Jake's as they cuddled. There was a bite in the air as October approached.

"Fall is heading our way," he said, and she nodded, absently smoothing her hands over the contours of his muscled back. Too spent to move, not wanting to speak, she savored the heady sensation of contentment, loving the feel of his smooth skin beneath her palms.

Stirring heavily, he rolled off her, dragging her against him. "I think that was a good call in giving those boys a second chance."

He picked up her hand and placed a kiss on her

palm. His mouth was moist and warm and slightly swollen, and she drew her thumb across his bottom lip, thinking about the care he'd taken with her. "They're going to be on manure duty in the arena for a few days, but I agree. It was the right thing to do. Mike is such a gentle soul and although Clay has enough attitude to spare, he's also a good kid. I couldn't send them back."

He nodded and smoothed his hand across her hip. "I'll keep working with Clay. See if I can find out what's wrong. Something happened and I think I know who's involved."

"Who?"

"Henry Swango. I think he's pressuring him."

"For what?"

"That's what I'm going to find out."

"Maybe I should—"

He went rigid, then shook her a little. "No, Alanna. I think it's safer if I handle this."

"All right," she murmured, and he relaxed. Time passed as the room cooled and Jake got up and closed the window. He settled back into the bed, snuggling her up against him.

"Jake?"

"Hmm?"

She raised her head and kissed his jaw. "I decided on a property."

He propped himself up on his elbow. "Which one?"

"The one on Chase Road, with the three barns and ample land."

"The house needs work."

"I'm thinking I'll tear it down and rebuild what I want."

He didn't answer right away. His eyes roved over her face as if he was studying her features to remember when he wasn't with her. That thought stabbed her hard in the heart. "That works," he said, cupping her face, rubbing his thumb roughly over her jaw. He tilted her head and kissed her.

It was going to be a lot of hard work, but she intended to make it a success. Closing her eyes as he placed a string of kisses down her neck, she sighed.

"Alanna," he whispered, breathing deeply. "I'm probably going to be heading out of here soon."

Closing her eyes against the sudden burst of pain, she slid her arms around his neck and held on to him, the sense of loss so intense it made her shudder. She was well aware she hadn't yet told him about what had happened in Dallas when she'd gone to meet with Becca. He hadn't asked. Maybe he'd let it go because it was easier. Even now fear kept her from saying anything. "How soon?"

"A few days. Zorro is taking really well to the saddle and bridle. I think I'll be able to ride him soon. Once that's accomplished, he's pretty much good to go."

She wanted to ask him, but the fear kept her locked up. She didn't want to say goodbye. As if sensing a change in her, Jake tightened his hold, his embrace suddenly rife with tension. "I'm going to miss you like hell, babe," he said, his voice husky and uneven.

Her jaw locked against the ache in her throat, she tightened her arms, trying to will away the awful fullness burning in her eyes. She didn't dare think about how she would handle his absence. She would never get through the next few days if she did. Easing in a deep, shaky breath, she turned her face against his throat, trying to absorb as much of his warmth and strength as she could. Enough to get her through him leaving. Enough to hold her together.

Slipping her hand around his waist, tracing the thick muscle on the side of his hip, she ran her hand up his chest.

"I wanted to thank you, Alanna, for pushing me that day with Zorro. I realized what I have been doing for some time." His voice was quiet and thoughtful, full of gratitude. That's not exactly what she wanted from him, but for the first time in her life she'd experienced the fullness of what it meant to connect to a man as she'd connected to Jake.

He brushed back the hair at her temple, then lowered his head and kissed her.

"What's that?"

"Second-guessing myself." He rubbed a strand of hair between his fingers and gave her a small smile. "Not relying on my instinct. What I learned here will serve me well in other areas of my life, too."

She wanted to ask him what he meant, but it was as if the words were trapped in her throat. She tried to will away the fear, but it wouldn't let go. Neither of them spoke for several moments, content with gentle stroking and even gentler kisses. Finally, Jake said, "Also, thank you for listening and understanding about Matt."

She curled her hands around his biceps, her voice husky as she whispered, "I'm so glad I could be there for you, Jake."

Covering her mouth in a drugging kiss, she kissed him back, catching his nape and holding on.

Cupping his jaw, she stroked the curve of his cheek-bone with her thumb. She didn't know what to say, the thickness in his voice affecting her profoundly. He obviously didn't expect her to say anything. Catching her by the hips, he drew her fully on top of him, then settled her between his thighs, running his hands along her rib cage until he reached her breasts. His touch sent spirals of sensation through her, and Alanna closed her eyes, yielding to his mouth.

Was she just going to let him go?

Or was she going to find the courage to tell him what was in her heart? Trust him.

Two simple words.

A world of meaning.

Jake was in the barn the next day saddling Zorro for his first ride. The stallion stood steady and calm as Jake tightened the girth. Zorro wasn't going to compete or be used for pleasure riding. He was first and foremost a stud horse. But getting in the saddle and putting him through his paces would keep him in line and keep him from getting bored.

As he tightened the girth, his cell phone rang. "McCord," he said.

"Mr. McCord. This is Jeremy Bellows. I understand from my assistant you have been trying to reach me." The man's voice was deep and apologetic. "I'm sorry it has taken me so long, but I've been in rehab." His tone was matter-of-fact.

Jake explained why he had called and Jeremy confirmed Alanna's story fully.

"I've already returned the sheriff's call, as well.

I'm just sorry Alanna had to go through all of this when I could have cleared it up so easily."

He was relieved Bellows had come through for Alanna and the evidence proved that she was innocent of threatening her father.

After Jake hung up, he led Zorro from the barn and set his foot in the stirrup. "Okay, boy, here we go." He pushed up and swung his leg over the animal's back. Zorro shifted and that was it. Jake nudged him into a walk, then a trot. As he passed people they were giving him warm and incredulous looks.

For the first time in years, he felt a deep sense of accomplishment. Something that had been lacking for so long. He took Zorro out of the stable yard and down the road and then leaned over the horse's back and gave him his head.

With a happy snort, Zorro took off, racing across the pasture like a bullet, his mane and tail flying. Jake whooped and urged him faster, eating up the real estate. There was one thing and one thing only that he and Fowler Colton could agree on. This stallion was going to make an excellent stud and add to the Colton stock immeasurably.

As he trotted the horse back to the stables, his only regret was now he could report to Fowler that his horse was no longer an unruly rogue, his job here was done. Both his jobs here. The only dangling thread was Henry. Jake dismounted in front of the barn and unsaddled, rinsed off and groomed Zorro before turning him out into the corral.

He watched the horse race around, whinny to some mares in the nearby paddocks and generally enjoy himself. When Jake called, he trotted over to where he stood at the fence. "You aren't so scary," he murmured as he rubbed his face.

"You did it," Dylan said as he climbed up on the fence with Jake. Slapping him on the back, they stood there for a few companionable minutes watching the horse.

Bidding Dylan goodbye, he climbed down from the fence and headed for the arena. Before he could slip inside to find Alanna, his cell phone rang.

"McCord," his boss said. "We just got the call from the sheriff that Alanna Colton has been cleared of threatening her father and since you haven't turned up any evidence that she had a hand in his disappearance, we're pulling you out."

"What about Henry Swango?"

"We're going to assign another Ranger to him. We still feel you could benefit from some more downtime. Report to me at nine sharp tomorrow for a debriefing, then you can head home."

"But he killed Tim. I want him," Jake argued, fury igniting. "He killed that rookie in cold blood. I was the one who let him go in. His blood is on my hands."

"No, Jake," his boss's tone was fierce and sympathetic. "The blood is on whoever killed Tim. It wasn't your fault he died. You did everything by the book."

"That's cold comfort," he said.

"I know, but if Henry is responsible, we'll get him. You have my word. Now stand down. We want you back here tomorrow." When Jake didn't respond, his boss said, "That's an order, Ranger."

"Yes, sir," he said.

As he hung up, bitterness making him swear under his breath, he heard someone shout Alanna's name. It sounded like Fowler. With all his protective instincts rising, Jake entered the arena as Fowler, dressed in a pearl gray suit and matching Stetson, marched up to Alanna. "Why the hell do I have to hear you're buying property from one of Dad's friends?"

She lifted her chin, her eyes flashing. She handed the horse she was just about to mount to Tamara and tried to draw her brother toward the office, but he wouldn't budge. "I don't need your permission to buy property."

"What is this about?" he growled.

"You know what it's about," she growled back. "You forced my hand. I'm going to leave Colton Valley Ranch and start my own stables. I have too much respect for myself to stay here and be treated like I don't make a difference."

Ever since Jake first met Fowler, he'd never seen the man so caught off guard or speechless. He sputtered and then said, "You can't leave."

"Why?" She threw her hands into the air. "You don't need me. I overtrain horses. Don't know when my own stock is ready for auction. Take on too many training jobs and am generally a pain in your butt. Did I leave anything out?"

Jake walked up. "Only that you're quite amazing."

Fowler whirled and his face contorted in rage. "You. This is none of your business. You were hired to train that stallion. Is he ready to go to stud?"

"Yes, he's ready."

Fowler hadn't expected that answer. "I'll be the judge of that." Fowler stalked off, then turned. "This isn't over, Alanna."

Alanna shook her head, then touched Jake's arm.

"I got an apologetic call from the sheriff. Mr. Bellows corroborated my story. Ella has disappeared, too. So, I'm in the clear."

"That is good news." He took off his hat and fingered the band. "Alanna," he said. "I've got to leave tomorrow." He would make a clean break of it. When he told Alanna who he really was, she was going to get hurt. He didn't want that, wished he could avoid it altogether, but in all conscience, he couldn't leave here without her knowing the truth.

"What? So soon. Jake, no." She wrapped her arms around his neck and held on to him with a fierceness that made his heart falter. "I want you to come work with me when I go out on my own," she blurted out.

He dropped his hat as his arms tightened convulsively around her. Faced with the reality of his decision, he closed his eyes. "That's a complicated request," he breathed and looked away. "I'm not sure working for—"

"No, I didn't say *for* me. I said *with* me. I'm offering you a partnership if you want it. You are so good with horses, magical. I was wrong about you, so up on my high horse. You take something natural and turn it on its ear. You believe in me and respect me. I want you there."

He cupped her face, his heart aching. "I can't give you an answer right now," he said. "I really need to talk to you. In private."

She released a sigh, telling him she was disappointed he didn't jump at the chance and it hurt like hell. She cupped her palm against the back of his hand where it lay on her cheek. "Jake, I wasn't just offering you…a partnership in business."

He closed his eyes then and pressed his forehead to hers. "Alanna, you astonish me one minute, then clip my legs out from under me in another."

"Then say yes," she pleaded.

"I can't. Let me explain. Could we go to your office?"

"No. We can talk here and get this all out in the open." She resisted his pull. "I like getting my way. I'm definitely a spoiled princess about this. It's just I've realized something and I'm a little scared about that, too. I treated you badly, but my only defense is I'm not used to being without armor. I'm not used to opening myself up to anyone. I never have. I have had two marriage proposals and they were wonderful with flowers and extravagant dinners. I thought I was in love with those men, but I know now I hadn't even come close." She looked away, the fear escalating in her. "Not even close." Alanna closed her eyes and pressed her hand to his chest, her fingers clenching in the fabric of his shirt. "I learned a hard lesson with my family that keeping my guard up was tantamount to survival.

"When I was in Dallas, I thought I saw my father. I chased him down in the street and discovered it wasn't him. It shook me up so badly, made me feel so utterly exposed and vulnerable. That's why I acted the way I did with you. My family taught me to be tough in a tough world. But there is also love. It's below the surface, but it's there. I don't doubt that. But because I had to build walls, I had acquired a kind of internal toughness.

"Then there was this cowboy who walked into my arena with a beautiful blue roan, confident, oh so handsome, the kind of warmth in his eyes that scared the hell out of me. And he got down to a difficult task. A task to tame a rogue stallion, and along the way, he taught me about courage and vulnerability. He taught me about deep, abiding trust."

"Alanna…dammit." He paced away in agony, his shoulders stiff. His hands running violently through his hair, the agony in him expanded. What he said next was going to shatter her trust, cripple her. After all they had been to each other these past weeks, this would effectively tear them apart. And, dammit, her heart was hanging in the balance.

"Alanna, for the love of God—"

"I'm in love with you, Jake."

His brain ground to a rushing halt at her words and his throat cramped up. He watched her with an intensity as his heart broke. He'd known, but he felt like he was on a runaway train and the track was running out. There was no way he could explain his way out of this or make this right. He was going to lose her. It was a fact, but one he had to live with. Hurting her was the last thing he wanted to do, and the joy of winning this woman's love was overshadowed by this secret between them. He stared at her for an instant longer, and then he closed his eyes briefly, crossed the few feet separating them and grabbed the back of her neck. He hauled her into his arms, his unchecked strength nearly crushing her. He didn't say anything for the longest time. He just held her as if he couldn't let her go, knowing Alanna was holding on to him for the last time.

Finally, he let all the air out of his lungs, and with unsteady fingers, he swept her hair back from her face. "Listen to me, Alanna," he said, his voice rough and unsteady. "Listen. You need to think about this, babe. Don't do something you're going to regret later. I need to talk to you about something, now," he said fiercely. "Not here out in the open. Can we go to your office?"

Suddenly the door opened and then slammed.

Alanna's face changed from confusion at his response to alarm. "Fowler?"

"You hack!" He heard before he turned around. Fowler advanced on Jake, his face contorted in an ugly sneer, cradling his hand against his chest. Buck was trailing behind him, giving Jake a warning look.

Jake faced Fowler, who went toe-to-toe with him. Fowler jammed a finger into his chest. "That horse isn't tamed! He bit me!"

Jake stood his ground, angry his discussion with Alanna got interrupted and tired of taking orders from a man who had no respect for anyone. "He was fine when I left him. Maybe he just doesn't like you."

Fowler's eyes narrowed dangerously and he yelled. "You're fired! Get off this property."

Alanna wedged herself between the two of them. "Fowler, you can't do that. He worked miracles with that horse. This isn't right."

"Alanna, stay out of it!" Fowler said, pushing her to the side.

"Jake!" Mike Jensen shouted as he ran into the arena and skidded to a stop beside him. Panting, he grabbed Jake's arm in a frantic grip.

"What is it?"

"Clay...he's gone!" Mike said, the concern for his friend evident.

"Gone?" Jake said in confusion. "Where?"

"I don't know. Mr. Colton ordered Clay to saddle Zorro, but he bit him. He threw the reins to Clay. He just got this look on his face. You know the one when you know someone is just at the end of his rope. He mounted Zorro and rode off."

Jake grabbed Mike's shoulders. "Holy hell! Clay's on Zorro?"

"Yes. He seemed real broken up."

"About what?" Jake shouted.

"I don't know!" Mike shouted back.

"Which way did he go?"

"Toward the lake."

"I'll have that kid's hide. If anything happens to Zorro," Fowler said.

Jake took off at a run with Alanna on his heels. He headed straight for the tack room. He grabbed his saddle, blanket and bridle. Alanna caught his arm. "I'll come with you."

"No." he said, his concern for Clay almost overriding how pissed off he was at the kid for such a reckless act. "Your brother's fit to be tied. You stay here and calm him down. I'll find Clay and bring that fool kid back and we'll get this all sorted out."

He went to Valentine's stall and quickly and efficiently saddled the gelding. He led him out of the barn and mounted.

"I'll find him," he said and kicked Valentine into a gallop as he raced out of the stable yard and onto the road that led to the lake. Sitting deep in the saddle, one with the horse as the gelding's powerful muscles moved beneath him.

Broken branches and flattened grass showed Jake

the way Clay hand gone. He urged Valentine on, feeling the horse bunch under him as he jumped an old log at the gallop, his hooves kicking up dirt and chunks of grass.

The wind whipped by tearing at his hat. In the distance he saw a black horse galloping full out as the rider on his back urged him on.

"Ya!" he said, giving Valentine a kick with his heels, and the blue roan increased his speed. Zorro was fast, but Valentine had the kind of stamina and speed bred into Ranger horses to go the distance. The black stallion was no match for him. He lost sight of Clay as he topped a rise and descended down the other side. As Jake hit the top of the hill, the Lone Star Lake glittered a deep blue and spread out before him. Clay had taken Zorro along the shore and was heading for the far side toward the dock where Jake had confronted Marceline.

"Clay," he shouted again, but again the kid ignored him.

With pounding hooves and another burst of speed, Valentine closed the gap between them. He raced after the stallion as they both skirted the lake.

"Clay!" Jake shouted. "Stop!"

Clay either didn't hear him or had no intention of stopping.

Valentine pulled out yet more speed and Jake gained on him now only about a length away. Clay looked over his shoulder and saw Jake.

"Leave me alone!" he shouted.

Jake came alongside Clay and yelled, "Stop, Clay. We can figure this out!"

"No! He's going to hurt her. I've got to get out of here. Keep her safe!"

Jake leaned over and grabbed Zorro's bridle and immediately pulled back to slow his own horse.

Their speed decreased by increments until Jake brought both Zorro and Valentine to a halt. He dismounted and went between the heavily breathing animals and pulled Clay out of the saddle.

"Are you out of your mind? You could have been hurt. You could have hurt the horse."

He shook Clay who dropped his head, despair radiating out of his eyes.

"I had to," he shouted, his head coming up as he struggled out of Jake's grasp and made a run for it. Jake swore under his breath as he went after Clay and wrestled him to the ground. Lying heavily on him, he straddled the kid when he started to fight.

"Stop it. Tell me what's wrong!"

Clay covered his eyes, his chest heaving, his voice thick. "You can't help me. He's going to hurt her if I don't do what he says and… I can't. I don't want to be that guy anymore. I just want to keep her safe."

Jake pulled down his hand and shook him again. "Who's going to hurt whom? Clay, tell me right now. I'm a Texas Ranger! I can help you!"

Clay stilled and his breath hitched in his throat. He stared up at Jake, hope springing there. He clutched at Jake, his words filled with a powerful fear. "Are you really a Texas Ranger?"

"Yes. Now tell me, Clay. I'll help you."

"I thought you were a cop the minute I laid eyes on you."

"Clay. We don't have time for this. Who gave you that black eye? Who is threatening you?"

"Henry. He said he'd hurt Daisy if I didn't get out of this program and get back to Dallas. He wants me to sell drugs for him. He's been smuggling them through the Colton ranch right beneath their noses."

"How?"

"In the hay. He showed me to get me locked in when I agreed to help him."

"You know where they are?"

"Yes!"

Jake hauled the kid up, realizing this was even more dangerous than he'd thought. "Show me."

Chapter 16

The crisis with Clay aside, Alanna had stood and watched the man she'd only come to realize moments ago, a man she adored, loved and didn't want to lose, ride heroically and confidently away. He'd been trying to tell her something and now she was terrified at what that was. What had she expected? He would fall into her arms and pledge to her that he loved her, too. Well, yeah, that is what she'd hoped. Now there was something he was keeping from her. He'd tried to get her to go with him to her office for privacy before they were interrupted. What was it he wanted to say?

He didn't love her?

"Miss Colton?" a tentative voice broke into her thoughts.

Alanna pulled her gaze from the now empty pasture as Jake had disappeared to find Daisy standing next to her. The young daughter of their apartment cook, Ellen, stood there, her face white, her mouth trembling. "What is it?"

"I know why Clay ran off," Daisy said, her voice wobbly.

"You do," Alanna said, clasping the girl's shoulders. "Why?"

It was clear the girl was terrified. She looked around with the look of a child checking under her bed for the bogeyman and said, "He's in trouble. You need to help him."

"What kind of trouble?"

"There's a man here who is threatening him and he wouldn't tell me why, so I followed them last night. There are drugs on the ranch."

Anger rushed through her and she clamped her jaw so hard, she felt the pressure all the way to the top of her head, a load of adrenaline dropping into her stomach like jet fuel. "What? Where? Show me!"

Daisy headed in the direction of the barn where Zorro was stabled. They entered the dim interior and Alanna was running on anger and adrenaline. How dare someone use her stables for drug smuggling!

With determination and hope, they headed down the alleyway as Daisy led her to the loft and Alanna followed her up the stairs into the hot, dusty hayloft.

Bales and bales were stacked up there and the loft to the outdoors was open, the view of the pastureland and the purple-hazed shadow from the overcast day. A pallet of bales waiting to be unloaded and stacked swung just below the frame on a heavy rope and pulley, intermittent creaking and the muffled stamping and snorting of horses below them breaking the eerie silence. Bracing her hand on the side of the open door, she looked down. It was quite a drop with more hay to be hauled up on the winch.

"Where are the drugs?" Alanna said, her voice naturally hushed as Daisy wrung her hands.

Her eyes shadowed with worry, Daisy whispered, "Do you think Clay is okay?" Her voice filled with both concern and affection for the boy.

Alanna hugged her hard. "Jake will find him. I'm so sure of that." She clasped Daisy's shoulders and said, "Show me where the drugs are."

Daisy went over to the hay and with plenty of grunting, tugged out one of the heavy bales. When she had it on the floor, she pulled a small penknife out of her pocket and cut the yellow twine wrapping the bale.

The sun came out and shone through the wide opening, the climbing dust motes creating a shimmering haze between Alanna and the door. A big black barn cat materialized through the nonexistent barrier, like a shape coming through a waterfall, and Alanna watched as Daisy knelt down, part of her mahogany hair blazing in the shaft of sunlight, the red highlights burning in the bright light. Alanna's breath ceased as she pushed apart the hay to reveal four plastic-wrapped white bricks.

The cat wound herself around her legs, momentarily distracting Alanna. To get the animal out of the way, she stooped and lifted it onto a bale, aware from her generous tummy, she was heavy with kittens.

The cat arched its back, then sat and began washing its face. Unconcerned with the terrible human drama unfolding before it.

The dread she experienced only moments ago compounding into something cold and heavy, her heart laboring as if she were wading through quicksand.

Then hard on the heels of dread came fury. She clenched her fists at the nerve of whomever it was that had decided to use her family's business as a way to smuggle and store this filth.

"Who is responsible for this?" she said.

"That would be me," someone rasped out.

This time it wasn't a cat who came through the waterfall of light. It was a man, his eyes glinting with threat and menace, a gun in his hand. The barrel pointed directly at her.

Jake hauled Clay to his feet. "You take Valentine. I'm not letting you back on that stallion."

"I already rode him. Besides, Zorro likes me." Clay walked over to Valentine. "He for sure does not like Mr. Colton," he muttered as he grabbed the blue roan's reins and flipped them over his head. With the ease of a seasoned cowboy, he mounted. The kid sure had learned a thing or two.

They road back to the ranch at a cantor, Zorro acted totally chill after the run-in with Fowler and the race from his corral. A good sign that he had settled into life here.

Jake was determined to bring Henry in today once Clay showed him where the drugs were stashed, knowing he was going to blow his cover. The kid kept glancing at him every so often as they rode, obviously absorbing the fact that Jake was a Texas Ranger.

"You're not in trouble, Clay," Jake said, giving

him a reassuring look. "But you might have to testify against Henry."

Clay glanced away, the muscles along his jaw tensing, his voice quiet when he said, "As long as Daisy is safe, I'll do anything to get that guy off the streets. He's an animal."

"You made the right choice here, Clay. We'll get him arrested and behind bars and you can get on with changing your life around."

He rode directly to the apartment, loosely tying the horses and ran up the stairs. Once in his apartment, he dug in his suitcase and found his gun case. As Clay's eyes widened, he pulled out his department issued SIG and shoved in the magazine, chambered a round, then thumbed off the safety. He picked up his badge and turned it over in his hands. This was it. Alanna was going to find out in the worst way that he was a Ranger. There was no help for it. He would have given anything to tell her himself before she saw him in action and knew without him owning up to it that he had been there to spy on her. He'd betrayed her even as he lay with her. Guilt twisted around him so hard, he clenched his teeth at the pain.

With resignation and pride, he clipped his badge onto his shirt and grabbed his cell. Dialing, he said, "Boss, I'm about to discover a cache of drugs Henry Swango has stashed on the ranch. I have an eyewitness. I need backup."

"Well, hell, son," his boss drawled. "That's good work. We've got the cavalry on the way."

"Roger that."

Clay's eyes, riveted to the star on his chest, said with awe, "Damn, you *are* a Texas Ranger."

"Let's go," Jake said, his voice filled with steel.

They went down the stairs and Jake asked where the drugs were.

"In Zorro's barn." Clay headed that way and Jake followed him. When they got to the doors, Clay went to open them, but they wouldn't budge.

"What's wrong?" Jake said.

"They're locked…from the inside."

Alarmed, he walked around to the other side of the barn, but all those doors were locked, as well.

"He must be inside," Clay said, a healthy dose of fear in his voice. "Jake," he said, grabbing his arm. "Henry has a backup plan."

"What's that?"

"He said he'd torch the place and all the evidence would go up in smoke. My God! There's like forty horses in there."

Jake's heart lurched.

Then they heard a soft muffled scream and Clay looked up toward the open doors to the hayloft. "That's Daisy!" he choked out. He ran to the bales, but Jake hauled him back.

"You stay put," he ordered. Tucking the gun into the small of his back, he climbed the bales and grabbed onto the pallet when he heard another voice.

"You're never going to get away with this."

His gut clenched in bone-deep fear.

Alanna!

"Who's going to stop me? Jake? Texas Ranger McCord? Did you hire him to spy on me?" At the widening of her eyes, he smirked. "That's right, I recognized him. Took care of one of his undercover baby Rangers. Should have seen the look on his face when I shot him in the chest."

He gestured with the gun, but she couldn't move, couldn't think clearly, couldn't decide on any course of action, because too many things were racing through her brain all at once. Jake? A Texas Ranger? Henry was a murderer and a drug dealer! Jake? Daisy was in danger!

"Come here," he said. She hesitated, not wanting to get within arm's length of him, debating for a split second whether to step back and rush out the door, but she couldn't because Daisy would be trapped with him.

"A bullet can move faster than you, Miss Colton. Don't even think about it," he said calmly as if reading her mind. The barrel of the gun moved toward Daisy.

"No!"

"Ah, I see we've found common ground."

As soon as Alanna was close enough, he shocked her by suddenly grabbing her hair and yanking her against him, her back to his chest. Her scalp on fire, an instant later she also felt the cold muzzle of the gun against her temple. His voice next to her ear made her shudder. "Don't get any bright ideas. I already have enough for both of us." His fist was still in her hair, and tears sprang to the corners of her eyes as he gave it a vicious twist. "Now, I will release you, and you will do as I say, when I say. Are we understood? I don't want to do anything to mar my ticket out of here." To punctuate his statement, he tugged her even more tightly back against him.

"Yes," she choked out.

"Good," he said with oily smugness, releasing her as suddenly as he'd grabbed her.

She staggered forward and landed hard on her hands and knees on the hay-covered wooden floor of the barn.

She met Daisy's eyes who, without moving her head, looked down at her hand, partially buried by the straw. She still had the knife she'd used to cut the twine. Her breath hitched and she nodded imperceptibly.

"Get up. It's time to go."

Still reeling from the information Henry had revealed about Jake and then Henry's sudden attack, she scrambled up, wanting to keep her eye on him at all times.

"Go? Where?"

"Somewhere I'll be safe. Then I'll let you go."

She faced Henry, whose back was to the open loft. The rope creaked and swayed, then she saw the glimpse of dark hair. Jake! Relief and pain swept through her, mingling with her shock.

She lifted her chin. "I'm not going anywhere with you," she snapped.

He reached into his pocket and pulled out a silver lighter. "You will unless you want it to get a little hotter in here." With a flick of his finger, a small flame flared.

Daisy moved. Raising the knife, lightning-quick, she stabbed Henry in the upper thigh. He cried out and the lighter flew out of his hand into the bale stack, immediately igniting the hay.

"You little bitch." He bellowed in pain and back-handed Daisy with the gun, clipping her temple. She flew back and didn't move.

"Daisy!" Alanna screamed, going to her, but Henry blocked her path. She sobbed once, going for the gun, but Henry fought her off while smoke started to fill the loft as more bales caught. He grabbed her by the hair and jerked her back, then shoved her forward as she lost her balance and she crashed so close to the burning hay that she got a lungful of acid smoke. Her legs shook violently beneath her, and she coughed violently.

Then Jake was there coming through the door. Alanna gasped. Henry, tipped off by her expression, whirled as Jake punched him in the face. They wrestled over the gun and Jake managed to knock it out of Henry's hand, but it was between her and the struggling men. They wrestled; both of them getting in blows to the face and body. The sounds of the horses squealing and kicking at their stalls filtered up from below as they got the first scent of smoke.

Clay materialized at the edge of the loft doorway, but Henry kicked him in the face and he disappeared from sight.

Alanna crawled across the floor on her hands and knees, reaching for the gun, but Henry and Jake knocked into her and she lost her grip.

Henry got the upper hand and shoved Jake so hard, he almost went out the opening, but at the last minute caught the side and teetered there.

Henry scrambled for the gun and brought it around just as Jake got his balance. The gun discharged and the bullet hit Jake. He grunted, stumbled and smashed his shoulder against the loft's wall, the impact a terrible thud.

"Jake!" Alanna screamed as blood blossomed. Jake clutched at his shoulder as Henry recovered and brought the gun up again. His face contorted in an ugly sneer. Spying a bale hook in one of the bales, Alanna snatched it and lunged off the floor and sank the business end of it deeply into Henry's back. He howled, trying to reach it as Jake pushed off the wall and slammed into him.

Knocking Henry right into the fire, an inhuman scream came from him as he reeled away. Clay, still dangling from the loft doorway, caught his ankle and sent him flying out the doorway.

There was a sickening scream and then a terrible sound of his body hitting the ground.

Clay pulled himself all the way up and rushed over to Daisy. Calling her name in an anguished voice, he scooped his hands under her, lifted her into his arms and headed for the loft stairs. Alanna ran to Jake and helped him up.

Together, panting from the smoke and heat, they pounded down the stairs. "Call for help," Jake said as Alanna ran for the locked stable door and lifted the crossbeam and threw them open.

Clay ran out and set Daisy down on the ground as hands came running.

"Daisy!" Ellen screamed as sirens sounded in the distance.

The roof of the stable was fully engulfed in flames as horses started running from the open stable doors. Alanna, careful of hurtling equine bodies, ran back inside and saw Jake, his shirt soaked with blood, running down the aisle, opening stall doors and herding horses out, yelling, "Ha!" The horses didn't need any more encouragement then as the animals, already terrified from the scent of smoke, headed for the open doors.

Clay was doing the same thing down the other aisle and Alanna started on the stalls closest to her. Smoke was pouring through the stable alleyway and Alanna started coughing, the air thick with a choking haze. She got turned around, not sure where the door was. Coughing harder, she leaned against the wall, overcome until a steely arm clasped her around the waist and hauled her against him, coughing deeply. He forced her to crouch where the air was clearer. Then he put his fingers to his lips and a sharp whistle pierced the air. She heard a responding whinny and then the sound of pounding hooves on concrete. The blue roan came rushing toward them through the swirling smoke. Jake grabbed on to the horse's saddle and dragged himself up. He reached down and, grunting in pain, hauled her across his lap.

"Let's get out of here, boy," he rasped to the horse, his voice weak.

Valentine shot down the alleyway, his innate sense of direction leading him to fresh air and the open stable doors. He burst out into the stable yard. Jake carefully held Alanna until she was safely on the ground. But Jake teetered, then fell, rolling onto his back as Sheriff Watkins, Texas Rangers, fire and EMT rolled into the stable yard, sirens flashing. Out of the corner of her eye, she saw Daisy sitting up, a bloody gash on her temple, but she looked like she was going to be all right as her mother supported her back. Clay kneeling beside her in the dirt, his face soot stained, blood streaked and dirty. His heart was in his eyes as he stared at Daisy.

The firefighters poured out of the first truck as a second one, the tanker, came to a stop. They connected hoses and got water on the blaze while Alanna looked down into Jake's pale face. He said softly as if his heart was breaking, "Alanna." He raised his hand, the backs of his fingers just brushing her cheek, his expression going very still. She held his gaze for a frozen moment, and then she abruptly looked away, an awful, shaky feeling sliding through her.

"Are you all right, babe?"

Her? Was she all right? He'd been shot, not her. He'd risked his life for her. She shivered, her chest suddenly aching. She didn't think she had ever loved him more than she did at that very minute, and Lord, but it hurt. More than anything, more than her next breath, she wanted to curl up in his arms and rest her head on his shoulder. She wanted to hold on to him and never let go. He closed his eyes, then passed out.

He couldn't be a Texas Ranger. He would have told her. He wouldn't have kept that information to himself. He couldn't be there under false pretenses to spy on her. No.

She wouldn't believe it. Maybe Henry was mistaken. But her breath caught in her throat, her heart suspended when she saw his badge. It was clipped to his chest. The evidence that he was exactly what Henry said he was. She leaned forward and unclipped it, looking down at it as tears welled in her eyes and her throat tightened into a hard lump. Oh, God. Oh, God. This had all been engineered.

Her heart fluttering wildly in her throat, she stared blindly across the yard, her stomach rolling over. Lord, how was she going to get through this?

Before she had time to assimilate the fact that she'd been set up, EMTs grabbed her, giving her oxygen as another set started to work on Jake. She felt as though she was in a surreal daze as she watched them pull open his shirt, stem the flow of blood, hook up an IV and lift him onto a stretcher, then haul him away.

Fowler was there, gathering her up in his arms, murmuring her name, but she couldn't take her eyes off Jake's ashen face as they wheeled him to an ambulance. With the siren blasting and the tires sliding on the pavement, the ambulance took off.

Fear, rage, love and the need to protect him mixed into a terrible roll of emotions cutting through her. She had finally learned how to trust, had fallen deeply into love.

And the man she had given her heart to, the man she had just said she loved, had all along been betraying her. Even as he made love to her night after night, he was working against her and her family.

Had everything she'd felt for him been a lie?

An illusion?

And the trust she had given him lay between her as burned-out a husk as the barn behind her.

Betrayal bitter on her tongue, she tightened her hand around the silver star as the pin stabbed into her palm and blood trickled between her fingers.

Chapter 17

Jake floated, trying to anchor himself. His eyes fluttered open and the bright light from the window to his left showed an overcast day.

He licked his dry lips and when he tried to move tensed up with pain.

He'd been shot.

Alanna!

He tried to sit up and his boss said, "Where do you think you're going?"

Jake collapsed back onto the mattress and turned his head.

"Alanna?"

"She's fine and so are the two kids. They've been treated and sent home. The barn is a loss, but you got all their ponies out so no loss of livestock. Henry Swango is dead. Broke his neck when he hit the ground. Miss Colton's statement to us was that he had killed Tim Preston. He recognized you. He thought she was working with us to apprehend him."

"Except for the barn, best possible outcome. Henry got what he deserved and Tim got justice."

"No argument there. The doctor will be here shortly. When you're ready to be released, I'll be back to get you. Don't be a pain in the ass, and do what the nurses tell you."

"Yes, sir," Jake said, his voice flat.

His boss left and the doctor came in, a man in his forties with a pair of black-rimmed glasses, kind blue eyes and smelling of antiseptic.

"Mr. McCord, I'm Dr. Lambert. How are you feeling?"

"Sore, but glad to be alive."

He nodded and chuckled. "Yes, I'm sure. There's good news all around. The bullet didn't do any serious damage. It went through and through and completely missed any bone. You have some slight muscle damage that I repaired, but all in all, not bad. We cleaned and irrigated the wound and removed any foreign objects. I'd say we'll keep you for a couple of days and then you can finish your convalescence at home."

"Thanks, Doc."

"It's my pleasure. I've never met a Texas Ranger before, but let me say it's an honor."

Jake smiled and reached out his hand. The doctor shook it and then exited the room.

A few seconds later the door opened again and Jake said, "You forget something, Doc…" He turned his head and his brain froze as his words trailed off. Alanna stood there, her eyes bruised and red rimmed.

Dammit, the knowledge that he'd been responsible for making her cry cut through him with sharp regret.

"I came here to get an explanation. I want to hear it from you."

His breath hitched and he closed his eyes briefly before he met her sad and angry gaze. "I'm a Texas Ranger. I was sent in to Colton Valley Ranch Stables to keep you under close surveillance and discover any clues to the whereabouts of your missing father. I was supposed to get close to you—"

When she made a soft, painful sound, he paused. "Alanna, I got too close and then I couldn't pull away. It wasn't planned. It just happened."

"It just happened?" she repeated and swiped at her cheeks. "I trusted you," she said, advancing on the bed, shouting. "You betrayed me. Did you feel anything for me?"

"Yes, dammit. I didn't do this lightly, but I couldn't help myself."

"Right. And if you had found out I had done something to my father?"

"That didn't happen. I'm not going to project what I would have done in the future."

She talked right over him. "Would you have cuffed me yourself, booked me yourself and thrown me in jail?"

"Alanna, please, all I can say is I'm sorry. I couldn't tell you. It was my job!" he shouted back.

"Well, good. I'm glad we have that cleared up. You broke my heart and betrayed me all in the name of justice. Congratulations. I don't know who's worse. Henry…or you!"

She whirled and ran from the room. Shocked down

to the bone, a sick, hollow feeling settled heavily inside him. He realized he'd lost the best thing that had ever happened to him.

He rang for the nurse. When she came in he said, "I'm in pain."

She upped his pain meds, but nothing she had in the IV bag was ever going to dull the agony of losing a woman like Alanna.

After he'd gotten discharged from the hospital, Jake got into his own truck, his boss behind the wheel.

"Where's Valentine?"

"We shipped him back to TDCJ French Robertson. He'll be there waiting for you." He stared at him for a moment, then put the truck in gear and drove out of the hospital parking lot. "You look like hell, McCord," he growled.

Jake felt like hell. Jake stared at him, his expression fixed and controlled; then without a flicker of emotion, he said, his voice flat, "Thanks."

"This have anything to do with the pissed-off Alanna Colton and her visit?"

"No comment." It had taken practice, but he'd learned to shut down and disconnect. He used his professional training to accomplish it. All it took was focus.

"All right, taking the fifth is your prerogative. I know that assignment turned out to be more than you bargained for, but for what it's worth, you acted beyond the call of duty"

Jake groaned. "Does that mean—"

"Yup, boy howdy, we're giving you a commendation for heroism. And, for that matter, so did Valentine."

"You giving my horse a medal? He deserves it. I don't need it."

"Doesn't matter and, yes, we're giving him a medal, too. You're getting it and you're going to look proud while we're pinning it to your chest."

Jake sighed. They rode in silence for a while, and then Jake said, "Boss, you been at this a long time. You ever think about getting out?"

"Yeah, once when a bust went bad and I lost my partner. That was tough going, but they don't make sissies Rangers," he said, giving Jake a quick glance.

"No, they don't," he agreed.

After they pulled up to his place near French Robertson, Valentine gave him a deep, joyous whinny from the corral. He walked over to the fence as the roan galloped to the rails seeking a rub. Jake pressed his forehead to the gelding's face and closed his eyes and took comfort from his four-legged friend.

"Jake, rest."

"Boss, I lost my badge."

"I'll get you another one."

"Don't bother... I'm out."

"What? Jake—"

"I'll train a replacement, then attend the ceremony, but after that I'm gone."

His boss left, not happy with Jake's decision, but he wasn't the one Jake cared about.

Being holed up in the house would drive him stir-crazy and a terrible restlessness came over him. He'd already ditched the sling, his arm painful, but he'd been kept in the hospital mostly due to the smoke inhalation, his lungs a little raw still. He got into the car, propelled by a force he couldn't name, he ended up in front of Jennifer Preston's little white house.

He got out of the car and went up to the porch. Knocking on the door, he heard the sound of a baby crying inside. He took off his hat and fingered the brim.

The door opened and Jennifer stood there.

"Jake?" she said, a catch to her voice, and then she reached up and wrapped her arms around his neck. "It is you. Come in," she said warmly. He entered the house and saw Tim's daughter in a playpen. Jennifer bent down and picked her up.

"This is Emily."

Jake reached out and smoothed his hand over the baby's downy hair and her satiny cheek. She reached up and curled her tiny little hand around his finger. His heart tightened. She turned her head and looked at him and he was struck at how much she looked like Tim. In her, Tim lived.

"Sit down. Can I get you anything?"

"Coffee would be welcome."

"I just brewed a pot." She set Emily back into the playpen and he followed her to the bright, airy kitchen where she poured him a cup of coffee.

They settled on the living room couch. Emily was sleeping soundly. He gave Jennifer the time to tell him how she was doing, that her mother had been there when Emily was born, how she had cried and cried when she'd held her for the first time. It was like holding Tim again. She was her blessing.

When his coffee was almost all gone, she said, "What brought you by?"

He looked away to gather his composure. "I wanted to let you know the man who killed your husband is dead."

"Jake…"

"He died as a result of drug dealing. I didn't kill him, but I knew you'd want to know. Closure is a powerful thing."

She nodded and slipped her hand over his. "Yes, Jake. Closure. Tim wouldn't want you to blame yourself. He was doing what he loved and I'm proud of his courage, his dedication and his drive to make a better world for our daughter. I hope this gives you some measure of peace."

He found as he drove away from Jennifer Preston's pretty little house that, in fact, it had.

Getting back behind the wheel he drove to Dallas. Pulling up outside a blue clapboard house on the outskirts. He got out of the car and smelled the faint aroma of beef sizzling on a grill. Skirting the house, he came around the corner, spying a man sitting at a picnic table drinking alone out of a long-necked bottle.

At the sound of Jake's approach, he turned his head and surprise flashed across his face, then concern. "Jake!" he said in a deep baritone. "What happened to your shoulder?"

"I got shot."

The man half rose and Jake waved him off. "I'm fine. There won't be any permanent damage. It won't affect my duty."

He relaxed back down onto the bench and Jake, bracing his good hand on the table, wedged himself onto the seat.

The man got up and threw another burger on the grill and closed the lid.

"What brings you here?"

Jake's gaze never wavered.

"Matt, Dad."

His dad's face went slack, his eyes shuttering. He looked away and took a swig of his beer. "Jake, please."

"Please what?"

"Let it go?"

"That's the trouble. I can't."

He took a few more swigs of his beer until Jake knocked the bottle off the table. "Tell me, Dad. Why don't you go to Matt's grave?" He went to get up and Jake said, softly. "Dad, please. I'm begging you. I need to know. Don't you even care? He was sixteen…" His breath hitched and he bowed his head, his shoulders slumping.

His father's eyes gleaming in the dim light from the porch, he blinked rapidly and looked away. "It's not that I don't care, Jake, son…" He rubbed at his eyes, his voice thick. "It's that I can't bear it. I failed him so miserably and it's all my fault that he's in the ground. If I hadn't pushed so hard, he'd be here doing whatever the hell he wants to do."

"Come with me now, Dad."

For a minute he sat there lost in his own grief and sorrow. When he raised his head, he nodded. "All right."

Not understanding why, his father stopped and picked up some flowers; they ended up at a set of stone gates. Driving through, he parked on the side of the paved road and they got out. Jake's boot heels sunk into the ground as he and his dad walked to the headstone. Setting the flowers down in front, he brushed off the granite.

There had been a time when Jake couldn't bear to go there, either. Before Alanna and the way she'd healed his heart. Even though now it needed a different kind of mending, the only kind of mending she could do, he came to grips with his love for his brother, came to terms with his loss, realizing he had done everything in his power to save him.

"Thank you for coming with me, Dad. It means everything."

He nodded. For a minute they stared at each other and Jake said, "I miss him so much."

"I know, son. I know." He reached out and clasped the back of Jake's neck and Jake grabbed on to his dad's forearm, squeezing tight.

As they left the graveyard, his dad said quietly, "What else is on your mind?"

"I'm quitting the Rangers. I'm burned-out and tried too hard to be what you wanted. I followed in your footsteps willingly, but I want something different now. I need peace, Dad. I owe that to Matt. That honesty. I've made mistakes and some of them will haunt me for the rest of my life, but maybe some way, somehow I can find middle ground where I can find my own forgiveness and sleep at night."

"Jake, you don't have anything to be sorry for. You were there for him when I wasn't. It all seems so pointless now. Just know I'm so damn proud of you in whatever you do. That's never going to change. Do what you have to do."

"They're giving me a commendation before I separate. Would you attend?"

His dad bowed his head and then met Jake's gaze. "Hell yes. Does it have anything to do with you getting shot?"

"Yeah, everything." He closed his eyes, thinking about one of those mistakes, one he couldn't fix. One of the ones where finding middle ground would be a good start. He'd lost something so precious and irreplaceable. Alanna's love. She made that abundantly clear.

I don't know who's worse. Henry...or you.

He would never forget how she'd looked when she'd said that. Heartbroken. He'd done that to her, and guilt and regret scored his insides.

Three weeks later, he was packed up and ready to leave TDCJ French Robertson prison and quitting had been the easy part. Leaving Valentine behind, that was almost as hard as losing a partner in the line of duty. He loved that blue roan and it was as if he knew Jake wasn't going to be back. He hung his head and refused to come when Jake was ready to leave. So he slipped through the fence and gave his stalwart companion some carrots, a few sugar cubes and a pat goodbye.

Thankfully, when he lost it over a horse, he was miles away.

There would be the ceremony and then after that it would be official. He'd stayed on at French Robertson prison to train his replacement. He pulled up in front of his dad's house. He'd stay there until he found a job.

The rain outside Meddlesome Butterfly's big picture window kept pedestrians off the street, but when a cab pulled up and a woman got out in a pricey rain-coat and a pair of gorgeous heels, Alanna recognized her sister Piper.

She dashed inside, handed off the raincoat and in her purposeful but definitely sultry way of power walking through the restaurant caused plenty of ap-preciative looks from the male patrons in the place.

"Sorry I'm late. Hard to get a cab on a day like today." She leaned in and gave Alanna a hug and quick kiss on the cheek.

"How's things in corporate America?" Having lunch with Piper wasn't out of the ordinary, but she'd noticed her sister had been hovering for oh, the last month. Ever since she'd come home from the hospital and locked herself in her room to cry out her despair and disappointment. She nursed her broken heart with some damn good Scotch and lots of mindless TV.

The waiter placed menus in front of them and Al-anna picked hers up.

"We'll have two martinis, dirty, olives," Piper said when the waiter prompted them for drinks.

She smiled and laughed. "You know Colton Incor-porated." Piper looked over her menu. "It's run with an iron fist with Fowler at the helm." She dropped her eyes and was quiet for a second, then said with-out looking at Alanna, "He's still royally pissed at you." She looked up then to gauge her sister's reac-tion, then leaned over and lowered her voice. "And, he asks about you every day."

"He does not," she said with a dubious look at Piper.

"Does." Piper nodded vigorously. "Big brother is worried about you."

"Why doesn't he just apologize and give me what I want, then?" Alanna groused as the waiter interrupted and they gave him their order.

Piper took a sip of her martini. "Beats me. Pride. Ego. Arrogance. Fear?"

"All of the above," Alanna said, and they both laughed.

Fifteen minutes after Piper took the last bite of her meal and set down her fork, she said, "Are you really going to sign those papers at the end of the month? Leave the stables?"

"Yes. I have to, Piper." Alanna had thought long and hard about her decision. Even with Jake out of her life, she knew his advice was sound. The only way to get the respect and support she was entitled was to show Fowler she deserved it.

"I guess I understand, but it won't be the same."

"No, it won't," Alanna said with a sigh. She looked up and her heart stalled in her chest. A man had walked in with dark hair and sexy broad shoulders, a gray Stetson on his head. When he turned, her stomach dropped. It wasn't Jake.

Piper followed her line of sight, then sighed dramatically. "How long are you going to torture yourself and him?"

Alanna stiffened. "Piper, drop it."

"No. I don't think I will. Look, you have always been kind to me, Alanna, and I've never really been able to repay the favor."

Fortifying herself with a deep breath, Alanna said, her voice soft, "You don't have to repay me."

Piper's eyes went tender. "I know that, but in this case, I can do something for you."

"What?"

"Tell you to get your head out of your ass," she said, oh so casually.

She huffed a tight laugh and shook her head. "He was here to spy on me, on our family."

"To find out who harmed Dad. I don't know about you, but sounds to me like he's the good guy here. Didn't he save your life?"

"Piper." Alanna felt stripped to the bone.

"Yes, I'm playing the he-saved-your-life card." She paused, then sighed heavily as if she was talking to a thickheaded idiot. "Yes, he was undercover. But it was for his job and he risked everything to fall in love with you. Sounds more like a keeper to me. Think about what would have happened if he never came. Henry Swango would have used our business as a drug smuggling operation. He could have hurt one of us. But he didn't because a Texas Ranger protected you and all of us by risking his life."

Alanna tried to tune her out because she was making some really good points and her heart was ready to say to hell with being angry and pissed at him.

Piper snapped her fingers in Alanna's face. "Listen to me, dammit! Really, Alanna. If I were you, I'd ask him to marry me."

"What?"

She released a long-suffering sigh. "Stop pretending you aren't crazy for him. I saw it that day he had lunch with us and Whitney went all crazy on you. The way you two looked at each other." She fanned herself. "Damn." She caught her gaze and held on to it. "Fess up. You still love him." Alanna couldn't speak, she couldn't utter the lie. "That's what I thought. Jake Mc-Cord has it bad for you. Head over heels bad. How many times in your life have you really fallen in love? Your trust in him wasn't shattered. If anything, he proved himself every step of the way. Anyway…" She reached into her purse and pulled out a stapled sheaf of papers and threw down a printed article. "They're giving him a medal. Commendation for heroism. By the way, it's not his first one." This time her voice got quiet. "He's leaving the Rangers, Alanna. He had to give up Valentine. That must have killed him." Alanna's eyes filled as her sister went on. "It's all there in the article. I've got to get back to work. Trust in him, Alanna. I would love to see you happy."

She sat there for a full ten minutes after her sister left. Everything she said hit Alanna straight in the heart. She reached for the chain around her neck where she'd hung his badge. It was warm from her skin. She curled her hand around it. Haunted by regret and guilt, wishing she could undo what she had done to him, especially what she'd said to him in that parting shot. *My God, that was the anger talking.* If she could take it back she would in a heartbeat.

The picture of him in the article showed a man scored with pain and marked by sorrow, and thinner. Much thinner. Her sorrow spilled over, and she covered her face with her hand. *What had she done to him?*

The thought of him holed up somewhere alone, without even Valentine to keep him company, with no one to hold and comfort him, was more than she could handle and something broke loose in her.

She blinked back her tears. Reaching for her cell, she put the phone to her ear and said, "Hello, Senator Stillwater. It's Alanna Colton calling."

The day of the ceremony dawned bright and clear. The senator had come through for her in one of the favors she'd discussed with him. One of them was to get tickets to Jake's ceremony. The other one, he was still working on.

Alanna had arrived early so she could choose a seat that wasn't conspicuous. The ceremony started on time and she looked and looked, but Jake was nowhere to be found. Valentine was there, but Jake's medal was given to his father.

As soon as the ceremony was over, she approached Mr. McCord and said, "Excuse me. Could I have a moment of your time?"

He turned with a smile on his face that faltered when he recognized her. "Miss Colton. What can I do for you?"

Oh, this was going so well. "I wanted to talk to Jake. Do you know where he is?" His mouth tightened. "Just so you know. I won't take no for an answer. I'm in love with him, Mr. McCord. I made a foolish mistake and didn't trust him. I want to find him and tell him. Now, will you help me, or not?"

This time, his eyes softened and he smiled.

Jake swung the lariat over his head, one, two, three revolutions and threw the rope, snagging the steer on the first try. "Hold," he ordered, and the quarter horse by the name of Cactus performed beautifully, stopping dead, planting his front legs and snapping the rope taut. Jake was already out of the saddle and tying the steer with quick, agile precision.

He turned to praise the horse and his words died on his lips.

Alanna stood by the cow pony looking as beautiful as he remembered. She was starring in every dream he had. He blinked a couple of times.

"Cat got your tongue, cowboy?"

The gleam of amusement in her eyes made his heart roll over and hope spring up. But still he couldn't say a word.

He'd quit the Rangers a little over a month ago, had blown off the medal ceremony and had taken a job with an outfit who trained ropers. It was a beautiful spread on ample acres, nothing compared to Colton Valley Ranch Stables, but decent and the pay was excellent. The owner had hired Jake on the spot and he loved every minute of the work. The only thing he missed about being a Texas Ranger was Valentine.

His knees weak, he couldn't move a muscle and his throat was so damn tight he still couldn't speak.

The amusement in her eyes faded and uncertainty came over her face. She took a step toward him, and a wave of stunning reaction slammed through him. Covering his face with his hand, he took a heaving breath, the emotion too intense to hold in, relief and something raw breaking from him. She closed the distance, her voice going soft and husky.

Clasping his hand, she removed it from his face. "I got you, cowboy. I got you," she said. He caught the back of her neck, pulling her toward him.

"Dammit, Alanna, what the hell took you so long?" he said, shaking because he was so glad to have her back.

When she slid her arms around his neck and hung on to him with fierce determination, he returned the favor, hanging on to her with every ounce of strength he had. He lost his ability to talk again, it was just too overwhelming.

"Jake," she said, her voice filled with aching regret. "I'm sorry for what I said to you in the hospital. It was out of line and very untrue. I didn't mean it. I was just hurt and angry."

He nodded. "Tell me you didn't just come here to…apologize."

"No. I didn't come here to just apologize. I simply can't live without you, cowboy. So tell me you forgive me for hurting you. My plan is to never do that again."

He slid his fingers into her hair and drew her head against him, then began stroking her jaw. "Ah, darlin'," he whispered, his voice rough with emotion. "My forgiveness is yours. You just made my life."

"The feeling is mutual, Jake. You just made mine."

He took a deep breath and said, "I love you, Alanna Colton."

"Well, fancy that. We're so in tune." She cupped his face between both palms. "I love you, too, Jake McCord. Now, let's go home."

He closed his eyes. That sounded so damn good.

"Wait a second, are you giving me a job?"

She laughed. "Do we need to negotiate terms?"

"I guess I would have to weigh the pros and cons." Her eyes narrowed with twinkling lights. "They're paying me quite a good salary here."

She leaned over and whispered a figure in his ear and he choked. "That's a lot of zeros, darlin'."

"You're worth every penny."

"What are some of the other pros?"

"Sleeping with the boss every night. Waking to her every morning. Mrs. Morely's cooking."

"Those are tempting. Cons—she snores, hogs the covers and the dessert, and uses all the shampoo."

"I do not," she said indignantly, swatting at him, but he caught her hand and whirled her around.

"All right, where do I sign?"

She pointed at her mouth and Jake bent her back and took her laughing lips.

Epilogue

"Wait, Alanna." Fowler came through the door, dressed in an impeccable charcoal-gray suit with exquisite Western design, a pricey black Stetson on his head and even more-expensive boots on his feet. Jake rose, but Alanna touched his arm to get him to sit back down. She was the one who rose. Becca gave her a wry smile and the seller frowned.

Alanna was downtown at Becca's building about to purchase the land and the stables to go out on her own. She felt the terrible resistance to opening her own business and leaving her family-run stables. But, she felt she didn't have any choice. Respect was too important to ignore.

Charlie Hanson's real estate agent took one look at Fowler Colton and sighed. "Miss Colton, is there a problem?"

"No, there isn't," she said, turning to her brother. "Fowler, you have no right to disturb this meeting." She folded her arms and gave him a strong, no-nonsense look. There was no way he was going to intimidate her.

"You don't need to go through with this, Alanna. Colton Valley Ranch Stables can't do without you."

"What?" Startled, she looked at Jake, and a sardonic smile crossed his face.

"You heard him right, darlin'," Jake drawled.

"We don't want you to go. You belong at the helm and I was an ass to suggest anything else."

"You're admitting you were wrong?" She felt damn giddy inside.

"Yes, I don't like being wrong." He flicked his gaze to Jake. "About anything. McCord," he said, nodding.

"Colton," Jake responded, that bad boy gleam in his eyes. He was enjoying this.

"So, this meeting is over?"

Alanna held up her hand. Leave it to Fowler to try to railroad her. "Not just yet. I have complete control of Colton Valley Ranch Stables."

"Yes," Fowler said.

"Including financial?"

"Yes, sister," he said with a sigh. "Including financial."

"Can I—"

"Get that in writing. Yes." He reached into the front pocket of his suit jacket and pulled out a set of folded papers.

"That's not what I was going to say." She smiled. "I was going to say, 'Can I trust you?'"

Jake rose and stood close to her. "I think that would

be a yes," Jake said, breathing in her ear and making her shiver.

"What he said," Fowler said.

She turned to Becca and Charlie. "Uh, let's talk about how I'm going to compensate you for taking up your time."

"*Tsk, tsk.* I would have been happy to fix a tray for you, Miss Alanna."

"I wanted to do it for Jake, Mrs. Morely, but thank you."

Mrs. Morely gave her an indulgent smile. "So good to have you blissfully happy."

"It's good to be blissfully happy. If it wasn't for Daddy still missing, everything would be completely wonderful."

Mrs. Morely nodded and squeezed her arm.

She eased into the room, then crossed to the bed and set the tray on the floor. She threw back the curtains and heard Jake growl from the bed. "For God's sake, woman! Are you trying to blind me?"

Bracing her arms on either side of his head, she brushed a kiss along his jaw. "I brought you breakfast in bed."

Alanna felt him smile as he ran his hand under her robe and up her rib cage. "That's some service."

Grinning, she nipped his bottom lip, then looked down at him. "I think you're taking the boss for granted there, lazybones. We have a shipment of horses coming in today. The first of my barrel racer stock. I'm so excited."

"What did you bring me?" He rubbed his hand up and down her rib cage, then stroked the indentation between two ribs with his thumb, amusement glinting in his eyes.

"Cranberry scones and café au lait. You'll have to extend your pinky when you drink it. It's French."

He laughed, deep and low, caught a handful of hair and pulled her head down, then kissed the side of her neck, his mouth hot and moist and erotically searching.

"Jake," she whispered, her tone a little breathless, a little urgent.

Releasing a long, tremulous sigh, he pulled one of her arms free, then drew her down on top of him, dragging her hair back from her neck before giving her another kiss.

Weakness flooded through her, and Alanna rolled her head, the feel of his mouth against her neck sending shivers up and down her spine. He let her go and slipped out of bed and she had to gather her composure.

"Alanna."

She opened her eyes and looked at him, saturated in sensation, her pulse thick and heavy. He was staring at her from the open bathroom door, his wrist braced on the frame, his face taut, looking hot, bothered and all desperado. He was all naked male, aroused, barely restrained. He grinned at her, and Alanna's knees went weak and then weaker.

"Let's get dirty while we get clean, babe."

Unbearable feelings swelling up in her chest, she moved away from the bed and reached for her belt. Without breaking eye contact with him, she gave him everything she had and he absorbed it from across the room. She undid her robe, then let it slide from her shoulders.

A muscle jerked in Jake's jaw, and he came toward her, his hot gaze drilling into her. Reaching her, he fingered his Ranger badge. She still wore it around her neck. "This looks better on you than it ever did on me," he whispered. Gripping the back of her neck, he took her mouth in a kiss that paralyzed her and made her knees turn to jelly. Expelling a ragged breath, he swept her up, then turned toward the bathroom.

Much, much later, she got word that the trailer had pulled into the stable yard. As they stepped out of the house, a wisp of wood smoke greeted them, the scent lingering in the air. Jake grabbed her hand and she stuck the other one in her pocket, the tang of fall and the chill mixing with the lingering smoke. Inhaling deeply, she savored the smell. God, but she loved fall, especially like the one they'd had this year. A true unseasonably warm fall with vibrant colors, clear skies and mild wind that had no force to detach the leaves. It was her favorite time of year.

They followed the trail through the copse of oak and pine to the arena, the dry grasses beside the trail rustling against her jeans. The horse trailer carrying six horses was parked in front of the arena and Alanna could barely contain her excitement.

Senator Stillwater had come through for her on her second request.

"Get in there and get those animals unloaded," she said to Jake.

"Yes, ma'am."

The back had already been lowered and Jake methodically and quickly untrailered five of the six horses. He went to go up the ramp for the sixth horse, but he stopped dead, turned to look at her.

"Alanna, how? What the hell?"

"Did I mention the Colton name has some pull with Senator Stillwater of the state of Texas? I called in some favors. One was to get tickets to your medal ceremony. The other was to get the Rangers to release Valentine…to you."

He dropped his head, overcome with emotion. She could see him fighting for, then regaining his composure. He turned and walked down the ramp and swept her up in his arms. "I love you for this. Thank you for him. He means the world to me."

"What's the fun of having all this weight to throw around and not using it?" She cupped his jaw. "He's all yours."

He went into the trailer and led Valentine out and the grin on Jake's face was all worth it. He walked over to her, and Valentine nudged him in the back and he stumbled forward. "He wants me to ask you something."

"He does?"

"Yeah." Valentine nudged him again, and Alanna laughed. "Holy hell, you're pushy, Val," Jake said.

"You'd better get on with it."

He took her hands and brought them to his lips. "I don't have a ring and I don't have anything prepared, so I'll keep it simple. Will you marry me?"

Valentine draped his head over Jake's shoulder. "Hey, stop horning in on my proposal."

Alanna kissed the roan on his nose, then said, "Yes, I'll marry you. Ring or no ring. Speech or no speech. It is quite simple. It's love."

* * *

Alanna stood with Jake in Tiffany's as he slipped the engagement ring on her finger. "It's beautiful, Jake."

She kissed him and they left the store arm in arm. He stopped her on the street and kissed her again.

She wrapped her arms around his neck, the noon lunch crowd parting and moving around them, and she got a tingling sensation. She opened her eyes, turned her head and froze, her heart in her throat. Across the street, she saw her father dressed in a ratty gray, ill-fitting sweat suit, sunglasses and a—what the hell—New York Yankees cap? The light on the corner changed to green and traffic started to move, blocking her view. She slipped out of Jake's arms and went to the curb, waiting in agony for the constant flow to clear.

"What's wrong?" Jake said, following her gaze across the street.

Finally, the light changed back to red and all the traffic stopped moving, but when she searched, he was gone. Her heart in her throat, her shoulders slumped and tears threatened.

Had the same thing happened to her that had happened when she'd been in Dallas to see Becca? Was she mistaken?

No. This time she was sure.

"Alanna?" Jake prompted.

"I thought I just saw my father."

"What? Are you sure?" Jake said, scanning the other side of the street.

"Yes, but how could that be?"

Later on at home, sitting at the dinner table, she

related what happened. All her siblings turned to look at her.

"It had to be wishful thinking," Fowler said, leaning back in his chair.

"Not possible. If Eldridge was walking around downtown Dallas, free of his assailant, he'd have shouted for help or gotten home," Piper said, and T.C., Reid and Zane agreed.

Whitney sighed heavily. "I just want my Dridgey-pooh back. I miss him so much."

"Maybe his assailant was walking beside him, a gun pressed against him?" Marceline suggested.

"No, there wasn't anyone near him. But I must be mistaken. My Texas Rangers–loving dad would never be caught dead in a Yankees ball cap. Right?" She could second-guess herself all night, the incident with the bald man on Pegasus Plaza still fresh in her mind. Maybe it *was* wishful thinking.

They all shook their heads in agreement and Jake covered her hand, her engagement ring shining in the light. She so hoped her dad was safe and would come back to them. She wanted to share her good news with him. Introduce him to Jake.

Right. Her dad dressed like a bum and wearing a Yankees cap…*but*…this time, she was *positive* it was him.

* * * * *

MILLS & BOON®

INTRIGUE
Romantic Suspense

A SEDUCTIVE COMBINATION OF DANGER AND DESIRE

A sneak peek at next month's titles...

In stores from 8th September 2016:

- **Still Waters** – Debra Webb *and*
  Navy Seal to Die For – Elle James
- **Army Ranger Redemption** – Carol Ericson *and*
  Kentucky Confidential – Paula Graves
- **Cowboy Cavalry** – Alice Sharpe *and*
  Dust Up with the Detective – Danica Winters

Romantic Suspense

- **Operation Cowboy Daddy** – Carla Cassidy
- **Colton Family Rescue** – Justine Davis

Just can't wait?
Buy our books online a month before they hit the shops!
www.millsandboon.co.uk

Also available as eBooks.

MILLS & BOON®

18 bundles of joy from your favourite authors!

2 free books

Get 2 books free when you buy the complete collection only at
www.millsandboon.co.uk/greatoffers